P9-CLD-236

## Praise for the novels of
### *New York Times* bestselling author Sharon Sala

"Skillfully balancing suspense and romance, Sala gives
readers a nonstop breath-holding adventure."
—*Publishers Weekly* on *Going Once*

"Vivid, gripping...this thriller keeps the pages turning."
—*Library Journal* on *Torn Apart*

"Sala is a master at telling a story that is both romantic
and suspenseful.... With this amazing story, Sala proves
why she is one of the best writers in the genre."
—*RT Book Reviews* on *Wild Hearts*

"Sala's characters are vivid and engaging."
—*Publishers Weekly* on *Cut Throat*

"Veteran romance writer Sala lives up to her reputation
with this well-crafted thriller."
—*Publishers Weekly* on *Remember Me*

"[A] well-written, fast-paced ride."
—*Publishers Weekly* on *Nine Lives*

"Perfect entertainment for those looking for a suspense
novel with emotional intensity."
—*Publishers Weekly* on *Out of the Dark*

Look for Sharon Sala's next novel available soon from MIRA Books.

# SHARON SALA

# FAMILY SINS

MIRA

**MIRA**

ISBN-13: 978-0-7783-1968-9

Family Sins

For questions and comments about the quality of this book, please contact us at
CustomerService@Harlequin.com.

www.MIRABooks.com

**Printed in U.S.A.**

For some people, family is everything.
They learned early on that nothing on earth matters
more than the confidence that comes from
knowing you belong—and knowing you are loved.

But there are others who bear the burden
of their blood and spend most of their lives
putting permanent distance between themselves
and the people with whom they share a name.

I dedicate this book to the people who are wise enough
to find their tribe among a circle of friends
and the places life takes them.

To the misfits in all of us.

# FAMILY SINS

# *One*

Stanton Youngblood was running for his life, desperate to elude the man behind him. Moving uphill had afforded him the cover he needed, but now the man was catching up and Stanton was lagging from exhaustion. All he kept thinking about was Leigh, getting home to Leigh.

*Leigh. Oh God, my sweet Leigh. This can't be happening. I do not want to die.*

Every footstep was an effort now. His side was burning, his legs were shaking, and his lungs felt like they were going to explode. He could actually hear the man crashing through the brush and trees behind him, which meant he was getting closer.

There was no time to turn and look. He knew who was chasing him, and he knew why. This day had been more than thirty years in the making, but he wouldn't have done anything different. His beautiful Leigh was worth everything.

Even this.

And the moment he thought it, a bullet ripped through his back. The shot was already echoing down the mountain as he began to fall. He had a moment of overwhelming despair, and then everything began happening in slow motion.

The gray squirrel leaping from one tree to another seemed suspended in midair. The flock of birds taking flight from the sound of the gunshot moved like a kite just catching the wind. The flash of sunlight was a laser beam as it came through the forest canopy into his eyes.

And then he was down and his line of sight was the forest floor. Something sharp was poking the side of his face. Breath caught in a sob as a rush of blood flooded his mouth.

*Oh God.*

He gave in to the inevitable as the pain began to fade. His vision was beginning to blur. He blinked, and as he did, a tiny striped beetle with crab-like pincers came into focus. He watched it crawling on top of a pile of leaves and then saw the tail of a black snake as it slithered away.

A dog howled from somewhere nearby, and another answered, and then another, and he heard the footsteps again. But this time they were running away.

He could no longer feel his legs. He didn't have enough air in his lungs to call for help. With the last of his life quickly fading, he pushed away the leaves from beneath his outstretched hand and scratched a name into the dirt.

* * *

Leigh Youngblood was in the garden behind her house hoeing weeds from the long rows of green beans. It was a repetitious job that required no thought, so she let her mind wander as she worked, thinking of the life she and Stanton had carved out for themselves on this West Virginia mountain.

Never once had she regretted giving up her family's wealth and prestige to marry Stanton. The Wayne family from which she'd come held sway over most of Eden, the city in the valley below. Her family's rage and disdain for what she'd done back then had known no bounds. They'd threatened Stanton's life. They'd laughed and jeered at her, saying how far she would fall and how the two of them would fail. But loving Stanton was beyond her control. He was the beginning and the end of her world, and so she'd walked out of the good life and into his arms. Thirty-five years later they were still on the mountain, loving and thriving, and still proving all of them wrong.

Of their five sons, Samuel, Michael and Aidan were married and living close by. They had one grandson and another grandchild on the way.

Bowie was their oldest, but after the love of his life turned him down when he was younger, he'd left the mountains for the oil fields, mostly working on offshore rigs down south. He came home for Christmas every year but had never put down roots anywhere else.

Jesse was their youngest. He'd gone to war with

plans of making the military his career, only to be sent home from what the war had done to him. Brain-damaged beyond repair, he would live out his life with the mind of a ten-year-old boy.

Leigh loved and supported them all, accepting their rights to strike out on their own as they saw fit, just as she had done.

She paused long enough to pull up a clump of grass from beneath the beans, and as she did, a tendril of her hair slipped free from the band holding it out of her eyes and proceeded to dangle in front of her face. She pushed it back as she tossed the grass clump out of the garden, then stopped to wipe away a bead of sweat. She was about to reach for the next clump of grass when she heard the crack of a gunshot, and then the echo as it bounced from peak to peak off the surrounding mountains.

Startled, she spun toward the sound just as a flock of birds took to the sky. Noting the direction, she thought of Stanton. He would be taking that route home, but he hadn't taken his rifle. He'd only gone to visit his sister, who lived down near the lake.

Then she heard a dog howl, followed by another and another, and for a second she was so scared that her heart actually stopped. She didn't know what had just happened, but something told her it wasn't good. She dropped the hoe in the dirt and started walking toward the front yard.

Her son Jesse was sitting in a rocker on the porch, staring off into the trees.

"The war's a-comin'," he said, as she walked past him.

"Stay here," she said, and when he started to get up and follow her, she turned and screamed, "Stay here! Get in your chair and don't move until I get back. Do you understand?"

He was startled and a little upset that she'd yelled, but he minded her instantly and sat back in the chair.

"Stayin' here," he said, and started rocking.

Leigh was so scared she was shaking. She was afraid to leave Jesse and afraid not to go. She looked back at the forest, willing Stanton to come walking out into the sunlight with a logical explanation for what she'd heard.

When his face suddenly flashed before her eyes, her heart dropped. Stanton must be in danger. She started running into the trees, leaving home behind for whatever awaited her below. She set her path in the direction of where she'd seen the birds take flight and wouldn't let fear lead her astray. She was a woman known for keeping a cool head and today would be no different, but she ran without thought for her own welfare, ignoring the brambles that caught in her skin or on her clothes, stumbling more than once on her downhill race to find the man who was her world.

All she needed to know was that he was okay, but she wasted no breath calling out his name. If the gunshot she'd heard had been a poacher's bullet, she didn't want to stumble into something and make it worse, and so she ran, ignoring the bramble vine that ripped the band from her hair. She ran without caution, falling more than once on her hands and knees, and once flat on her belly, causing her to lose her breath. She didn't know she was crying until she felt the tears roll across her lips.

It was the sunlight coming through the canopy onto the back of Stanton's red plaid shirt that she saw first. She stopped in midflight and screamed his name.

"Stanton! *Stanton!*"

Any second she expected he would lift his head and tell her it was just a broken leg or that he'd simply taken a fall. But when she was only a few feet from where he was lying, she stopped as if someone had shoved a hand against the middle of her chest.

He was dead.

She knew that from the bullet hole in the back of his shirt and the amount of blood on the ground beneath him. She fell to her knees from the shock, and then, when she couldn't get up, began crawling toward him. The lack of a pulse was confirmation of what she already knew, and still she ran her fingers through his hair, through the long tangled strands, sobbing as the tendrils curled around her fingers. Tears continued to roll as she rocked back on her heels, searching the surrounding trees for signs of a poacher, and yelled out, "Are you still here, you bastard? Are you too scared to come out and admit what you've done?"

Then she noticed the odd crook of Stanton's right arm and traced the length of it to the finger pointing at the word he'd scratched into the dirt.

Sound faded. Thought ceased.

A thousand images of the past thirty-plus years with him flashed through her mind, followed by shock and then disbelief.

"No! No, no, no, they didn't! They *wouldn't*! Why? Why *now*?"

All of a sudden she was on her feet, her heart pounding in growing rage. Then she threw back her head and screamed. Once she began, she couldn't stop. One scream rolled into another, making it hard to breathe.

Nearby, dogs heard her, heard the devastation in her screams, and started howling. Then other dogs—dogs farther up the mountain and dogs farther down—heard and followed suit, until they were all howling in concert, understanding with their animal senses what humans had yet to discern.

Death had come to the mountain.

Samuel Youngblood had the strong bones and features of his Scottish ancestors, and looked like a mountain man with his long hair and simple clothes, but looks were deceiving. He made his living as a small business investor and a day trader, but being inside so much on pretty days like today was wearing, so he'd taken the day off to relax.

He was just getting ready to mow the yard when his hunting dogs began to howl. He looked back toward their pen and frowned. Not only were they all howling, but they were extremely agitated, which was highly unusual.

His wife, Bella, came out onto the back porch, shading her eyes as she looked toward the pen.

"What's wrong with those dogs?" she asked.

"I don't know, but it's not just ours. Listen. Can you hear them?"

She tilted her head and then frowned.

"They're howling all over the mountain," she said.

"Something's wrong," Samuel said. "Bring me my rifle."

"What are you going to do?" she asked.

"I'm going to take Big Red and find out what happened."

She ran into the house as he headed for the dog pen. He grabbed a leash, clipped it on to his best tracker's collar and headed back to the house.

Bella came out carrying the rifle and his phone as he was tying back his hair at the nape of his neck.

"I know the signal's not good here, but you might need it," she said, then handed him the rifle and dropped the phone in his shirt pocket. "I love you, Samuel. Be careful."

"I love you, too, honey. I'll be fine." Then he let the leash out as far as it would go and tightened his grip as Big Red took the lead and began pulling him up the mountain.

Michael Youngblood had gone to his brother Aidan's house early that morning to help him set up some new software on his home computer. Aidan was a website designer. Michael was in IT for a large computer company and, like Aidan and their other brother, Samuel, worked from home. All three men bore the traces of their Scottish ancestry with pride and kept their hair long.

They were still in Aidan's office when they began hearing the distant sounds of dogs howling. Before they could comment, the dogs that were penned up out back began to howl in return.

"What the hell?" Aidan said, and got up from his computer and walked outside, with Michael behind him.

The moment they exited the house they heard the sound of distant howling.

"Sweet Lord, it sounds like every dog on the mountain is howling," Michael muttered.

Aidan walked off the porch and then out into the yard, looking for smoke or a sign of something off-kilter, but all he could see were trees. He was just about to go back inside and call his mother when he realized there was another sound beneath the howls.

His heart skipped a beat.

"Michael! I hear a woman screaming."

Michael frowned. "Can you tell the direction?"

"No. I need to get my dog. Tell Leslie to give you my rifle," Aidan said, and headed for the pen as Michael ran back into the house.

Like Samuel, Aidan had hunting dogs—good trackers when they had a scent to follow. He wasn't sure if his dog would lead them to the source, but they were about to find out.

Within minutes, he and Michael were in the woods, following Aidan's dog Mollie down the mountain. He didn't know whether she was following the sound of the dogs or the sound of the screams, but she was running full tilt. If he hadn't had her on a leash, she would have run off and left them.

Samuel heard the woman screaming about ten minutes into the search. He knew now that Big Red was following her screams rather than the howls, because the farther they ran, the louder her voice became.

When he stumbled into the clearing and saw his mother, and then his father's body on the ground, he thought he was dreaming. Then Big Red began to howl. At that point he tied the dog's leash to a tree and ran toward her.

"Mama! Mama!"

Her screaming stopped the moment she heard her son's voice. Then she realized what was about to happen and leaped across Stanton's body before he stepped on what Stanton had scratched into the ground.

"Stop!" she cried, and then leaned her forehead against Samuel's chest and began to shake. "He's dead, Samuel, he's dead. Someone shot him in the back."

He looked down at his father in disbelief, trying to wrap his head around the fact that his father was dead. Tears rolled.

"Mama, what happened?"

She pulled out of his arms and pointed down.

"I don't know why this happened, but your daddy named his killer before he died."

Samuel looked down, saw the word and frowned.

"Wayne? Wayne who? Who do we know—"

"No!" she screamed. "Not Wayne *who*! My family. *Those* Waynes! Oh my God, they finally did it. They killed him, just like they threatened they would."

Within seconds Michael and Aidan came running into the clearing. Aidan tied Mollie up and then ran to join their mother. The shock of finding out it was her screams they'd been following was horrifying, and then they saw their father's body.

Aidan leaped forward as if he'd been launched, screaming, "Daddy! No, Daddy, *no*!"

Samuel turned and caught him.

Tears were running down Michael's face as he took his mother into his arms. "What happened, Mama?"

"I don't know," she sobbed. "I was in the garden. I heard a shot, and I don't know how to explain it, but I knew. I ran until I found him." She pulled out of his arms and shoved her fingers through her hair, as if trying to gather her thoughts. "Did one of you bring your phone?"

All three of them pulled their phones out of their pockets.

"Not sure we can get a signal here," Samuel said.

"You don't need a signal to take pictures. Take pictures of your daddy, your daddy's hand, and then the name he scratched in the dirt before something happens to it. Someone in my family did this."

Aidan looked down, saw the name and all of his father's blood that had seeped into the ground beneath him, and then staggered away and threw up.

Leigh had set aside her grief. It was rage carrying her through this tragedy, and when Aidan got sick she strode after him, impatience in every step.

"We have no time for this," she said, as she grabbed his ponytail and held it back.

Even in anger, she was tending her own as she held his hair back away from his face while the spasms rolled through him.

Aidan took a deep breath and then straightened up, wiping his mouth with the back of his hand.

"I'm sorry, it just... I can't believe... Why, Mama? Why?"

"I don't know, but I *will* find out which one of my siblings did this, and I *will* make them sorry they were ever born."

The three brothers stared at her then, magnificent in her grief with the glare of the sunlight behind her, and her hair all wide and tangled around her scratched and bloody face. She looked like a warrior woman from another time.

Michael glanced at Samuel and then pointed at his father's body.

"You two take the pictures. I'm going to try calling the constable."

Leigh stood to one side, watching the proceedings without voicing the obvious.

Life as they'd known it was over.

Walter Riordan was in his twenty-fourth year of serving as county constable. He'd seen a lot of the sad side of life, but when he got a phone call from Michael Youngblood and heard the details of what had happened, his heart sank. Incidents like this one were how blood feuds began. Michael gave him the GPS readings from his phone, which gave Riordan a clear location.

"It will take us at least thirty minutes to get there," Riordan said.

Michael looked back at his mother, who was standing guard over their father's body.

"We're not going anywhere," he said, and disconnected, then ran back to the scene. "I spoke to Constable Riordan. It will be at least thirty minutes, maybe more, before they can get here."

Leigh thought about Jesse alone at their house.

"Samuel, please call Bella and ask her to go stay with Jesse."

"Yes, ma'am," he said, and then started walking until he had enough bars on his phone to make a call.

Bella answered on the second ring. "Hello?"

"It's me," he said.

"Are you okay? Did you find out what happened?"

He tried to say it without breaking down, but the truth was too appalling.

"Daddy's dead. Mama found him in the woods, shot in the back. He scratched the name 'Wayne' in the dirt before he died."

Bella gasped, and then started crying.

"Who's Wayne? Why would someone kill your daddy?"

"Mama says it's someone from her family. She's gone all quiet. I've never seen her like this. It's nothing but pure rage."

"What can I do?"

"Mama asked if you would please go to the house and stay with Jesse until we can all get back."

"Yes, yes, of course. I'll leave right now. Oh, Sammie, this just breaks my heart. I'm so sorry."

"So am I, honey, so am I. I'll see you there later."

He disconnected and hurried back to his mother. "She's on her way. What do you need me to do?" he asked.

She pointed into the woods.

"Take Big Red. See if you can find where the killer stood. It has to be in that general direction. If Red can catch the scent, set him on it and see how far he'll take you."

"Yes, ma'am," Samuel said, and ran for the dog, then headed into the woods as Michael and Aidan called their wives with the news. Like Bella, the other two daughters-in-law headed to the home place to be with Jesse.

It didn't take Samuel long to find his daddy's footprints because he recognized the boot tread, and even less time to find where the killer had stood when he shot him. He searched around the area and found an ejected cartridge. Rather than pick it up and possibly ruin a fingerprint, he marked the spot with a small pile of rocks, took a picture of the footprints, then set Big Red on the scent and held tight to the leash as the dog headed down the mountain.

It was easy to follow the trail because the killer had been running and making no attempt to hide his tracks. Samuel took note of the length of the stride as he paused more than once to take pictures.

Within ten minutes Red stopped and yipped. He'd lost the scent. Samuel followed him as he began circling the area, trying to pick it up again. The ground was hard and rocky beneath the trees, and when Samuel finally saw tire tracks from a motorcycle, his heart sank. The shooter was gone. The hunt was over. He pulled in the leash and then stopped.

"That's good, boy. That's good," he said, patting the big hound. "Let's go back. Let's go find Mollie."

The dog trotted beside Samuel as they headed back up the mountain, his tongue hanging. When they crossed a small creek Samuel stopped to let Red drink. A little rabbit hopped farther back into the brush, and a pair of squirrels scolded from the canopy above their head.

Samuel took a couple of steps upstream from Red and squatted down beside the trickling water to wipe the sweat from his face. As he leaned over to sweep his hand through the water, he caught a glimpse of his reflection. He'd always taken great pride in looking like his father, but now it was a reminder of their loss. He set his jaw as he sloshed the water on his face. Tears were rolling down his cheeks as he stood, mixing with the water droplets as he started back up the mountain with his dog. By the time he got back to the murder scene, cops were everywhere, and the ache in his chest was firmly entrenched.

Leigh's silent vigil over Stanton's body ended when the constable and his men arrived. Once she had given her statement, she had to watch from a distance as the crime scene investigators began taking pictures of everything from the name that he'd scribbled in the dirt to the position of his body. When the medical examiner rolled the body over and realized the shot had been a through and through, the crime scene officers began looking for a bullet, hoping it had hit a tree.

When Michael and Aidan offered to help look, their offer was rejected, so they went to stand beside their mother. They stood for a few moments before they realized she was too quiet, and began to get concerned.

Leigh's expression was evidence of her contempt as she watched the officers stomping around the area and examining the trees in search of the missing bullet.

"Both of you, please, go help those fools find the bullet. It's going to help us name the killer."

"We offered. They told us to step aside."

"Oh my God," she muttered, as she ran a shaky hand through her tangled hair.

"You don't think they'll find it?" Michael asked.

She pointed.

"No. Just look at them. They can plainly see where Stanton is lying and a direct line of shot would be there." She pointed toward the northeast. "And yet look where they're at."

Aidan frowned. "I don't care what they said. I'm going to help search. This is ridiculous."

"I'll go with you," Michael said.

They were on the other side of the clearing when

Samuel came up behind his mother. He tied Big Red up and then slid a hand across her shoulder.

She spun immediately.

"Anything?" she asked.

"I found a cartridge casing, and then the trail ended a ways down. He got away on a motorcycle."

"Where's the cartridge?" she asked.

"I marked the trail and let it lie. I figure the crime scene investigators will need to bag and process it."

Leigh paused for a moment, staring up at her second son, then she cupped his face. Her voice shook as she spoke.

"You and Bowie look so much like your daddy."

Samuel pulled her into his arms.

"We love you, Mama. We'll all be here for you and Jesse. Always."

She drew a slow, shaky breath. There were tears on her face when she pulled away, but the fire in her eyes was even brighter.

"Do you have Bowie's number on your phone?"

"Yes, ma'am. Do you want to call him?"

He watched a muscle jerk at the side of her jaw and then the tears began to fall in earnest.

"I can't say the words yet. Will you call him for me? Tell him I need him. Tell him I said to come home."

"Yes, I'll call. I have to go find a signal. I won't be long."

Leigh watched him walking away and for a moment could almost imagine it was Stanton.

*Oh my God. Stanton. How am I going to live life without you in it?*

# *Two*

Samuel tried to call Bowie but had to leave a message for him to return the call, then headed for Constable Riordan instead.

"Sir, I have some information for you."

"I'm listening," Riordan said.

"I took my dog and trailed the shooter all the way down the mountain until the trail ended at a set of tire tracks. It was some kind of motorcycle. I took pictures of the tread and of his footprints. Give me a number and I'll send the pictures to you. Also, there's a spent cartridge in the brush where the shooter stood. If you'll get one of your investigators to follow me, I'll show him where it is. I marked the spot without picking it up."

Riordan's eyes widened.

"Good job," he said, and then added, "I'm sure sorry for your loss. Stanton was a good man."

Samuel's eyes were glassy from unshed tears, and his chest was so tight it hurt to breathe.

"Yes, sir," he said, and waited.

The constable called out to one of the investigators, who came on the run.

"What's up?" the man asked.

"This is Samuel Youngblood, one of the victim's sons. He found a spent cartridge. Follow him to bag it."

"Yes, sir," the investigator said, and took off after Samuel, who was already walking away.

Despite being frowned at for interfering, it was Aidan who located the tree where the missing bullet was lodged. He turned and called out, "Here! I found the bullet."

A couple of the investigators came running, one with a small handsaw and the other right behind him carrying his evidence recovery kit.

Aidan watched them saw a notch out of the tree with the bullet still in it.

"Why didn't you just dig it out of the tree?" he asked.

"It can ruin the striations," the investigator explained.

"Ah, makes sense," Aidan said, and watched them bag it up, tag it and enter it into evidence.

Bella Youngblood was relieved to see Jesse sitting on the porch when she drove up and parked. He was rocking too fast, which told her he was nervous, but at least he was still there.

She got out and hurried up the steps. "Hi, Jesse."

He nodded. "Hi, Bella. Mama told me to stay here. The war's coming," he said.

Bella was a tall, buxom blonde and used to Jesse's ways. She knelt in front of the rocker and patted his knee until he looked into her eyes.

"Are you hungry, Jesse?"

He nodded.

"Want to come into the house with me? You can show me what you want to eat."

"Mama's gone. She told me to stay right here."

"She'll be back," Bella said, then stood up and opened the front door. "She won't care if you come inside with me."

Jesse got up and followed her into the house.

They were frying bacon for sandwiches when Maura and Leslie walked into the kitchen. Maura was six months pregnant, and Leslie was carrying her eighteen-month-old toddler on her hip.

When the baby saw Jesse, he squealed.

A big smile broke across Jesse's face, and in that moment they could see the man he'd been.

"Hey, it's my little buddy," Jesse said, and sat down immediately and held out his arms.

Leslie laughed, leaned over and kissed Jesse on the cheek, and then handed over her wiggling toddler.

"Johnny sure loves his Uncle Jesse," she said.

Jesse looked up at her. "Jesse loves Johnny, too."

"I know, honey," Leslie said, and then quickly turned away before she started to cry.

None of them wanted to let on that anything was wrong and get him upset, so there was no mention of what had happened or the sadness they were all feeling.

"Are you guys up for a BLT?" Bella asked.

Maura shook her head.

"No thanks. I was eating soup when Michael called. I'm good."

Leslie held up her hand.

"I was feeding Johnny when Aidan called. He's eaten, but I haven't. I would love one if there's enough."

"Yes, there's enough," Bella said, and added a few more strips of bacon to the skillet.

"Ow, ow, ow," Jesse said.

The baby laughed.

They all turned to look. Johnny had his little fists wrapped in Jesse's long brown hair, and every time Jesse made a face and cried out, the toddler pulled his hair.

"Don't let him hurt you," Leslie cautioned.

Jesse pulled the baby to his chest. "It doesn't hurt," he said, and rubbed the baby's curly head, then looked at Leslie. "Long hair, too?"

Leslie nodded. "Yes, Johnny's hair will get long like yours."

Jesse nodded. "Daddy says 'Youngblood tradition.'"

The women's eyes welled with tears.

"You're right. It *is* a Youngblood tradition."

"Like Samson in the Bible," Jesse added, and hugged the little boy again.

Bella swallowed back tears. "There's enough

bacon fried to start making sandwiches. Maura, get the bread and mayo, and, Leslie, would you please slice up a couple of tomatoes, and then put ice in the glasses and pour some sweet tea?"

The young women set about their tasks, but their hearts were heavy. These moments here with Jesse were the calm before the storm. Once Leigh returned and the truth of their lives was out in the open, nothing would ever be the same.

The killer rode the motorcycle like a bat out of hell, taking all the back roads down the mountain to the Wayne family lake house. He rode straight into the detached garage and parked against the wall behind a half-dozen ATVs, grabbed a rag hanging from a nail and wiped the bike down to remove any fingerprints, then covered it with a tarp.

The walk to the lake house was brief, and once inside, he got the cleaning kit and set about breaking down the rifle. By the time he was through cleaning it and then wiping it free of fingerprints, no one would know it had been fired. It would be back in the gun case with the others, with no one the wiser.

When the job was finished and the gun replaced inside the case, he locked up and left. After one swift glance around to make sure nothing was out of place, he drove away in a dusty black Lexus.

Leigh watched them putting her husband in the body bag, and when they zipped it up, she pressed her fingers against her lips to keep from screaming as they took him away.

When Samuel touched her shoulder, she turned to him with purpose.

"Samuel, I need to borrow your phone. I have to call your Aunt Polly. That's where Stanton went this morning. Then I need to call your Uncle Thomas. Stanton's sister and brother need to hear what happened from me."

Samuel took out his phone and checked the signal.

"The signal is good here. Their numbers are in my contact list if you need them."

"I know them," Leigh said, and wiped her hands on her pants before she took the phone from his hands.

Samuel kissed the side of her cheek and then walked a distance away, giving her some privacy to make the calls.

Leigh called Stanton's sister, Polly Cyrus, first. Her thoughts were in a jumble as she tried to figure out how to tell her without screaming, and then Polly answered and Leigh's eyes immediately filled with tears.

"Hello?" Polly said.

"Polly, it's me, Leigh."

Polly laughed. "Honey, I know your sweet voice."

"I have something to tell you, and I don't know how," Leigh said, and then started to cry, soft, near-silent sobs.

Polly's heart skipped a beat, and then she started to panic. Leigh was not the crying kind.

"Honey, just spit it out. What's wrong?"

"Stanton's dead."

Polly gasped and then moaned.

"No, no, no. He was just here. What happened? Was it his heart?"

Leigh took a breath and then choked on her sobs.

"No, he was murdered. Shot in the back on his way home." As she told Polly the rest, Polly went into hysterics.

"I'm sorry. I'm sorry," Leigh said. "If I could, I would die for him. I don't know why it happened."

Polly was sobbing. Leigh had started to hang up when Polly's husband, Carl, took the phone.

"Leigh! What the hell happened? Polly's done lost her mind."

Leigh told it all over again, and Carl groaned.

"Sweet Lord, I am so sorry, honey. I'm so sorry. What can we do for you?"

"Nothing. I just had to tell you myself. Now I've got to call Thomas."

"Do you want me to do it for you?"

Leigh wiped her eyes and then her nose on the back of her sleeve.

"Yes, I want you to, but I have to be the one to do it. I think Stanton's family deserves to hear this from me."

"All right, then, but we'll be coming over to your house soon."

He disconnected, which left Leigh with one more call to make. She punched in the numbers, dreading this call the most, because Thomas sounded so much like Stanton when he spoke.

Thomas Youngblood answered on the third ring.

"Hello, Samuel. How's it going?" he said.

Leigh sighed. She'd forgotten she was using Samuel's phone.

"Thomas, it's me, Leigh. I'm just using Samuel's phone."

Thomas laughed.

"Well, you're a lot prettier than my nephew, so that's fine with me. What's going on?"

"Is Beth there with you?"

"Yes, do you need to talk to her?"

"No, I called for you. I just wanted to make sure you weren't alone."

She heard him take a quick breath, and when he spoke again, his voice was deeper, even a bit nervous.

"What's wrong, girl?"

She started all over again, saying the awful words: Stanton is dead. She ended by explaining what had happened, and that she bore the blame because it was someone from her family who'd done it.

Thomas was crying, but the whole time he kept trying to reassure her. Finally he handed the phone off to Beth.

"Leigh, it's me. I am so sorry. I can't believe this happened, but we'll get justice for Stanton. We'll be over to the house in a while."

"Okay," Leigh said, and started to hang up, but Beth stopped her.

"Leigh?"

"What?" Leigh said.

"I just want you to know how much we love you. You won't go through this alone. You have a mountain full of people who love you and Stanton. We'll stand beside you all the way."

"Thank you," Leigh said. "I love you, too."

She disconnected and then waved at Samuel. He and his brothers came back on the run.

He could tell how hard it had been for her to make those calls. Even though he was broken up about the loss of his father, he was struggling with how to help her first. He picked a piece of vine from the tangles of her hair and then cupped the side of her cheek.

"Hey, Mama, how about I run up to the house and bring back Bella's car so you won't have to walk?"

Leigh glanced back into the clearing, to the huge dark blot on the ground where Stanton had bled out, and then shook her head.

"I need to be gone from this place. I'll walk. Will you all walk with me?" she asked.

They gathered around her then, like the little boys they'd once been, fussing for a place in her arms. Only this time, they were the ones who were holding on to her.

"Yes, we'll walk with you. I love you, Mama, and I am so sorry," Samuel said.

"Love you, Mama," Michael said, and slid his arm across her back. "Yes, we'll walk with you. Just lean on me."

Aidan cupped her face and then kissed her forehead. "We love you. Let us be strong for you this one time, okay?" he said.

Tears rolled down her face as her gaze moved from face to face, and then back to Samuel.

"Did you call Bowie?"

"Yes, ma'am, but he was unavailable. I left a message for him to call me."

She nodded, leaned against Michael's chest and reached for Aidan's hand, and then said in a soft, shaky voice, "I want to go home."

They started up the mountain with Michael and Aidan on either side of her, as Samuel led the way with the dogs. Despite Leigh's determination to walk, she kept stumbling, until finally Samuel turned around, handed the dogs off to Michael and picked her up in his arms. She never said a word. She just leaned her head against his chest and let him carry her home.


The sisters-in-law had cleaned up the kitchen and were doing their best to keep Jesse entertained, but he was bothered, and they knew it. He kept walking out onto the porch and then back into the house. Finally they all decided to sit outside with him, and once he settled in his rocker, he seemed to calm.

Jesse was the first to see his brothers walking up the road. He abruptly stood.

"Mama's not walking," he said.

Before they could stop him, he was down the steps and running toward his brothers with a long, loping stride.

"Oh, boy," Samuel said. "Mama, you need to wake up. Jesse's coming."

"I wasn't asleep," Leigh said, and quickly wiped her eyes as Samuel set her on her feet.

"Are you okay?" Michael asked.

Leigh fixed him with a look. "Are you?"

"No."

She reached out and squeezed his hand. "Sorry. I've been emotionally gutted. I lose my manners when I feel threatened."

"We know, Mama. Don't apologize to us. Just brace yourself for Jesse."

Leigh turned around just as Jesse came to a skidding stop and took her in his arms.

"Mama? Are you hurt?"

She took a slow breath, and then took his hand and laid it against her chest.

"No, I was just tired, and Samuel carried me so I wouldn't have to walk."

Jesse wrapped his arms around her and rested his chin on the crown of her head.

"You are my mama. Did I make you sad?"

She knew he'd seen the tears in her eyes, and she hugged him fiercely.

"No, my sweet boy, you did not make your mama sad. Come walk with me. I need to talk to you." She then took him by the hand and led him toward the house, talking all the way.

The brothers watched, but their hearts were breaking. They knew the minute their mother cupped Jesse's face that she was saying the words. And they knew from the way Jesse flinched and doubled over as if he'd just been gut-shot that one of the legs to his world had just been cut out from under him.

"God Almighty, why is this happening?" Aidan asked, his voice thick with tears.

Samuel shook his head and then swiped a hand across his face, and when Jesse fell to his knees, he started crying again.

Michael wiped his tears and grabbed the dogs' leashes.

"I'm gonna tie them to the porch. You guys go help Mama with Jesse."

Samuel took two steps forward, and then his phone began to ring. He looked at it and groaned.

"It's Bowie. You all go on. I need to do this alone."

They patted him on the shoulder and then walked away.

Samuel cleared his throat and then answered. "Hello."

"Hey, brother! It's me."

"Bowie, I'm not going to beat around the bush. We have bad news."

There was a moment of silence, and then Bowie spoke, but this time the delight was gone from his voice.

"What's wrong?"

Samuel tried to say the words, and then the crying got the better of him.

Bowie Youngblood couldn't remember seeing Samuel cry after he'd turned eighteen. Now he was scared.

"Is it Jesse? Did something happen to Jesse?"

"No, it's Daddy. He's dead, Bowie. Mama found him shot in the back."

Bowie's knees went out from under him. He sank down into a chair inside the office on the drilling platform and then curled his fingers around the arm of the chair.

"What? What did you say?"

Samuel sighed.

"Daddy's dead. Mama said to call you. Mama said to tell you to come home. She needs you."

"God in heaven," Bowie whispered, and felt like he was going to throw up. "How did it happen? You said someone shot him? On purpose?"

"Yes. He scratched a name in the dirt before he died."

Bowie tried to speak, but the words wouldn't come.

Samuel kept talking.

"The name was Wayne. I didn't get the meaning, but Mama did. She's certain the killer's someone from her family."

The shock of that reality transformed Bowie's sorrow to instant rage. He stood abruptly.

"Why now? That was more than thirty years ago. What the hell's happened now to start this up again?"

"I don't know. It just happened a few hours ago. We just got Mama back to the house. She's telling Jesse now, and I have a feeling it's going to be a long night here."

Bowie glanced at the clock. It was just after 3:00 p.m.

"I don't know how long it will take to get a chopper

out here to pick me up, but I'll be there as soon as I can. Tell Mama I'm on the way. Will one of you come into Eden to pick me up when they drop me off?"

"Yes. I will. I'm so sorry to be calling with such bad news," Samuel added.

"I'm sorry, too, for all of us," Bowie said. "I love you, Samuel."

"Love you, too, bro," Samuel said.

The call disconnected, and Samuel was still standing there, staring at the phone, when he heard footsteps and looked to see Bella coming toward him. He walked into her arms and came undone.

Bowie came out of the office leading with his chin, and headed for the boss.

"Claude! Claude!" he yelled to be heard over the noise on the drilling rig.

Claude Franklin turned, saw the look on Bowie Youngblood's face and knew something was wrong. He headed toward him at a trot.

There were tears still on Bowie's face when he grabbed Claude by the arm.

"I need a chopper, ASAP. My father's been murdered. There's going to be hell to pay on the mountain. I need to get home as soon as possible," he said, then began to explain.

Claude was speechless. In his whole life he'd never known anyone who was murdered, and to hear Bowie naming the other side of his family as the ones responsible was beyond understanding.

"Go pack. I'll get you a chopper, son. Just get your head on straight."

Bowie nodded and took off toward their sleeping quarters, the long black braid hanging down his back bouncing with every step.

By the time Bella and Samuel got back into the house, it appeared that Leigh's momentary weakness had passed in her need to care for her youngest son. She was sitting at Jesse's bedside, waiting for his meds to kick in as he cried himself to sleep.

The longer she sat, the angrier she became. By the time Jesse fell asleep, she was so mad she was shaking. She went through the house in search of her boys, calling them by name.

They came rushing out of the kitchen, thinking she needed them to tend to Jesse. He was a big strong man and, due to his head injuries, was hard to handle when he got upset, but when they saw she was alone they slowed down.

Leigh put her hands on her hips.

"I'm going to Eden. I want the killer to know before he lays his head on a pillow tonight that his days are numbered. Will you go with me?"

"Yes, ma'am," they said in unison.

"What about Jesse?" Michael said.

"I gave him one of his pills. He's sound asleep."

"Do you want to change clothes or anything?" Samuel asked.

Leigh looked down at the shirt and jeans she'd been wearing in the garden. They had blood all over them. She thought of the scratches on her face and realized she hadn't even pulled the leaves out of her hair, and then let it go.

"No. I'm not changing anything. I'm not hiding the hideousness of what was done."

"You can ride with me," Samuel said.

"Aidan and I will follow you in my SUV," Michael said.

"Bring your rifles," Leigh said.

Bella gasped.

Maura and Leslie looked anxious.

"Do you think you're all in danger?" Bella asked.

"No, not unless we turn our backs," Leigh snapped, and then grabbed her purse and the keys to her Jeep. "We won't be long. Jesse isn't going to wake up, so don't worry."

"We're not afraid of him," Maura said, and hugged Leigh.

"Be careful. All of you," Bella said, as she hugged Leigh, too.

Leslie kissed her mother-in-law on the cheek and then squeezed her hand.

"Scare the shit out of them, Mama."

"I fully intend to," Leigh said, and went out the front door with her sons behind her.

She tossed the keys to Samuel and then got in the passenger seat as he slid behind the wheel.

Moments later they were gone.

Henry Clayton had been the police chief in Eden for more than fifteen years. He'd just gotten off the phone with Constable Riordan, who'd filled him in on the murder and the name Stanton Youngblood had scratched in the dirt before he died.

Clayton was shocked. He'd gone to school with Stanton and had always thought of him as a friend. He didn't know what to think, other than that the Wayne family held sway over the town and nearly everyone in it, including him. The constable was in charge of the case, but he would be depending on Clayton for assistance when the investigation got under way. Before Clayton could formulate a plan for himself, he heard the sound of vehicles coming down Main very fast, and when he began to hear constant honking, he frowned.

"What the hell?"

By the time he got out to the street, a crowd of people were gathering to see what was happening.

The two vehicles he'd heard speeding and disturbing the peace were now illegally parked in the middle of the street.

He was all ready to start issuing citations when he realized whose vehicles they were. His pulse kicked into high, and he began to sweat.

It was already beginning.

Leigh Youngblood got out first and stopped just shy of the sidewalk, fixing Henry with a cold, angry stare. When her sons fell into step and fanned out behind her with fire in their eyes and their rifles cradled in their arms, Henry felt like a cornered rat.

"Mrs. Youngblood, what—"

Leigh raised her arm and pointed straight at him. Henry had to look twice to reassure himself the only thing she was pointing was her finger. He was horrified at how many of the townspeople were gathering behind her. Now he had to be extra careful of what he let her say and do.

"You don't talk. You just listen." Leigh's voice was loud and carrying, but she sounded entirely rational. "My husband was murdered this morning."

The gasp from the crowd was loud but brief as they quickly silenced themselves to hear what else she had to say.

"Someone shot him in the back. But there's something the killer doesn't know. Stanton named his killer before he died. He scratched the name Wayne in the dirt!"

Leigh's voice was shaking, but her rage remained strong.

"My people! My family! They took the man I loved away from me, just like they swore they would do years ago."

Henry blustered, "But that was so long ago, surely you don't—"

"You doubt the last word of a dying man?" Leigh demanded. "No matter. We didn't expect anything more of you than this. You are bought and paid for by the Waynes just like half the people in this town. So I'm giving fair warning to you and to them. I will find out which one of them killed my husband, and when I do, they will pay."

Then Leigh turned around and walked between her sons to face the crowd.

"Yes, look at me. Look long and hard, all of you. As for my so-called family, if any of you are hiding in the crowd, you best take a look, too, because this is what the devil looks like when he's on your heels. When I find which one of you did this, you will wish you'd never been born. There isn't enough money between you and God to buy your way out of this."

Michael walked up to flank his mother on her left. Samuel and Aidan stepped into place on her right, and then Samuel slid an arm across her shoulders and raised his voice.

"The back-shooting coward and the family who harbors him best remember, you won't catch us unarmed again."

Leigh lifted her chin as she stared at the crowd. She stared them down until they began looking away.

"I think we're done here," Leigh said.

"Yes, ma'am," Samuel said, and slipped a hand beneath her arm, then escorted her to the Jeep and seated her inside.

Samuel led the way out of town with his brothers behind him. He didn't speak until they were all the way out of town. He looked at his mother. Her jaw was set. Her eyes were clear, and her gaze was fixed on the road in front of them.

"Mama."

She answered absently without shifting her gaze. "What?"

"I am very proud to be your son."

Leigh nodded, squeezed his arm and then took a deep shuddering breath.

He caught movement from the corner of his eye and quickly shifted his gaze. Her feet were on the dash, her elbows resting on her knees. She took another breath, covered her face with her hands and moaned.

Breath caught in the back of Samuel's throat as her shoulders began to shake and she started to cry— harsh, ugly sobs ripped from the depths of her soul.

"Oh my God, oh my God, Stanton Lee, how am I going to live without you?"

Samuel didn't talk, and he didn't touch her. This grief was for her alone.

# *Three*

By a twist of fate, Leigh's sisters had been in the crowd. Nita Garner and Fiona Tuttle were older than her and rarely gave her a thought anymore, but that was obviously about to change.

Since Nita was divorced and Fiona widowed, they alternated their residences between the family estate in Eden and their apartments in New York City. They had been in Eden for nearly two months and, to pass the time, were redecorating parts of the mansion. On a whim, they had taken the day off for their own mini-makeovers and were just coming out of the local day spa on their way to have lunch when they'd been alerted by the honking.

"What on earth?" Fiona muttered, as she stopped and turned around.

Nita pointed at the woman in the passenger seat of the front vehicle racing up the street.

"Oh my God! Is that Leigh?"

Fiona gasped. "Yes, I believe it is."

They stopped to stare, and when they saw the two vehicles stopping in the street in front of the police station, they stayed to watch.

They hadn't seen their sister up close in years and were horrified by the condition of her hair and clothing, but when they saw the men getting out with her and realized they were her sons, they were stunned. They would not have known their own nephews if they'd passed them on the street.

They weren't the only ones who were curious about the racket, and when a crowd began gathering, they stood at the back out of curiosity. Then Leigh began talking, and when they heard the rage and the pain in her voice, and the accusations she was making, they left in a rush, frantic to get back to the family and find out what the hell was going on.

The fact that the crowd was still milling and talking when they tried to slip away set them at a disadvantage. They knew when people began calling out to them that this was going to get completely out of hand. By the time they got in Fiona's car and drove away, they were nearly in tears.

"What in the world do you suppose has happened?" Nita asked.

Fiona shook her head.

"Who knows? I haven't heard a single member of the family even say her name in years. Now this. It makes no sense," she said.

Nita pulled out her phone.

"What are you doing?" Fiona asked.

"I'm calling Blake. If he's not home, he needs to get there."

"If you're going that far, then tell him to gather the whole family. This is a mess that's not going to go away soon," Fiona said.

"Right," Nita said, and waited for Blake to pick up.

When he finally did, his voice was terse and distracted. "What do you want, Nita? I'm about to take a conference call," he snapped.

"Get home. Now. And make sure everyone else is there, too. We have a huge problem."

Blake shoved his chair back from the desk and stood abruptly.

"What are you talking about?"

"Leigh and three of her sons just drove into Eden in a rage. Someone murdered her husband today. He wrote his killer's name in the dirt before he died."

"What does that have to do with us?" Blake asked.

"The name he wrote was Wayne. Leigh just called us all out in front of Chief Clayton and half the town, and pretty much promised to send the killer to hell."

Blake gasped. "Son-of-a-holy-bitch! You cannot be serious."

"I do not make jokes about the family skeletons. Get everyone home. Fiona and I are on the way."

She hung up before Blake could argue and then dropped the phone in her purse.

They rode for a few moments in total silence, and then Fiona sighed. "I can't believe Leigh would think any of us capable of that."

Nita snorted.

"Get serious. Father already threatened to do that very thing, and Blake and Justin backed him."

"But that was ages ago, and Father is dead," Fiona said, and skidded through the turn into the open gates at the entrance to the Wayne estate.

"Uncle Jack is *not* dead, and they don't call him Mad Jack Wayne for nothing. For that matter, Blake and Justin have more or less turned into Daddy," Nita said.

"What possible reason would they have to do that after all these years? I don't believe this. There has to be an explanation. Besides, our family law firm can destroy them in court. That could just as easily be the first name of a man we don't even know."

Nita looked up at the looming three-story mansion and shifted nervously in her seat.

"Leigh was scary, wasn't she?"

Fiona sighed.

"Yes. With the scratches on her face and arms, and all that blood on her clothes, she looked like she'd been in a war, not to mention her sons were very protective of her."

"And those sons are absolutely gorgeous," Nita drawled.

Fiona gasped.

"Seriously, Nita! That sounded incestuous."

Nita glared.

"It was just a comment about their physical appearances. I didn't hit on them, for God's sake."

Fiona wheeled the car beneath the portico and

slammed on the brakes, then looked up in the rear-view mirror.

"Charles is right behind us, so I guess Blake is calling in the family as you asked," she said.

Blake's son, Charles, had just turned twenty-one and was constantly teased by the family that he drove like an old man, never speeding. He was a stocky, muscular young man, more like his mother's people than the Waynes. After he'd turned sixteen, he'd chosen to live with his father instead of his mother, who'd returned to her family home in Florida. Charles had his eye set on a future in the family conglomerate. As he pulled up beneath the portico, he noticed his aunts were still in the car beside him.

He greeted them as they all got out together.

"Hey, Aunt Fee, what's all the rush about getting home?"

"You'll find out soon enough," Fiona said, and led the way into the house.

Within minutes Justin arrived, and Blake was right behind him. As they were pulling up to park, their Uncle Jack came around the corner of the mansion with a tennis racket in one hand and a bottle of water in the other. He was the CEO of Wayne Industries and their father's youngest brother. It was the first day he'd taken off in ages, and it appeared the moment he had, they'd all left, too.

"What in the world's going on?" he yelled. "What are you all doing here? Why aren't you at work?"

"You'll find out soon enough," Blake said, and led the way into the house.

They went to the library because it was always where the family gathered, usually for festive occasions, although this was anything but.

Nita was pacing in front of the French doors that led out to the tiled terrace, and Fiona was already nursing a whiskey and Coke when they walked in.

Charles was pouring a Coke over ice for himself. He hadn't thought much about the phone call to go home until he realized his aunts were nervous. Then, when his uncles suddenly appeared, he set the drink aside and stared. He'd never seen everyone in such a state.

Blake and Justin had entered in tandem, well-dressed executive look-alikes. All the Wayne men took after their mother in looks, which was unfortunate, because their mother, God rest her soul, had been a skinny blonde with small features and a less than defined chin, while the girls took after their father—black hair, high cheekbones, pretty features and dark flashing eyes. Nita and Fiona had been coloring their hair for years, and until today, when they'd seen Leigh and that mane of wild, dark hair with only hints of gray, had all but forgotten what their natural color used to be.

Jackson Wayne strode into the library in his white tennis shirt and shorts, tall and tan and obviously angry. "Well, we're here!" he said, glaring at Blake. "What the hell's so damn important?"

Blake pointed to his sisters.

"It's their story to tell," he said.

Nita looked at Fiona.

"You tell them," she said.

Fiona nodded. "Stanton Youngblood has been murdered."

Charles frowned. "Who's Stanton Youngblood?"

Blake frowned back at his son and then realized he was within his rights to be confused. Leigh's name was rarely mentioned in this house, and Charles had been born long after all of that embarrassment had faded away.

"He's your Aunt Leigh's husband," Blake said.

Jack waved his tennis racket over his head.

"What does that have to do with us?"

Fiona sighed.

"Less than an hour ago, Leigh and three of her sons came into Eden driving all crazy on their way to the police station. When she got out she was covered in blood, her hair was all wild and tangled, and her sons were right behind her, armed to the teeth. She confronted the chief and told him that Stanton had been murdered. He supposedly scratched the name of the killer in the dirt before he died."

"Sweet Mother of God," Justin muttered. "It takes you forever to tell anything. Just get it said."

"The name he wrote was Wayne. Leigh called us out in front of the chief and the whole town. She said one of us killed her husband and when she finds out who it is, they will wish they'd never been born, or something to that effect."

Justin wiped a shaky hand across his face. Leigh

was his twin, and as loyal to her family as he was to his. Imagining her like that felt weird.

Jack was furious. "She can't just come out and accuse someone without evidence!"

"Well, there is the fact that Stanton wrote our family name in the dirt before he died," Nita drawled. "And there is that other fact that our family already threatened to kill Stanton years ago, so trying to claim innocence puts us in an awkward position. What I want to know is, what the hell's been going on in this family that I don't know about?"

Blake frowned. "Are you insinuating that one of us did this?"

Fiona looked at Nita.

Then Nita looked at Blake and shrugged.

"I wouldn't put it past us."

The silence in the library was shocking. Someone in the family had finally said aloud what they all thought about the others. The Waynes weren't known for pulling punches or playing fair. They'd been taught from an early age that success was worth whatever it took to achieve it.

Jack Wayne shoved a hand through his shock of white hair and then pointed the tennis racket at Blake.

"Call the law firm. Get Ed Beale out here ASAP. I'm going to take a shower. I'll be back down shortly."

He strode out of the library, banging the tennis racket against the chair, then the doorway, then the hall table and then up the balusters as he went upstairs, cursing every step of the way.

Everyone was looking at Blake, waiting for further directions, but he was too pissed to care. He'd had to cancel a conference call, which was probably going to nix the deal he'd been about to seal, and all because of his crazy-ass sister. He stomped out of the room to go call their law firm, leaving the remaining family members on their own.

Charles was silent. He wasn't upset about a dead man so much as wondering if this was going to become a media circus. He'd known his Uncle Justin had a twin sister and that she was persona non grata for shaming the family years ago, but now that she'd been introduced into the conversation, he was curious about her.

"So, Aunt Fiona, what does Aunt Leigh look like?"

Fiona shrugged.

"She looks like a Wayne."

Nita shook her head.

"No, she looks better. As much as I hate to admit it, she looked like some Amazon warrior standing in that street. She was always pretty, but today she was absolutely beautiful. Even covered in blood, she was magnificent, and her sons are all well over six feet tall and movie-star handsome with those wide shoulders, long legs and all that hair. I swear, they are something to behold."

"What do you mean by all that hair?" Charles asked.

"Their hair is as long as their mother's. Stanton's always was, too," Nita said.

Justin had always been self-conscious about his lack of a manly chin, and to hear that all Leigh's sons had what he coveted pissed him off.

"They probably look like a bunch of hillbillies."

Fiona rolled her eyes. "Shut up, Justin. I've heard all I want to hear about Leigh and her sons. Someone murdered her husband. That's what we need to be concerned about, and if any of you know anything about it, now's the time to speak up so we can formulate a plan."

Charles picked up his Coke and headed for the door.

"Well, it certainly wasn't me. I'm just now hearing that these people even exist, so I hardly have a reason to want one of them dead," he said, and left the room.

Justin's face flushed.

"I'm going to pretend you did not just seriously ask me if I killed a man," he snapped, and walked out behind his nephew.

Nita looked at Fiona. "Did you do it?"

Fiona rolled her eyes. "I don't know how to shoot a gun. You're the one who beats everyone at target shooting. Did you do it?"

Nita giggled. "No, silly. I wouldn't have had the faintest idea where to find him, even if I'd wanted him dead."

Fiona shrugged. "Someone's lying," she said, and walked out of the library, leaving Nita on her own.

Nita glanced at the liquor cabinet and then headed to her room. Getting sloshed would serve no purpose other than a temporary fix to this horrible news. She was getting a headache, and needed to take one of her pills and lie down.

Bowie was packed and waiting at the helipad for the incoming chopper. He'd showered after removing his work clothes and unbraided his hair to wash it. All of his brothers' hair had a curl to it, like their father's. His hair was like his mother's—straight, and so dark a black it almost looked blue, growing from a widow's peak at his forehead and hanging well below his shoulders. Because it was still wet and drying, the ocean breeze was rolling it into tangles, but he didn't care. He didn't know what strings his boss had pulled to make this happen so quickly, but he was grateful.

Word about what had happened to his father had spread quickly on the rig. He'd been working with the men on this shift off and on for about a year and considered most of them friends. One by one they'd gone looking for him to express their condolences. Bowie was touched, but the sympathy made it hard to maintain control over his emotions. It had been a little over an hour since he'd talked to Samuel, and in that short time he'd lost one of the most important people in his world.

As children, they'd always known their daddy would keep them safe at night, and as they'd grown older, Daddy had taught them how to keep themselves safe during the day. He'd seemed larger than life then, and even though Bowie had grown bigger and taller than his father, right now his world was shattered. He could only imagine how his mother was feeling.

All of a sudden Claude yelled down at him from above and then pointed to the north.

"Bowie! Incoming!"

Bowie saw the helicopter in the distance. And so it began. It was time to call Samuel.

The phone only rang twice before he heard his brother's voice.

"Hello. Bowie?"

"Yes. The chopper is landing in a few. I can't give you an exact time frame for the trip from offshore Louisiana to Eden, but I'm guessing something between two and three hours. You'll have to come to Eden to pick me up at the helipad."

"I'll call Chief Clayton to let him know. Unless I send you different info, consider yourself clear to land there," Samuel said.

"Will do," Bowie said. "How's Mama?"

"Chin up. All business. Taking care of Jesse. Ready to shed blood. Devastated. Broken."

Bowie sighed.

"Damn it. Is there anything new?"

"Well, Mama got a notion to call out her family in the middle of the street in front of the police station. Michael and Aidan and I went with her—armed, at her request. It was a show of force, but also a visual of a family united. Half the town was there. She's given the killer the only warning they'll get. She pretty much promised to take them down."

"Good. Wish I'd been there beside you guys."

"You're on the way, and that's enough. Safe flight. See you soon. I'll be waiting, and don't be surprised if Mama wants to come with me."

Bowie took a deep breath, thinking about that first moment and seeing her face.

"Whatever she wants."

"That's where we're all at right now," Samuel said.

The chopper was overhead now, and the noise was deafening.

"Gotta go. Chopper's here. See you soon."

Bowie disconnected, dropped the phone in his jacket pocket and picked up his duffel bag.

The chopper landed. Bowie tossed in his bag, then took a seat beside the pilot and put on the extra headset.

"Ready?" the pilot asked.

Bowie gave him a thumbs-up.

And then they were gone.


"Was that Bowie?" Leigh asked, as she saw Samuel slip his phone back in his pocket.

"Yes. He's on his way, Mama. He's got a chopper bringing him straight here. I'm going into Eden to pick him up in a couple or three hours."

"I want to go, too," she said.

The other brothers heard the news, and when it was finally time for Samuel to head down the mountain, the rest of them loaded up, including Jesse, and followed behind him.

Stanton's brother and sister and their spouses were

still at the house to take care of things. The men had volunteered to do the evening chores, while the women moved to the kitchen to begin making supper for everyone. Their church family had already heard the news and had begun bringing food to the house so the cooking would be minimal.

The ride down was fairly quiet. The closer Samuel got to town, the faster he drove. Bowie was the oldest and the missing piece to the family that Leigh needed.

He glanced up in the rearview mirror at Jesse, who was sitting quietly in the backseat of Samuel's pickup. Jesse seemed calm, but it was always hard to tell.

Leigh was in the front seat beside him. Her hands were in her lap, clenched into fists. There was a muscle jerking at the side of her jaw, but she had dressed up for Bowie in one of her church dresses and had tied back her hair. If it hadn't been for the raw scratches on her face and arms, no one would have guessed they were a family in crisis.

They drove into town without the fanfare they had created earlier in the day, and then turned off Main toward the hospital. There was a block of parking spaces in front of the helipad where Samuel parked to wait. Michael and Aidan pulled up beside him. They all rolled down their windows to let in the evening air.

Leigh couldn't focus. Her thoughts were filled with horror. She knew in her heart that her last day of true happiness had ended with Stanton's last breath. Yes, she would go on, because that was the burden of the living. And, yes, there would be laughter again one day, and there would be times of calm, and times she felt peaceful in her heart. But it would be the absence, the longing, the loneliness, that would be with her always. She took a deep breath and tried not to cry. She was holding on so tight for so many when all she wanted to do was weep.

The sounds of kids playing nearby and a dog barking at a passing car made everything seem so ordinary. She heard a siren somewhere off in the distance. The police were at work. An ambulance pulled out from one of the bays behind the fire station next door and took off with lights and sirens running.

Jesse leaned forward and touched Samuel's shoulder.

"Someone's hurt," he said, pointing to the ambulance as it turned a corner and drove out of sight.

"Looks like it," Samuel said.

Jesse looked at his mother.

"Mama, do you reckon I better say a prayer for them?"

Leigh turned around, reached for Jesse's hand and gave it a squeeze.

"I think that would be a fine thing for you to do, son."

And so they sat in the swiftly fading light with the breeze on their faces and aches in their hearts, listening to the sweet halting words of a gentle, broken man.

# *Four*

Talia Champion heard the news about Stanton Youngblood's murder when Erin McClune, the hospice nurse, came to check on Talia's father. Erin was a tall, pretty blonde with strong arms and a gentle heart, and she wasted no time talking about what she called "the showdown" in front of the police station.

Talia was shocked by the news, and saddened to learn that the man she'd once thought would be her father-in-law had been murdered. Then the reality of what that meant hit her. The family would gather. There would be constant turmoil until the killer was found. And knowing that family like she did, she was sure Bowie Youngblood was already on his way home.

It had been over seven years since she'd refused his marriage proposal and ended the joy in her life. It made her stomach hurt just thinking about seeing him again, even from a distance.

She glanced in on her father, grateful Erin was

there tending to him for now, and decided to take a quick break. She poured herself a glass of sweet tea and went out on the back porch for a breath of air. After his years of suffering, her father's Alzheimer's was finally taking him down. As she sat, she thought back to the night she'd learned her father's fate, and then leaned back and closed her eyes, remembering what else that realization had meant to her world.

Talia was dividing the last of her birthday cake for their dessert that night and thinking to herself that nineteen didn't feel any older than eighteen, when her daddy came in the back door from work.

"Hi, Dad," she said.

"Hi, baby, did you have a good day?" he asked, as he hung his cap and work coat on the rack by the back door.

"I guess. I did laundry all day," she said, and then smiled.

"I need to talk to you," he said.

She was wondering what she'd done that had upset him as she took a seat at the kitchen table, and then she looked at his face. There were tears in his eyes.

She started to panic; even before she asked, she knew it had to be bad. Daddy never cried.

"Daddy? What's wrong?"

He reached for her hands and held them—almost as if he needed her strength to say what had to be said.

"I'm sick, girl. And I'm not gonna get better. In fact, it's gonna get worse, much worse. I wish to God it wasn't happening. I am so sorry this burden has fallen on you."

From the moment she'd heard him say I'm sick, she'd been shaking.

"What's wrong, Daddy? What is it?"

Marshall Champion shuddered. What he was about to say was terrifying, and saying the words aloud would validate the truth of what he aleady knew.

"I have Alzheimer's disease. The doctor reckons I've had it for a couple of years now."

Talia gasped. She couldn't focus. She couldn't make a sound. She looked at her father as if seeing him for the first time and was afraid—afraid of what he would become.

He kept talking.

"I've got my pension coming from the railroad, and I'll start drawing my Social Security this year, but today was my last day at the gas station. I'm making too many mistakes. I reckon what's coming in will be enough to put me somewhere when the need comes, but I'll have to depend on you to do all that, and I'm so sorry."

Now Talia was holding on to her father's hands in desperation. Life had been so perfect. She and Bowie were finally out of high school and getting ready to go away to college together. She was already toying with the idea of being his wife for the rest of their lives. She had to talk now. *Please, God, let it make sense.*

"It's not your fault, Daddy, and of course I'll be

here for you. Don't ever apologize about this to me again, okay?"

Marshall nodded as the tears rolled down his face.

"You are a good girl, honey."

She took a deep, painful breath and smiled around the heartache.

"You are a good father. I've been blessed."

Marshall nodded, then turned her loose, patted her hands and stood up.

"Well, now, I'm glad it's been said. I'll make supper tonight, okay?"

"I've already got it going," she said. "Just go wash up. It should be done in about thirty minutes."

Her hands were shaking as she watched him leave the room. Still reeling from the news, she began grasping at straws, trying to figure out how to make this work and still have her life with Bowie. Her thoughts were chaotic as she reached for her laptop.

She'd been researching colleges, and now she began researching nursing homes instead, checking them for costs and levels of care. It didn't take long to learn that not every nursing home would even take Alzheimer's patients, and the ones that did were nowhere near Eden and unbelievably expensive. She was beginning to research nursing homes that took Medicare and Medicaid patients when she heard the shower turn off.

Her dad would be back soon, expecting supper on the table, so she shut down the laptop and got up to finish the meal.

They ate in near silence, both of them uncertain

how to have a normal conversation when the rawness
of a death sentence was still on the table.

The next few days passed slowly as the shock
wore off. Talia spent every free moment on the computer or the phone, looking into different facilities
with increasing dejection. The longer she searched,
the more obvious the answer became. With no insurance and not nearly enough money for care, she had
no other option but to take care of Daddy at home.

The night Bowie got down on his knee and offered her the world, she turned him down.

She gave up the love of her life for the man who'd
given her life.

When the dog next door began to bark, Talia
turned loose of the memory and opened her eyes.
Lengthening shadows were a precursor to nightfall.
Nearly one more day behind them. She and her father had ridden this hell together, and it was finally
coming to an end.

While the disease had destroyed her father both
physically and mentally, it had taken a toll on her,
too. She had no future, no hope for one, and no plans
for what she would do after his imminent death. She
was so used up that she just wanted to sleep until she
either woke up or she didn't.

She thought about Bowie again, letting her mind
wander to the possible scenarios where they might
meet. He would likely be here far longer than the
usual brief trip home at Christmas. During those
trips he always spent all his time at home on the

mountain, and even though she'd known he was up there, she'd never had a fear of running into him after she'd moved herself and her father into town. Bowie didn't hang out in town, and she no longer had any reason to be up on the mountain.

It hurt to think about what she'd done to him. It made her sick to her stomach, and she often lost sleep thinking about what might have been. But this news about his father's murder changed her anonymous existence. What would she do if they came face-to-face?

The gentle sway of the porch swing was soothing, and while she couldn't hear what Erin was saying to her father, she could hear the murmur of her voice. Marshall had long since lost the ability to communicate, but it didn't deter Erin. She was all about spreading light and love to all of her patients, whether they could answer her or not.

It was less than an hour away from nightfall when Talia began hearing the distinct sounds of an approaching helicopter. Living so close to the hospital, it wasn't unusual, but it always gave her the urge to say a prayer knowing someone was in crisis. She'd watched plenty of times as patients from the hospital were wheeled out to the helipad and loaded into the Life-Flight choppers.

Curious as to what was happening now, she got up and moved to the edge of the porch. It wasn't like she would be able to see who they were picking up, but she could say a prayer for safe travels.

It wasn't until the chopper began landing that she

realized it wasn't from Life-Flight. She squinted, trying to read the logo on the side, but she couldn't. Then the door opened on the passenger side, and when she saw an oil company logo, her heart skipped a beat. When two very long denim-clad legs suddenly appeared below the door, she shivered. She couldn't see his face, but she didn't have to.

*It was Bowie!*

Then she saw people getting out of several cars parked on the street in front of the hospital, and when they all began walking toward the helipad, she knew they must be some of his family. A moment later she recognized his mother, and then his brothers. She watched Bowie duck beneath the rotors as he headed toward them. The sight of him after all these years hurt her heart. Unwilling to torture herself any longer, she went back inside as his family welcomed him home.

Bowie looked out the window as the chopper was landing. He could see his brothers in their cars looking up through their windshields. Coming home because of a death in the family had been the farthest thing from his mind when he woke up this morning, and yet here he was, about to face the truth.

The moment the pilot was down he thanked him, removed the headset and got out. He stopped to grab his duffel bag, and when he turned around, his mother was coming toward him.

Leigh felt like she was in a living nightmare. She knew that was her son, but it was like looking at

Stanton. She swallowed past the knot in her throat and kept moving.

The downdraft from the rotors was whipping her hair to the point that the ribbon she'd tied it back with came undone and blew away. Now all of her hair was windblown and flying about her face, while the blast flattened her dress to her body, outlining her long legs and slender torso.

Bowie couldn't see her expression, but his heart was pounding so hard it hurt to breathe. Facing her was going to be the worst. He knew the loss of their father was an amputation of part of herself. The chopper was already in the air and leaving as Bowie dropped his duffel bag and caught her on the run, hugging her close.

"Mama, I am so sorry," he said.

Leigh shuddered as her fingers dug into his forearms.

"He's gone, Bowie. They killed him."

Tears were running down his face.

"I know, Mama, but we'll figure it out together, just like we always do, right?"

And then they were surrounded by his brothers hugging him and crying, and then hugging him some more.

Leigh stood aside and watched.

As children they'd been like a litter of playful puppies. As teenagers they had bonded in a way not all brothers can. And now they were together again, gathered in grief.

*Oh, Stanton. Look at them. Look at what we made*

*with our love. They are all I have left of you, but they*
*don't belong with me. How do I learn to live without*
*you and still take care of Jesse on my own?*

When they started home, Bowie sat in the backseat with his mother, giving Jesse the front seat beside Samuel. He took his lead from her, and when she
immediately clutched his hand as they drove away,
he held on tight, sensing her need for an anchor.

Jesse kept up a running list of questions for Samuel, which left Bowie and Leigh able to sit in comfortable silence. Once he glanced over at her and saw
tears running down her face. He undid his seat belt,
slid his arm around her shoulder and pulled her close.
She leaned into the curve of his body and closed her
eyes. She hadn't stopped crying, but it didn't matter
anymore. She wasn't crying on her own.

Halfway up the mountain Samuel turned on the
headlights, piercing the growing darkness as they
went higher and higher, until he tapped the brakes
and turned up the driveway leading to the family
home. When the headlights swept across the front
yard, it was obvious there were more people there
than when they'd left.

"Who's here?" Jesse asked.

Samuel patted his brother on the leg.

"I don't know, Jesse. How about we go see?"

"Yes," Jesse said, and got out, but then, when he
would have run toward the porch, he stopped and
went back to open the door for his mother. "Good
manners, right, Mama?"

Leigh touched his cheek.

"Yes, son, good manners always matter."

Bowie shouldered his duffel bag and steadied his mother's steps as they climbed the stairs and went inside.

The ongoing conversation instantly stopped as they walked in, and then started up again as everyone stood up to welcome Bowie home.

He saw his Aunt Polly and Uncle Thomas and their spouses, a good half-dozen cousins about his age, and the preacher from the family church. He glanced at his mother to see if she was upset by all this chaos, but she'd turned into the perfect hostess, and was quietly seeing to everyone's comfort and talking to her daughters-in-law about food.

When Leigh saw all the food from family and friends it seemed to settle her concerns. Home was familiar. Home and family were the comfort she would need tonight.

It wasn't long before she picked up her grandson, Johnny, and began carrying him around on her hip like she'd done when her own boys were small, taking comfort in being able to meet his simple needs. When Bella and Maura announced dinner was ready, Leigh went into the kitchen with Johnny to get him fed first. Leslie already had a plate filled with things he would eat. Leigh asked if she could feed him, and Leslie quickly found them a seat in the kitchen and left them on their own.

Bowie was thinking Johnny had been a baby in

arms when he'd seen him last, and now he was walking and saying words.

But while Johnny was eating well, he noticed his mother wasn't. Her plate was untouched. He understood her lack of appetite, but he didn't want her to faint on them later, so he brought her a piece of cake and sweet iced tea.

"Thank you, son, but I'm not hungry," she said.

"Just a few bites," he said, and walked away.

Later, he noticed she'd drunk the tea and some of the cake was gone, too.

He went back into the living room with a piece of pie and a refill of his own iced tea, found a chair out of the way and let the conversation roll over him while trying not to think of why they were all there.

He finished the pie and was thinking about sleeping in this house tonight without Stanton, when something he heard his Aunt Polly say stunned him.

"It's so sad," Polly said. "I heard Talia finally had to call in hospice. She's been a faithful daughter, for sure, tending to him like that on her own."

Her sister-in-law, Beth, nodded in agreement.

"You know my granny passed the same way. When they get to that point, there's nothing you can do but wait it out at their bedside."

Bowie was speechless, and then his need to know more drove him to ask, "Aunt Polly, are you by any chance talking about Talia Champion?"

She nodded. "Yes, her father's Alzheimer's has just about run its course."

"How long has he been suffering from it?" Bowie asked.

Samuel knew the moment Bowie spoke what he was thinking. They'd all wondered what had happened between Bowie and Talia, but it wasn't their way to intrude on each other's personal business.

"If I had to guess, it's probably been something like six or seven years, at least," Samuel said.

Bowie's eyes widened as he thought about what that meant, and then he got up and stepped outside onto the porch.

The night was quiet. The sky was dark—not even a sliver of moon to mark the passing of time. Lights from inside their home spilled out through the windows, painting oblong patches of yellow-gold on to the simple wooden porch.

An owl hooted from a nearby tree. Somewhere on the mountain, someone was running their hounds. He could hear the dogs yipping as they struck a trail, and he remembered nights like that with his brothers and their dad. It hurt to think all of that was gone.

Sick at heart about his father, and confused by what he'd learned about Talia, he closed his eyes. Away from home, he'd dreamed of nights like this, lying in bed with the windows up, letting in fresh air and falling to sleep so close to heaven.

He heard the door open behind him but didn't turn around. And then he felt a hand on his shoulder and heard Samuel's voice behind him.

"Are you okay?" Samuel asked.

"Talia never left Eden?"

Samuel sighed. He'd guessed this was what had driven Bowie out of the room.

"No."

"Why didn't any of you tell me?" Bowie asked.

"Tell you what, brother? We didn't know what broke you up. Why would we suddenly butt into your business? It's not our way, right?"

Bowie sighed.

"She turned down my proposal and led me to believe she just didn't want to get married. I knew I couldn't live here and see her every day, so I left."

"You never saw her after that? Not even when you were home?"

Bowie shook his head. "I did drive past their place once, but the house was empty. I thought they'd moved away."

"She moved into Eden to make it easier for her to take care of him."

Bowie took a slow, shaky breath. "Where does she live?"

"On the street behind the hospital and fire station. It's directly behind the helipad, a small white house with black trim. I think she drives a blue Ford Taurus."

Bowie listened but said nothing.

"Are you going to go see her?" Samuel asked.

"I don't know. There's too much else going on," Bowie said.

"Her father is dying, Bowie. She's alone. The least you could do is stop by to pay your respects."

Having said what he'd come to say, Samuel went back inside, leaving Bowie on his own.

In the space of one day, Bowie had learned of his father's murder and Talia's lie. It was a hell of a lot to consider.

Finally everyone had gone home, and Leigh was seeing to getting Jesse settled in his bed. Bowie could hear his mother explaining all over again why Stanton wasn't going to come tell him good-night. Taking pity on the both of them, Bowie got up and went down the hall to Jesse's room.

"Hey, brother," Bowie said. "I'm about to head to bed and wanted to come tell you good-night."

The grateful expression on Leigh's face was hard to miss.

"Thank you," she said, softly.

"Why don't you go shower first, Mama? I'll shower after you're done."

"Yes," she said, then leaned over and brushed a kiss across Jesse's forehead. "Sleep well, honey. Mama loves you."

Jesse smiled.

"Love you, too, Mama."

Leigh gave Bowie's hand a squeeze as she walked past him and out of the room.

Bowie sat down on the side of Jesse's bed. It was hard to look at him and know the injuries he'd suffered in battle had left him with the mind of a child.

"Do you want me to read to you, Jesse?"

Jesse nodded, and pointed to a stack of books on the bedside table.

Bowie saw one with a bookmark and guessed someone had been reading that one to him. He smiled when he saw it was a biography of Daniel Boone.

When Jesse was a kid in elementary school the class had studied Daniel Boone, and once he learned the famous frontiersman had been from Kentucky, he'd come home with a head full of dreams about killing bears and living in a log cabin and hunting for his own food. He played at that until he outgrew the pretend phase of youth.

"That one," Jesse said. "Daddy's reading it to me." Then his lower lip quivered as tears suddenly rolled. "Daddy can't read to me anymore. Daddy is dead, Bowie. Daddy went to heaven like my friends in the war."

Bowie patted Jesse's arm and handed him a tissue to wipe his eyes.

"I know, man. We're all sorry. We're all sad. But let's read a little bit more tonight. Daddy would want you to hear the rest of the story, right?"

"Yes. I'm ready," Jesse said, and turned over on his side and closed his eyes.

Bowie felt like crying all over again. Instead, he began to read. As he did, he heard the water come on in the bathroom down the hall and knew his mama was probably in the shower.

Bowie knew when Jesse fell asleep because his lips parted and his breathing settled. He set the book aside, taking care to mark the place, and made sure the night-light was on before he left the room.

As he was walking down the hall, he paused. His mother was still in the bathroom, and he could hear her crying. Sympathetic tears blurred his vision. His heart hurt. Without the experience of living with the love of his life, he could only imagine how she felt.

Immediately, he thought of Talia. He thought he'd gotten over her rejection of his marriage proposal—until today. At the time he'd had anger to help him move on. But if her father's illness was why she'd rejected him, she'd only had the lie and the burden of her father's future. Had she been able to move on, or had the deception and the years of tending her father broken her spirit? Samuel was right. He would have to go see her. But his first priority was to the family and finding his father's killer.

Every light in the Wayne mansion was on. From a distance it appeared there was a party going on, but inside it was far closer to a wake.

They sat around the dinner table, glaring at each other, wondering who was to blame for the current disruption of their lives. Being under suspicion for murder was horrifying. They hadn't yet been contacted or questioned by the county constable or the local police, but, as their lawyer had warned them, it was only a matter of time.

He'd ordered every one of them to make sure they had an airtight alibi for the time between eight and ten this morning, then ordered them all to keep their mouths shut in public and feign surprise that anyone had taken the accusation seriously.

The only two out of the whole family who *actually* had an airtight alibi were Nita and Fiona, because they'd been seen in and around Eden all morning. But they were part of the Wayne empire, and depending on what they knew and when they'd known it, it might not be enough to eliminate them from guilt. The sins of a family like theirs could be hard to live down.

Jack Wayne's thick shock of white hair was, at best, rarely contained into a regular style, and tonight, thanks to the number of times he'd run his fingers through it in frustration, it looked more like the fanned-out head feathers of a pissed-off cockatoo.

He was stabbing at the food on his plate and poking it into his mouth in short, jerky movements while glaring at his relatives around this table. His nephew Blake had the same expression of flaring indignation. Jack didn't know if it was all a show, or if Blake was as upset as he was. What really ticked him off was that his nieces and nephews were looking at him suspiciously, too. The only person who knew the truth wasn't ready to talk—might never tell unless forced. What was bothering him was why it had happened. There had to be more of a reason than some old threat.

They were down to dessert when there was a knock at the door. Jack looked up from his pie à la mode and waved his fork in the air.

"Who the hell comes calling unannounced at dinnertime?" he roared.

Nita laid her fork on the plate.

"It's probably Andrew. I invited him for dessert earlier. After this morning's events, I felt it best to carry on as a family, as if none of this shit was happening," she drawled, giving all of them an accusatory look before excusing herself. "I'll be right back. Have Cook send out another piece of pie and a cup of coffee, please."

Jack shoved his hand through his hair again and then rang for the cook as his niece left the room. He was in no mood for a social evening with Nita's latest lover. She'd brought this one with her from New York but at least had the good sense to put him up in a hotel in town. Last time she'd brought a lover home from one of her travels, she'd put him up in the mansion and he'd stolen some of the family silver when he left.

Nita was all but bouncing on her toes as she strode down the hall toward the foyer. She had just turned fifty, but she would never admit it. She was a sexual woman and unwilling to live her life without a man in tow. She heard the butler answer the door, then heard Andrew Bingham's voice and shivered, thinking about how good he was in bed.

He met her with a smile and a kiss midway between the foyer and the dining room.

"Um, peach pie?"

She smiled. "À la mode."

He groaned. "Dessert and you? My day just keeps getting better."

She rolled her eyes.

"Well, the day has gone to hell for us," she said, and slid a hand through the crook of his arm and led him back down the hall.

"I heard," he said. "I assume the mood is less than jovial tonight."

"You've got that right. Just don't bring it up. Brag on the coffee, instead. It's one of Uncle Jack's favorite blends."

"Will do," he said, and then they walked into the dining room.

"Good evening, all. Hope I'm not too tardy. I hear the peach pie à la mode is amazing tonight."

Fiona smiled politely.

"Do join us. Cook outdid herself tonight on the crust."

"Good evening, Andrew. You almost missed dessert," Jack muttered.

"It took a while to get through all the traffic," Andrew said, and then looked nervous, realizing that was something he shouldn't have mentioned.

"What traffic?" Blake asked.

Andrew looked at Nita and shrugged an apology. "The traffic outside your front gate."

"What the hell are you talking about?" Blake said.

"The, uh, crowd of people. I might have seen a few picket signs."

Blake abruptly stood. "There are people picketing outside our front gate?"

Nita sighed and took another spoonful of ice cream before it melted.

Afraid to take a bite of pie for fear someone would slap it out of his mouth, Andrew put his hands in his lap and nodded.

"What the fuck do the signs say?" Justin asked.

"I only got a glimpse of one. It might have said something about being above the law."

"I'm going to call Henry Clayton," Blake snapped. "What the hell good did it do putting him in office if he can't protect us?"

He stomped out of the room.

Jack threw his napkin down on the table and followed him out.

The rest of them looked at each other in disbelief.

Andrew pulled the dessert plate closer and took a big bite, just in case it was the only one he got.

# *Five*

Henry Clayton was at home soaking his foot, glad that the earlier chaos the Youngblood family caused when they came to Eden had ended without bloodshed.

He had an ingrown toenail that was killing him, and when he'd pulled off his boot tonight, he'd noticed that it was swollen and inflamed. He'd had visions of a doctor's office and needles and getting part of the toenail removed, and decided to make an antiseptic foot soak in hopes that would take care of it.

He'd been soaking his foot for the better part of an hour, and the water was just beginning to cool when his cell phone rang. He reached past the reading lamp to grab it.

"Hello?"

"Henry! This is Blake Wayne. I want this crowd of rabble removed from my property ASAP."

Henry swung his foot out of the water, splashing it everywhere as he launched himself out of the chair.

"What people? What crowd? I don't know what you're talking about."

"Well, you *should* know. You're the police chief. I don't know who all is involved, but if I find out names, they're going to be sorry."

"Okay, okay, I hear what you're saying," Henry said. "But where are they? What are they doing? Are they destroying your property or what?"

"No. They're in the street outside the front gates."

Henry's gut knotted.

"And what, exactly, are they doing?"

"Standing there. Protesting."

"But why?" Henry asked.

Blake roared, "I don't give a fuck *why*. I want them gone! Do we understand each other?"

"Yes, sir, and—"

The line went dead in Henry's ear.

He hung up, cursing his toe and the fact that he'd ever let himself become involved with the Wayne family. They were ruthless when things didn't go their way.

He dried off his foot, mopped up the splatters with the towel, and then put his uniform back on and headed out the door, pulling out his phone as he went.

Lonnie Clymer was the deputy in charge tonight, so Henry called his cell, taking care to keep this conversation off the radio. Henry was backing out of his drive as Lonnie answered.

"Hello, Chief. What's up?"

"What the hell is going on out at the Wayne estate?"

"Aw, just a few people walking around with signs about seeking justice for Stanton Youngblood."

Henry groaned. "And you let them?"

The tone of Lonnie's voice shifted to nervous.

"I didn't exactly *let* them, Chief. They just showed up. They're not making a sound. There's no shouting, no vandalism. They're just standing on public property holding signs."

"Did they get a permit to picket?" Henry asked.

"Well, no, but there's no law against picketing in Eden, so technically they're not doing anything wrong."

Henry groaned and disconnected.

Now his belly was hurting as much as his toe.

He drove without flashers or siren, because he hoped to clear them out without a fuss. He was stunned that this was happening. He couldn't remember anyone ever challenging any member of the Wayne family in any way—except Leigh, the one who got away.

He saw a small gathering, hardly more than a dozen people, standing beneath a street light as he turned the corner. They obviously saw him, but no one moved or even pretended to make a run for it. They just stood there holding their handmade signs, and as Henry got closer, he could read what they'd written on them.

*Justice for Stanton Youngblood.*

*Murder in Eden.*

*Shame to the Waynes.*

He groaned as he pulled up and got out.

"Whose idea was this?" he demanded.

They all raised their hands, refusing to let any one of them bear the blame.

Henry sighed. He wasn't about to give Blake Wayne their names, but he needed them gone.

"Look, I don't think I need to tell you that it's not a good idea to get on the wrong side of this family."

A small, clean-shaven man with dark, deep-set eyes stepped forward. He looked to be in his late forties and was holding a sign that read *First our land, then our lives.*

"They can't hurt us anymore," he said.

Henry frowned.

"Do I know you?" he asked.

"My name is German Swift. I was part of the crew that put the new roof on your house last year."

"Oh. Sorry. I wasn't home much when that was happening."

"No matter." German pointed to a skinny blond woman wearing threadbare jeans and a blouse. "This is my wife, Truva. My whole family has lived on the mountain above Eden all our lives. My wife and I were living in the home where I was born when she got cancer. About three years ago we took out a loan to pay hospital bills, but we got behind on our payments. It was all fine until recently, when the bank suddenly foreclosed and we lost our home. It had been in the family for over a hundred years. So you can threaten me all you want about what could happen from making an enemy of the Waynes and it won't matter, because we have nothing left to lose."

"Yeah, me, too," a man said.

"The bank foreclosed on *us*, too," a woman said, and started crying.

One by one, all the people there told the same sad tale.

Henry's frown deepened.

"I'm sorry, but I don't see what the bank foreclosing on you has to do with the Waynes."

"You would if you saw what's happening to our land," German said.

"Then tell me," Henry said.

"Take a drive up to the north side of the lake and check out the land they're clearing for that new resort. It all used to belong to us," German said. "Ask around up there. Find out who the biggest investors are."

"What does all of this have to do with Stanton Youngblood's murder?" Henry asked.

"Polly and Carl Cyrus. Thomas and Beth Youngblood. That's what," German said.

"I don't understand," Henry said.

"Then it's time you did your job and found out," German said. "We're going now."

And one by one, they laid the signs they'd been holding at Henry Clayton's feet and walked off into the night.

Henry sighed. This wasn't his case, and he didn't want any part of bucking the Waynes, but he'd grown up with Stanton. The man deserved his justice.

Henry began gathering up the signs and tossing them into the back of his cruiser. He would deal with them tomorrow. Tonight, he just needed to get home and take off his damn shoe.

The killer stood in the dark, watching from his bedroom window as the police car arrived and dispersed the protestors.

He was wondering who in Eden would have the guts to protest so openly, knowing full well what his family could do to them. Then he thought about the people who'd already been displaced. They had nothing left to lose, and obviously Stanton Youngblood had been their friend.

He frowned. Right now the family had only been called out by a grieving woman. But their lawyer had warned them that the authorities would soon be all over them. They would have no choice but to put up with the interrogations. The final word of a dying man was powerful.

He watched until the cop car was gone, and then stepped away from the window and sat down in the dark. He needed to think—to make sure there were no loose ends that would tie him to this. He was thoroughly disgusted that he hadn't gone to make sure Stanton was dead before he ran. He frowned, thinking back to the day's events. Even though he hadn't seen this situation coming, he still wouldn't change what he'd done.

Bowie woke up before daybreak to the sound of footsteps in the hall outside his room. He glanced at the time and frowned. It was barely five. He didn't have to look to know who it was. Every time he'd turned over in the night he'd heard movement somewhere in the house. His mother was struggling. They were all struggling. A death is one thing. A murder is another.

It had occurred to Bowie after he'd gone to bed last night to wonder if his mother could be a target, too. Until this was resolved, they needed to make sure she was never alone.

He heard a cabinet door bang and guessed she was starting her day, so he got up and dressed, then headed into the kitchen. She'd started the coffee-maker but not the food, and she wasn't anywhere in the house. He noticed the back door was ajar and walked out, guided by the light coming from the kitchen behind him.

She was sitting in the porch swing in the dark, with her hands pressed against her chest.

"Mama?"

Leigh looked up.

"Did I wake you?" she asked.

"No, ma'am. Are you in physical pain?" he asked, pointing at the way she was clutching at the blouse over her heart.

She shook her head and then patted the seat beside her.

"Come talk to me, Bowie. I need to think about something besides the hell we're living, if only for a moment."

He sat down beside her, kissed the side of her cheek and then pushed off with the toe of his boot, letting the swing rock them into daybreak.

"I'd talk about the scenery, but it's too dark to see it," he said.

"I couldn't lay in that bed alone," she said, and then started to cry.

Bowie groaned inwardly as tears welled.

"I can't begin to know what you're feeling, Mama. I grieve from the standpoint of a son, but I know he was your life and you were his. We love you so much. Just hang on to that fact while you find a new way to be in this world."

Leigh leaned her head against his shoulder for a moment before she could gather herself to speak.

"When did you get so smart?" she asked, and then felt him shrug.

"She didn't die, but when I lost Talia, I didn't know how to be here without her. I had to find new footing. It's why I left."

Leigh wiped her eyes and blew her nose as her mother instinct kicked in. This was something they'd all known, but since he'd never talked of it to them, they'd respected that choice. This opened the door.

"What happened, son? We wondered. All of us did. We were so sad for your heartache, but as sorry as we were to see you go, we understood."

"I asked her to marry me. She said no without an explanation. It was a shock, and it broke my heart. I grew up and got over it."

Leigh turned to him then, and even though it was dark, she saw enough—from the set of his jaw to the way he looked everywhere but at her—to know that wasn't true.

"Did you really get over it?" she asked.

"I thought so. Until I heard Aunt Polly talking about Talia and her dad."

"Are you going to go see her?"

Bowie was silent for a few moments.

"I think I have to," he finally said.

"What if you find out you still care for her?"

"It won't matter, not if she's moved on," he said.

"And if she didn't forget?"

"I'm not sure."

Leigh patted his hand.

"If you love someone with all your heart and you walk away, your life will never be as it was meant to be. You will always be unhappy. You will never be rich enough or successful enough to fill that void. Love matters, Bowie. It matters most of all."

He heard, but he didn't have the composure to comment.

His mother must have sensed his dilemma, because she changed the subject and kept talking.

"I'll need a lot of groceries in the next couple of days," she said. "If I make a list, will you go shopping for me? I don't want to go to Eden and face the comments."

"I'll do anything you need of me, Mama. It's why I'm here."

"Okay, then I also need one more favor."

"Absolutely. What do you want?"

"I want you to go to Talia's house, knock on her door and follow your heart to wherever it leads you.

But don't do this for me. Do it for yourself and for her."

The skin crawled on the back of Bowie's neck. It had taken him so long to bury that pain, but he knew she was right.

"I'll go," he said.

"Good," Leigh said, and then pointed toward the east. "Look, the sky is getting lighter. It will be daylight soon. Jesse will do the chores later if you'll go with him to make sure he doesn't hurt himself."

"Sure thing," Bowie said, and then thought about what would happen here when he was gone. "Can you take care of Jesse by yourself?"

Leigh tossed her head and then stood abruptly.

"I can do anything I have to. God gave Jesse to me twice. Once when he was born, and once when He saved Jesse's life. I've thought all night about this very thing, and I've come to a conclusion that gives me ease. God knew I was going to lose Stanton. That's why Jesse came home from the war this way. He knew I would need purpose or I would die from a broken heart. As long as I have Jesse, I have purpose. It isn't what I would have wanted, but it's what I have been given. I'm going to start breakfast. Biscuits or pancakes?"

"Biscuits, please. No one makes biscuits as good as you do."

Leigh ran her fingers through the thick length of Bowie's hair.

"I love you with all my heart," she said softly, and went inside, leaving Bowie alone in the swing.

\* \* \*

Talia's sleep was restless. She slept on a cot beside her father's bed, and every moan he made, every creak of the bed springs, had her up on her feet within seconds.

Before hospice stepped in, she'd been in constant fear that he would roll out of bed. Hospice had helped her get a hospital bed, and then she'd moved him from the bedroom at the back of the house to the living room up front. Now it was easier for her to care for him, and cook and do laundry, as well. And, with the hospital bed, she no longer had to be afraid he would fall.

Still, every sound he made had her up and checking to be sure he wasn't choking, or if she needed to change his diaper before he messed up his bed. Even though he was a shadow of his former self, he was still heavy. She didn't know how much longer she could hold on, and seeing Bowie after all these years had been a bitter reminder of what she'd lost.

After tossing and turning for hours, she got up and dressed, ran a brush through her hair and then tied it back out of her face. Her feet were dragging when she went to start the coffee. She needed to eat, but the thought of food turned her stomach, so she started the coffee and then went to check on Marshall.

His chest was barely moving, but his eyelids were fluttering. She wondered what he was seeing. Mama, she hoped, or maybe angels.

Daddy was dying.

She didn't want him to be afraid.

* * *

It was after ten when Bowie drove into Eden in Stanton's truck. It smelled like Stanton's aftershave, and there were bits of paper with notes he had written to himself all over the seat. Bowie picked them up and dropped them into the console without reading them. It was hard enough to accept he was gone without all the tangible bits and pieces he'd left behind.

Bowie had his mother's list in his pocket, but his thoughts were on Talia. If he was honest with himself, he was afraid—afraid to find out that her father's illness had nothing to do with her telling him no.

The supermarket was busy, and because he didn't know the layout of the store, it took longer than he'd intended to get everything. More than once someone stopped him to ask about his mother and send their condolences. After the sixth or seventh time he got cornered in an aisle, he understood his mother's reluctance to do this herself.

When he finished, he added a six-pack of root beer for Jesse and headed for the checkout lane with the shortest line to wait his turn. By the time he got checked out, his stomach was in knots. Going to see Talia was scary. It might put their past to rest or stir up things best left unsaid. It was all an unknown, and Bowie didn't like feeling uncertain.

He loaded all the sacks into the backseat of his dad's truck, and then got in and drove out of the parking lot. His heart was thumping all the way through town as the knot in his belly grew tighter. When he finally found the house he pulled in behind a blue Ford Taurus and parked.

His throat was dry. His hands were sweating. He wasn't sure how he felt emotionally, but it wasn't a comfortable feeling. Still, waiting wasn't going to make things any easier, so he got out and headed for the front door.

Talia was nearly finished bathing her father when she heard a knock at the door. She frowned as she glanced at the time. Erin was really early this morning. Maybe her schedule had changed. She dropped the washcloth back in the basin and drew the sheet up to her father's waist, then pulled the guardrail back up.

"Someone is at the door, Dad. I'll be right back."

She tucked a stray lock of hair behind her ear and smoothed her hand down the front of her shirt. It was wet in places, faded and old, but it served the purpose. She opened the door and then froze.

It wasn't Erin.

It was only a few seconds, but in the space of time it took for her and Bowie to meet each other's gazes, every moment of their past flashed before her eyes.

Then he spoke, and the shock ended.

"May I come in?" he asked.

She took a deep breath as the sound of his voice rolled through her. The urge to strip where she stood and lie down beneath him was so strong it made her ache.

"I'm bathing my father."

"I'll wait somewhere until you've finished…if you'll let me in."

She told herself to stay cool, stay calm, and then she stepped aside.

"If you insist," she said. "As you can see, Dad's in the living room, so feel free to have a seat on the sofa. I can hear you from there."

Bowie didn't know what he'd expected to see, but it wasn't Marshall Champion's frail, emaciated body laid out in that bed like a corpse. But instead of sitting down, he followed her back to the bed.

Talia was shaking, uncertain what to do. If she picked up the washcloth again he would see her trembling. She didn't want him to know he still had the power to touch her like that, so she grabbed the guardrail instead before she faced him across the bed.

"I am so sorry about your father," she said. "I was horrified to hear what happened. Please, give Leigh and your family my condolences. I would have taken food over, but as you can see, my time is not my own."

"Thank you, I will," Bowie said, unnerved by being in her presence.

It was impossible to ignore the changes in her appearance. Her hair was pulled back at the nape of her neck, and the lack of makeup made her look even younger than he knew she was, but the dark circles under her eyes and the huge weight loss were evidence of how hard this was on her. But he'd come to ask her a question, and he wasn't leaving until he got it said. Unconsciously, he leaned forward, as if shortening the distance between them would make her answer easier to bear.

"I just heard about your father."

It was all she could do to stand her ground when she wanted to run.

*Sweet Jesus, my worst nightmare is coming true. He's going to ask.*

Her knee-jerk reaction was to occupy herself with work so she wouldn't have to think, so she put down the guardrail and resumed her father's bath. She folded the sheet back so she had access to his right leg and fished the washcloth out of the water.

"Talia?"

"What?" she said, as she wrung out the excess water and began wiping the soap off her father's skin.

"When was your father diagnosed with Alzheimer's?"

"Years ago," she muttered, and rinsed the washcloth, then wiped all the way down to his foot.

"How *many* years?" Bowie asked.

She dried him, then pulled the sheet back over his leg.

"Oh, I don't know…maybe seven or so, but at this point it hardly matters."

Bowie had tried to fool himself, tried to tell himself he was over her—over all this—until now. Why did he feel like his whole future hinged on how she answered his next question?

"Is this why you wouldn't marry me?"

The question felt like a death blow. Without thinking, she put a hand to her heart, expecting to feel a mortal wound. Instead, all she did was leave a wet handprint on the front of her shirt.

Bowie knew he made her nervous. He also knew she wouldn't be afraid of him. He'd never done anything to her but love her, so it had to be because she was about to be caught in the lie that had ended them.

"What does it matter?" she finally said, and, to her credit, faced him, even lifting her chin as if she expected a blow.

"Matter? What does it matter?" he asked, and then circled the bed and took her by the shoulders. "I thought you didn't love me."

A soft moan slipped out of her mouth, the punctuation to an answer she couldn't voice as she dropped her head and closed her eyes.

"No. You don't get a pass on this," he said, gripping her shoulders tightly. The moment he did, he was shocked that he could so easily feel her bones. "I'm sorry. I'm so sorry. Did I hurt you? God, please tell me that didn't hurt," he whispered, and pulled her into his arms.

The shock of being held was second only to the fact that she was in Bowie Youngblood's arms. It was too much too soon. She didn't have time to block the flood of emotions and regrets.

One sob bubbled up, and the next one choked her. Before she could stop herself, she was crying.

Bowie had his answer, and it broke his heart. *She* broke his heart. All the time he'd wasted being angry and feeling used, he should have been at her side.

# Six

"You should have told me," Bowie said. "We could have figured some—"

Talia shoved him away. Her face was still streaked with tears, and her words came out in choked, angry sobs.

"We? What newlyweds get married like this? I would have had no time for you. There would not have been an 'us' or college. It would have been Dad and me, and you in a separate space in my head and heart."

"I just thought…there are places where…"

Again Talia reacted in anger.

"Stop talking!" she said, and then took the tail of her blouse and wiped the tears off her face.

When she did, he saw the hint of ribs and her too-tiny waist, and shut the hell up. It was blatantly obvious how ignorant he was of this disease and what she had endured.

She strode to the other side of the bed and finished bathing her father without looking Bowie's way again.

Afraid she would kick him out, he went over to the sofa and sat down, watching the gentle way she tended her father's body. When she began to roll him toward her so she could wash his back, Bowie jumped up and did it for her.

Too tired to argue and aware it would be to her father's detriment not to accept, she finished his bath, then began rubbing lotion all over his skin.

"Tell me when you're ready and I'll ease him back down," Bowie said.

"You can do it now," she said, and then proceeded to put lotion on the rest of his body, diaper him and cover him back up.

As she began gathering up the bath things, Bowie picked up the basin of water.

"Where do I pour this?"

"Bathroom is down the hall, first door on the left. Just pour it in the tub."

"Okay," he said, and started down the hall.

When he came back, she was gone. He followed the sounds of movement into the kitchen and then into the laundry room, where she was putting all the bath things and the dirty sheets she must have taken off the bed earlier into the washer.

"Is there anything else I can help you do?" he asked.

"I'm sorry I yelled at you," she said.

He hurt for the tremble in her voice. He'd caused it, and it made him miserable.

"It's okay. I didn't know what I was talking about. I've been known to do that. I'm the one who's sorry for thinking I could have fixed this for us."

She shut the lid on the washing machine, and then took a deep breath and looked up. She needed to be looking at him when she said this. He deserved that much.

"I already knew before you proposed that I was his only option. I had priced available long-term care facilities for Alzheimer's patients, only to discover they began at five thousand dollars a month. Then I looked into regular nursing homes. Most of them won't take Alzheimer's patients because they require too much care, and the ones who do are just as expensive as the others. They don't all take Medicare, and I couldn't afford to make up the difference at the ones that did. His retirement money wasn't enough, not even with his Social Security check added in. There were some nursing homes that would have taken someone like Dad and settled for whatever Medicare paid, but they looked like something from a horror movie. I wouldn't house a dog there, let alone my father. All I knew was that what I wanted had to take a backseat to what he needed. I was heartsick and didn't know what to do."

"And then I asked you to marry me," Bowie said.

"I panicked. I was angry at fate and sick at heart that I was going to lose you. I just said no, and then you were gone, and I told myself it was for the best."

Bowie didn't know what to say, but he knew how

he was feeling, and he needed to put some space between them before he said too much.

"I want to stay and talk more, but I have a carload of groceries for Mama, so I need to get back."

Talia stifled a groan. Was this where he told her it was too late? Her heart began to hammer. God, was this going to hurt as much as it had last time?

"I understand. Seven years is a long time. I'm glad you came by, though. I'm glad you understand, and I hope you don't hold it against me anymore."

Bowie frowned.

Was she trying to get rid of him? Did this mean it was too late for them to try again? He wasn't giving up on her yet.

"What would you say if I said I wanted to see you again?" he asked.

Talia's heart skipped a beat. "I would ask you why?"

"Because I do."

"That's not an answer, Bowie."

He was afraid to say what he was feeling, but when he saw the tears in her eyes, he took a chance that it wasn't too late and blurted out what was in his heart.

"I want back what we lost," he said.

Talia gasped, and then her gasp turned into a sob as she walked into his arms.

When Bowie pulled her close, the seven years apart disappeared. He knew the curves of her body, the catch of her breath and what turned her on. This was what had been missing from his life. This was why settling down had never mattered to him, and why he'd taken any job, wherever it was, without caring how far he had to travel.

He kissed the top of her head, then tilted her chin and brushed his mouth across her lips so sensuously that she turned to follow the motion, desperate not to lose the connection. The second kiss was a deliberate onslaught, filled with hunger for what they'd lost.

Talia leaned into him, remembering what it felt like when he was inside her, remembering how crazy they'd been making love. Seven long years of sadness and misery, and all it took to break the nightmare was his mouth on her lips.

The kiss lasted until they were both aching for more.

When Bowie finally let go, Talia was shaking.

"This happened so many times in my dreams," she said.

He took her hand and pressed it against his heart.

"Can you feel that? My heart is racing. I came home to such heartache, only to find a joy I thought was lost."

Before he could say more, her father let out a moan.

Talia flew out of Bowie's arms and headed to the living room on the run. Bowie was right behind her.

She leaned over the bed to check her father's pulse. It was the same, slow and faint. Relief settled her jumpy nerves as she leaned down to straighten his covers.

"He does this sometimes. Erin says he's not in pain. It just happens," she said.

"Who's Erin?" Bowie asked.

"His hospice nurse. She'll be here any time."

Bowie took that as his cue to leave.

"I know your time isn't your own, but may I have your phone number? As you can imagine, stuff is a mess at home right now, so I don't know how often I can get back here, but I have to be able to at least hear your voice."

Tears rolled down Talia's face as she gave him the number.

Bowie could hardly bear to leave her and was troubled by her tears.

"Talia, sweetheart, why are you crying?"

She felt her cheeks, her brown eyes widening in surprise when she discovered the tears.

"I didn't know I was," she said, and swiped her hands across her face.

"Where's your phone?" he asked.

She pulled it out of her hip pocket.

"Put my number in your contacts," he said. "And will you promise to call me anytime, for any reason?"

Tears rolled again.

Bowie couldn't bear to see her like this and once more took her in his arms.

"Baby…why?" he asked.

"I never had any backup before. I guess I'm just overwhelmed."

That hurt. He hadn't meant to, but the happiness she'd sacrificed had led to him abandoning her at her darkest time. All he'd known was that she'd shot down his dreams. There weren't enough years left in their lives to make up for what she'd suffered alone.

"We're both up to our necks with grief. Just know that whenever this is behind us, I'll still be here," he said.

Someone knocked at the door.

"That will be Erin," Talia said.

"I'll let her in on my way out," Bowie said, and then leaned in for one last kiss. Her lips were soft and a little damp from recent tears. It felt like he was walking away just as he'd found her again. He so didn't want to leave, but the nurse was at the door and the groceries were in the truck. "I'll call," he said, but Talia wouldn't let go.

"What?" he said.

"Thank you," she said.

He frowned. "For what?"

Her fingers tightened around his wrist.

"I've loved you forever, Bowie. Even when you were gone. Thank you for still caring enough to do this again."

"I guess I buried the memories so far down I forgot that caring was there. This feels damn good to me, too," he said softly.

It was the second round of knocking that ended the moment.

"Damn it," he muttered, and headed for the door.

The tall blonde looked startled to see a man in the house.

"I'm just leaving," Bowie said, then held out a hand. "I'm Bowie Youngblood."

"Erin McClune." She shook his hand.

"Nice to meet you," Bowie said, then looked back at Talia. "Remember what I said…call me anytime."

She nodded, and then he was gone.

Erin shut the door behind her and then stood there a moment with her hands on her hips.

"Spill it," she said.

Talia sighed.

"The love of my life. I didn't think I'd ever see him again." Tears were rolling again, but she didn't care. "He came back."

Erin sighed. "Come talk to me while I check on your dad, and I'll try not to hate your guts that he's already taken."

Talia followed her to the bed and then brushed her hand across her father's forehead. He didn't respond to the touch.

She looked at Erin. "He moaned a few minutes ago."

Erin was taking his pulse. When she finished, she made notes on his chart.

"He's getting weaker, isn't he?" Talia whispered.

Erin nodded.

Talia looked at her father and then leaned down and whispered in his ear, "Dad, you don't have to worry that I'll be alone anymore. Bowie came back for me."

The wind had come up while Bowie was at Talia's house. He could see storm clouds building over the mountain as he drove through Eden and knew it would be raining soon.

He stopped off at the police precinct to talk to Chief Clayton. His dad and Clayton had gone to school together, and despite the gossip about Clayton being in the Wayne family's pocket, it didn't deter him from believing the chief would be fair. It wouldn't take long to get an update, and he wanted to take any news home to his mother.

The receptionist looked up as Bowie entered. She knew before he got to her desk what he wanted, because she recognized him as one of Leigh Youngblood's sons.

"Is Chief Clayton in his office?" Bowie asked.

"Yes, but he was on a conference call. I'll have to check and see if he's finished. One moment, please."

Bowie watched her walk out of the lobby, heard a door open and close down the hall, and then the murmur of voices. She hadn't asked for his name, so he assumed she recognized him.

She came back a few moments later and stopped in the doorway.

"Chief Clayton will see you now. Follow me." Then she led the way to the chief's office and opened the door.

"Thank you," Bowie said, and walked in.

Henry Clayton was already on his feet and coming forward with his hand outstretched.

"Bowie, it's good to see you, though I'm sorry it's under these circumstances. It's a little bit disconcerting. You look so much like Stanton, it's eerie."

"So they tell me," Bowie said, and grasped the chief's hand.

"Take a seat," Clayton said.

Bowie eased into the chair across from the chief's desk, looked up at the framed photo of Clayton and Mad Jack Wayne, then shifted focus and leaned forward, his hands resting on his knees.

"I'll get right to it," Bowie said. "Our family is wondering where the investigation into our father's murder stands?"

Clayton flushed. He felt the heat rushing up his neck and on to his cheeks, and knew how that was going to read.

"Well, I can't really say, Bowie, because it's not my case. My authority and responsibilities end at the city limits of Eden, so—"

"But since the suspects live here, you surely know the status of the interrogations, right?"

"Yes, I would be kept informed of that, but to my knowledge they haven't begun that part of—"

The shock of hearing that sent Bowie to his feet. He was so angry, it was all he could do to keep from shouting.

"A dying man spent his last seconds leaving the family name of the man who killed him. That was a day ago, and no one's even bothered to talk to them?"

Clayton sighed.

"I'm really sorry, Bowie. I wish I had better news for you, but—"

"Save it," Bowie said. "Sorry to bother you."

He was gone before Clayton could get out of his

chair. He looked up at his framed credentials and then at the picture of him standing beside Mad Jack Wayne at a ribbon-cutting ceremony for the new jail, then picked up the phone and called Constable Riordan's private number.

Riordan answered on the second ring.

"Riordan, this is Henry Clayton. I have some information for you regarding the Youngblood murder."

"Anything you can tell me would be appreciated," Riordan said.

"Bowie Youngblood was just here and hot under the collar because no one had interviewed any of the Wayne family. That's an FYI, in case you get a call. Also, I got a call from Blake Wayne last night, demanding I run off the people who were picketing outside their property. When I got there, it turned out to be about a dozen or so people who'd lost their homes to that investment group that's putting up a resort down by the lake. I didn't get the connection, but there must be one. You should look into who the investors actually were. They said they all lost their homes to sudden bank foreclosures. I asked them what that had to do with Stanton's murder, and one man said, and I quote, 'Polly and Carl Cyrus. Thomas and Beth Youngblood.'"

"I don't get it," Riordan said.

"Well, just so you know, Polly Cyrus and Thomas Youngblood are Stanton's siblings. You might talk to them and see what they have to say. It could lead to some kind of motive."

"Okay, thanks for the info *and* for the heads-up," Riordan said.

"Hope it helps," Henry said. "I grew up with Stanton. He was a good man."

While Bowie was inside the police precinct, the wind had risen to storm-like proportions, matching the tumult of his own rage. He was nearing the city limits when he saw the looming roof of the Wayne estate off to the right, a visual reminder of the hold the family had on this town. The sight of his mother's grief-stricken face flashed before him, and on impulse he turned off the main road and drove down the street leading to the main gates.

He'd seen the three-story mansion many times but had never been able to picture his mother growing up there. He didn't intend to stop, but as he drove past, he saw a man and two women standing beneath the portico at the far end of the driveway, and he hit the brakes. He put the truck in Park and leaped out, heading toward the open gates with a long, steady stride. The wind tore through his hair and flattened his shirt against his torso.

He stopped only inches away from the property line and waited for the moment when they saw him, and when they did, he pulled the tie from his hair so they'd know who he belonged to, braced himself against the rising wind and stared at them in a gesture of defiance. A cold rage swept through him. His father was gone, and they were going about their business, seemingly without concern that one of their own was a murderer.

He watched the man take a few steps forward, and then both women grabbed him and pulled him back.

The man was shouting now, but the wind carried away the words. While Bowie couldn't hear what he was saying, from the way the man was behaving, he guessed it was a challenge.

Bowie sent back his own challenge, raising his arms, holding them level with his shoulders, as if to say, "Here I am. Come and get me."

That sent the man into a rage. He began waving his arms as both women grabbed him again and held him back.

Bowie hadn't accomplished anything, but he felt better for confronting the monsters, even in such a small way. Then he turned his back to the house with his arms still outspread while the wind tore through his hair. He stood there long enough for them to get the point, that while they'd shot his father in the back, he was making himself vulnerable to prove they didn't scare him.

After a few moments he dropped his arms, got back in the truck and drove away.

Justin knew the moment he saw the man at the gate and that long hair blowing in the wind that he was one of Leigh's sons. It pissed him off that he was there at all, and made him even angrier that his presence felt like a threat.

Justin shouted at him, and when the man didn't

even budge, he began shouting louder. When the man suddenly turned his back and stood there in an obvious reference to his father being shot in the back, Justin lost it. He was screaming curses, damning every Youngblood on the mountain and wishing them to hell, when the man left as abruptly as he'd appeared.

Nita and Fiona were vacillating between letting Justin make a fool of himself, and slapping some sense into him and dragging him inside. But they were saved the trouble of making the decision when Uncle Jack came storming out the front door in a rage. He grabbed Justin by the arm and yanked him around to face him.

Spittle was running from the corner of Justin's mouth, and he was so out of control it was unsettling. There was a moment when Jack hesitated to confront him, but then he remembered that he was the one in charge.

"There's a storm coming. Shut the fuck up and get inside. Now!"

Justin pointed up the drive.

"You don't fucking tell me what to do. You didn't see him! You didn't see what he did!" he screamed.

Jack slapped him across the face.

The shock of the blow sent Justin staggering backward.

"Don't ever raise your voice to me again," Jack said softly, then pointed to the door. "Get inside." Then he pointed at his nieces. "Whatever you're doing, do it somewhere else," he said, and followed Justin toward the house.

Nita and Fiona hurried inside before the rain began to fall, still pissed at being treated like children.

"Damn him," Fiona huffed. "*We* didn't do anything."

Nita shrugged. "With this family, we're always guilty by association." She paused a moment and then added, "That was one of Leigh's sons, wasn't it?"

"Most likely," Fiona said.

"What did you think when you saw him there?" Nita asked.

Fiona shrugged. "I don't know, maybe that he was curious."

Nita shook her head.

"No, that wasn't curiosity. He was standing like he was ready to fight, and then he raised his arms like he was about to be nailed to a cross. Damn it, he gave me the creeps. He might not have said anything, but he called us out again just like Leigh did. Those people don't mess around. If you piss one of them off, you get the whole nest in a stir."

Fiona stared at her sister like she'd suddenly grown horns.

"Piss them off? That's hardly the way I would describe murder."

Nita flushed. "Well, it wasn't me," she muttered.

"So you keep saying," Fiona said, and headed up the stairs to her suite.

Nita stood in the foyer, eyeing the oh-so-familiar elegance, and shuddered. She had a feeling in her gut that this was all going to come undone.

# *Seven*

Bowie drove home on autopilot.

He'd gone from elation at seeing Talia to unadulterated rage. He felt sick and completely helpless. His father was on a slab in the morgue, and no one had made a move to interview a single member of the guilty family.

He needed to talk to the county constable before he got home. Maybe things weren't as bad as they seemed. He pulled over long enough to Google the number, and as soon as his call was answered, he resumed driving.

"Constable's office. How may I direct your call?"

"Constable Riordan, please. This is Bowie Young-blood."

"One moment," the operator said, and put him on hold.

While he was waiting for the constable to come on the line, the first raindrops hit the windshield, splattering on the dusty glass, then turning into a muddy trickle that reminded him of Talia's tears. The wind picked up, whipping the tops of the trees and sending leaves flying into the air. He turned on the windshield wipers and tightened his grip on the wheel as Riordan's voice came over the line.

"Bowie, I see you made it home."

"Yes, sir."

"What can I do for you?" Riordan asked.

Bowie wasn't about to waste time on polite conversation.

"I guess what I need to know is, why hasn't anyone interrogated the Wayne family?"

Riordan wasn't going to tell him that Chief Clayton had called him, or that he'd already heard from the governor, warning him to tread lightly in the case. Even so, he had no intention of easing up on anything. He just had to be careful how he went about it.

"I wanted to gather every bit of information I could get from the autopsy and ballistic reports before I began, because we don't really have a motive. And since there are obviously a number of possible suspects, I need to go in prepared. We had the coroner expedite the autopsy because of the delicacy of the situation."

It was a slap in the face to the whole Youngblood family, and the anger in Bowie's voice reflected that.

"There's nothing delicate about my father's murder. He gave you the name of the guilty family, and it is your damn job to *find* the motive. I object to the fact that special consideration is being taken just to protect the rich and powerful."

"No, that's not what—"

Bowie quickly interrupted. "Yes, it is. Give me the respect of admitting that much, because we both know the truth."

Riordan sighed, and Bowie took that as a yes.

"When can our family get a copy of the autopsy?" Bowie asked.

"I don't even have a copy myself, and giving out a victim's information is—"

"Your 'victim' is my father. He belongs to our family, and everything pertaining to his murder is our business. If I get even a hint that there's going to be a cover-up, I will take this story to every news outlet in the nation. The Waynes are big shots, and big shots in trouble are always good for ratings."

Riordan's stomach rolled.

"There's no need to get defensive, Bowie."

"You misunderstand me, Constable. This isn't defense, it's offense, and you'll be in the spotlight right along with them. If you aren't physically at the Wayne estate tomorrow, ready to interrogate every last one of them, autopsy or no autopsy, I won't give you a second chance. I work for powerful people, too."

"It is against the law to threaten the office of the constable of this county, and you don't want—"

"I didn't threaten you at all," Bowie snapped. "I informed you of my intentions. It wasn't a warning. I thought I was doing you a favor in giving you a heads-up. There will be representatives from our family watching to see if you show up there tomorrow. If you don't, then we will assume other people besides you are running the show and act accordingly. I'll be in touch," Bowie said, and disconnected.

The rain was coming down so hard now that it sounded like hailstones against the cab. Bowie turned the windshield wipers on to the highest speed and put his phone in the console. That call had been as futile as his appearance at the Wayne estate. He'd accomplished nothing, but at least all parties involved now knew where the Youngblood family stood.

Riordan cursed beneath his breath. The call was nothing he hadn't expected, but all it had done was increase the pressure on him. Still, Youngblood was right. If this had been any other case, he would have been talking to the guilty family the same day the body was discovered. Instead, they'd had plenty of time to prepare their statements and get everyone's alibis straight. It had been an unforgivable move on his part, but it was too late to take it back.

"Damn it," he muttered. He glanced at the clock and realized he'd missed lunch, but he'd lost his appetite. He was retiring at the end of the year. Why in hell couldn't all this have happened after he was gone?

Bowie had his emotions under control by the time he arrived. Instead of parking in his usual place, he drove to the back of the house and up to the wide covered porch, parking right beside the steps.

His mother had obviously been watching for him, because she was wearing a waterproof poncho when she came out to help carry in the groceries.

"Stay on the porch, Mama. I'll bring the sacks to you," he said as he got out, then opened up the door to the backseat and began grabbing bags and handing them over.

Jesse came outside smiling and talking about the rain. Bowie handed a heavy sack off to him and sent him back inside with it. By the time they'd carried in the last of the groceries, Bowie was soaked to the skin, but he didn't care. The rain was emotionally cleansing. He moved the truck away from the steps, then ran up onto the back porch and began stripping down to his briefs so he wouldn't track water through the house.

Leigh came outside carrying a towel and a dry pair of pants.

"Your Aunt Polly is inside. I don't want you to give her a heart attack parading yourself through the house."

He grinned. "Thanks."

She eyed the smile. "You talked to Talia."

He nodded as he began toweling the rain from his body.

When he didn't elaborate, Leigh poked a finger against his chest.

"And...?"

He paused.

"And it was good… *We're* good."

Talia's eyes welled.

"Good for you, son. Life is too short to waste."
Then she went back inside, leaving him to dry off
and get dressed.

He could hear the women talking in the living
room as he walked in the back door. He slipped
through the kitchen and down the hall to his bedroom
without them knowing he was there. By the time he
got back to the front of the house, he'd plaited his
wet hair into one long braid and was wearing clean,
dry clothes. He needed to tell his mother what he'd
found out, and talk to his brothers about being in
Eden tomorrow morning to see if Constable Riordan showed.

He was walking into the living room when he
glanced out the front window and saw a truck coming toward the house.

Leigh walked up behind him and put a hand on
his back.

"It's Samuel. He texted me he was coming."

Bowie frowned. "It must be important to get him
out in weather like this. Is something wrong?"

"He came to take Polly home. Your Uncle Carl
twisted his ankle today and isn't able to drive."

"Oh, sorry about Uncle Carl, but I'm glad Samuel is here. I need to talk to the both of you before
he leaves."

Leigh rushed to open the front door as Samuel
came running through the rain. He leaped up onto
the porch, thankful to be out of the rain, and began

taking off his rain gear, leaving it beside the door before going inside.

"Hi, Mama," Samuel said, as he gave her a kiss on the cheek.

"Hi, honey. Did you have any trouble getting here?"

"No. The roads were clear. Other than the heavy rain, it's all okay." Then he glanced at Bowie and saw his wet hair. "You've been out?"

"In town. We need to talk," Bowie said.

"Come into the kitchen," Leigh said. "Polly is making coffee and cutting a chocolate pie."

They followed their mother into the kitchen and greeted their Aunt Polly with a hug.

"Can we help?" Bowie asked.

"I've got it," Polly said. "You boys take a seat."

They grinned at each other. For as long as the older generation lived, they were always going to be "the boys."

Once the pie and coffee were served and everyone was at the table, Bowie began telling them what he'd learned, what he'd done, and why he and his brothers needed to be at the Wayne estate tomorrow morning.

Leigh was unusually silent, but Bowie could tell something was running through her mind.

"I suspect Uncle Jack is pulling in favors," she finally said. "They'll try to buy their way out of the whole thing."

"It won't matter," Bowie said. "I've already warned Riordan that I'll give the whole story to the press. Rich people in trouble are prime news."

Leigh looked surprised, then nodded approvingly.

"Yes, that would stir things up," she said. "Good move."

"I wonder if they got anything from the ballistics report?" Samuel asked.

Bowie frowned. "What do you know about a ballistics report?"

"I found the shooter's shell casing at the scene. One of the crime scene investigators took it into evidence."

"Could you tell what caliber the gun was?" Bowie asked.

"It was a rifle," Leigh said. "I heard it. Nothing else sounds like a rifle shot."

Samuel frowned. "Looked like a 30-30 casing to me."

"If we knew that for sure, Michael could put his hacker skills to good use and see if any weapons of that caliber are registered to the Waynes."

"Dad had one once," Leigh said. "All of us kids got together and gave it to him for Christmas one year."

"Something to pass on," Bowie said.

Polly had been listening to the conversation, but she knew something the boys did not. She reached for a tissue in her pocket and dabbed at a fresh set of tears.

"Carl thinks it might have something to do with Stanton and Leigh paying off our bank loan, and Thomas and Beth's loan, too."

Bowie frowned. "What do you mean, Aunt Polly?"

"The bank began finding reasons to foreclose on all the outstanding loans down where we live. At least a half-dozen of our nearest neighbors lost their homes. We would have, too, if it hadn't been for your parents."

"Why?" Bowie asked.

"There's a big consortium gathering land to build a resort on the north side of the lake. Tourist business has really picked up in the last four or five years," Samuel said.

"Let me guess. The Waynes are investors in the resort?" Bowie asked.

Polly nodded. "And our land sits right in the middle of the project."

Bowie looked at Samuel.

Samuel shrugged. "It could explain why Daddy was targeted."

Bowie looked at his mother.

"Mama, did Daddy ever mention being concerned that paying off the loans could cripple the project?"

"No, and I wouldn't have put any of it together if it hadn't been for Polly."

"What will happen if they don't get your land, Aunt Polly?" Bowie asked.

"I don't know. Maybe the resort will have to be relocated," she said.

"Then that's motive," Bowie said. "I'm calling Riordan back and telling him about this. Even if he doesn't want to hear it, he needs all the information he can get to build a case against anyone from the Wayne family."

\* \* \*

Talia sat in the rocker beside her father's bed with a glass of sweet tea and a half-eaten cookie, listening to the rain blowing against the windows behind her.

Turbulent weather used to agitate her father, especially strong wind, but no more. Erin had told her before she left today that he was moving into the final phase. Talia wasn't sad to hear this. His suffering was heartbreaking to witness. The father he'd been was long gone. All she knew was he was finally going to be released from this hell. She'd cried all her tears as he'd suffered through this. She wouldn't be sorry when it was over.

The creak of the rocker was a comforting sound as she finished her tea and cookie. She had vague memories of being rocked in this chair when she was young. Her mother had died when Talia was ten, and with no one to talk to about the memories, she was beginning to forget things about her, too.

Before Bowie Youngblood had knocked on her door, Talia's future had been a blank. She didn't know how the timing of her father's imminent passing and the murder of Bowie's father played out in the universe, but she believed everything happened for a reason. The fact that they were both losing their fathers and regaining their relationship felt orchestrated by a higher power. All she knew was that she no longer felt dead inside. Knowing he still cared for her gave her the strength she needed to finish this journey.

A loud clap of thunder rattled the dishes in the

china cabinet behind her. She set her glass aside and got up to check on her dad. His lips were moving slightly, like he was talking, but no sounds were coming out. She wondered what he was seeing and who he was with. Were there angels standing around his bed waiting to take him home? She needed to believe there were.

As soon as she was certain the thunder hadn't disturbed him, she carried her glass back into the kitchen and put it in the dishwasher. It was almost eight o'clock. She wondered what was happening at the Youngblood house, then wondered how people coped when death came as murder.

She was thinking about Bowie and the sadness she'd seen in his eyes when her phone rang. She slipped it out of her pocket and, when she saw Bowie's name on caller ID, answered eagerly.

"Hello," she said.

"Hey, honey, it's me," Bowie said.

"I'm so glad you called."

"Is everything okay?"

She heard exhaustion in his voice, and she heard sadness.

"Nothing's changed, if that's what you mean. You sound like you've had a rough day," she said.

Bowie leaned back against the headboard of his bed and closed his eyes, enveloped in peace at the sound of her voice.

"I've had better," he said.

"I'm so sorry," she said.

He nodded.

Silence lay between them, as uncomfortable as the truth of what was happening.

Tears rolled down Talia's face as she stared at a water spot on the ceiling. "Erin said Dad's time is short."

Bowie heard the resignation in her voice.

"Are you okay? Do you need anything?" he asked.

"I am at peace, Bowie. You gave that to me today. I don't have the words to explain how much it meant."

He rubbed his finger between the frown lines above his nose, trying to rub away a headache.

"It was a healing time for me, as well."

"Then we were both blessed today," Talia said. "So that was the good part of the day. What else aren't you saying? There's something, because I hear it in your voice."

"The authorities have yet to question a single member of the Wayne family."

She gasped. "You aren't serious!"

"I wish I wasn't," he said. "When I found out, I left Chief Clayton and Constable Riordan with their ears ringing."

"I'm so sorry."

"So am I."

"It's because of who they are, isn't it? Is there anything you can do to force their hand?" she asked.

"I called my brothers. We'll be in Eden tomorrow morning to see if the constable shows up at the Wayne estate. If it's okay, I'd like to come by and see you later before I leave town. I know you're overwhelmed with responsibilities, but knowing there's still an 'us' doesn't feel real yet. I'd be happy with a hug and a kiss, and then I'll leave without complaint."

Her heart fluttered. Knowing there was an "us" was a big deal for her, too.

"I would love to see you. Come whenever you can. I'm not going anywhere."

"Then I'll see you tomorrow. Try to get some rest. I wish I was there to hold you."

Talia shivered. "I wish you were, too. One day soon. Good night, Bowie."

"Good night, Talia. Love you, baby."

Her eyes welled.

"I love you, too, Bowie. I always have."

She disconnected just as another clap of thunder sounded, followed by a bright flash of lightning. She jumped when she heard the crack and ran to the window to look out. Since she didn't see anything on fire, she went back to the living room to her father's bed.

She leaned over to stroke the side of his face and then gently patted his shoulder beneath the sheets.

"It's raining, Dad. Lots of thunder and lightning, but that's all. Everything is okay. I'm going to turn on TV for a bit, but I'll keep it low. I just want to keep an eye on the weather reports."

She turned on the TV at the other end of the room, then sat back down in the rocker. If there was a weather bulletin of any kind, she would hear when they signaled the warning. But she was so tired, and it had been a relief to hear Bowie's voice again so soon. She closed her eyes for just a moment during a commercial and fell asleep.

Jack Wayne had stewed all day about the dark cloud over the family name. Never in their history had they been faced with anything this vile. It wasn't to say that none of their ancestors had ever done anything like this, but they'd never been caught.

As soon as the cook served dessert and coffee, he pushed his aside. He slapped the table with the flat of his hand, rattling china and silver, and startling them all.

Blake looked up and glared. "What the hell, Uncle Jack?"

Jack looked pointedly at Justin and then addressed the room.

"Every one of you, save Charles, knew Stanton Youngblood, or at least knew who he was, so I want to know why you think he was worth killing."

Silence.

Nita's fork scraped the plate as she took a dainty bite of cake.

Her social faux pas made everyone turn to look.

She poked the cake in her mouth and then committed a second gaffe by talking with her mouth full.

"What?" she asked.

Fiona rolled her eyes.

Blake glared at his uncle again.

"You surely don't expect an answer to that question, do you? The only person with any knowledge would be the one who did the deed. And I don't know how the rest of you feel, but I wouldn't admit to a hangnail in front of any of you. I didn't do it, but if I had, I wouldn't trust one of you not to feed me to the lions of the law just to get this monkey off your backs."

Jack was taken aback. "You aren't serious?"

Blake gestured toward his family.

"Look at their faces if you don't believe me! Just *look* at them. They can't even meet each other's eyes right now because they know I'm right."

Jack leaned forward, staring intently at each one of them in turn.

"So who did it? If you won't tell me, how can I create the perfect alibi for you? I can, you know."

Silence.

Jack sat there for a moment and then delivered a question none of them had thought to ask themselves.

"Then answer me this…how many of you can account for your whereabouts on the morning of the murder? Were there witnesses? Who outside of the family can corroborate your whereabouts?"

Fiona spoke up at once.

"Nita and I were in town, and in and out of shops. Dozens of people saw us when we were being waited on," Fiona said.

"Yes, we talked to lots of people," Nita added.

Jack nodded, then glanced at Blake. "And you?"

"I was in and out of the office," he said.

"Out where?" Jack asked.

Blake sighed. "I was out at the resort site, but I was talking to people the whole time."

"How close is that to the murder scene?" Jack asked.

Blake shrugged. "I have no idea. I don't know where the man was killed, other than on the mountain."

Jack's gaze shifted to Justin.

Justin glared back. "What? Before, you slapped the shit out of me to make me shut up, and now you want me to talk? What if I don't want to?"

Jack shrugged.

"You were acting like a madman, screaming obscenities for so long I actually heard you from inside the house—even though the wind was already gearing up for the thunderstorm that's here now."

Blake and Charles looked as startled as they felt.

"You hit Justin?" Blake asked.

"No, I slapped him. If I'd hit him with my fist, he'd still be lying out there in the rain," Jack said shortly, and gave his great-nephew Charles a studied look. "It's already evident that you have more manly brawn than your relatives. Pity they took after their mother, God rest her soul. I sincerely hope you have more brains than the rest of them, as well."

Charles paled and then flushed. It was extremely embarrassing to be held up as an example to all of his elders, and he was pissed off at Jack for doing it.

"I'm sorry, but it's very rude of you to shame them and use me to do it. I don't appreciate it. It makes me feel like you're trying to drive a wedge between us," Charles said, and then set his cake and coffee aside. "Excuse me. I've lost my appetite, and I'm going to go see some friends."

He walked out without looking at anyone.

Blake sighed.

"Way to go, Uncle Jack," he said, then left the room, as well.

Justin shoved the last bite of his cake into his mouth and got up, chewing it as he left.

Jack was ticked off that he'd just been told off by the youngest member of the family, but he couldn't argue the point. There was even a part of him that admired the boy for standing up to him. No one else ever did.

He glanced at Nita and Fiona.

Nita set her fork aside and stared back.

"Are you going to eat your cake?" she asked.

Jack rolled his eyes, slid the dessert plate down the table like a hockey puck on ice and stomped out of the room.

Nita leaned over and caught the dish before it went off the side of the table.

Fiona grinned at her sister.

"Are you really going to eat a second piece of cake?"

"No," Nita said. "I just wanted to piss him off. He shouldn't have hit Justin."

"Oh Lord, Nita, someone had to. I've never seen Justin act like that in my life."

Nita shrugged, took her fork and raked it across the icing for one last bite.

"I love cream cheese frosting," she said. "I'm going to my room to watch some TV for a while. I'm keeping my own company tonight."

"Where's Andrew?"

Nita shrugged.

"I don't know, but when he called this evening, I told him I wasn't up for company."

Fiona arched a brow. "You don't care what he's doing without you?"

Nita snorted softly. "No, why would I?"

"You trust him that much?" Fiona asked.

Nita laughed.

"I don't trust him at all, but that doesn't have anything to do with our relationship. He has a hard dick and endurance. That's all the job requires."

Fiona blinked. "You never used to be so crude."

Nita laughed again.

"Oh, Fee…I was always crude. I just don't care enough to hide it anymore."

She started to leave the table, then stopped, went back for the cake and her fork, and took them with her.

Now Fiona was alone.

She looked about the beautifully appointed dining room, at the elegant table with dirty plates and cups scattered up and down the length of it, and realized the scene before her was a shocking analogy for the family: a beautiful setting with a scattered assortment of very expensive, very dirty plates and cups. Cook would wash all of this clean, but who was going to clean their souls?

# *Eight*

Charles had a raincoat over his dinner clothes and was heading out the door when his dad caught him in the hall.

"Where are you going?" Blake asked.

"Like I said, out with friends," Charles said.

Blake frowned.

"Be careful. There could be flooding on the roads."

"Yes, I will, and I'll be home late." Then he paused. "Can't you do something with Uncle Jack? He's getting on everyone's nerves."

Blake shrugged. "He's trying to protect the family."

Charles stood a moment, eyeing the serious expression on his father's face. "Are you worried?" he asked.

Blake frowned. "Hell, yes. This has the look of a nightmare for all of us."

"What happens if there's no one to pin it on?" Charles asked.

"What do you mean?" Blake asked.

"Well, if everyone has an alibi that can be confirmed, then what happens?"

"Hell if I know," Blake said. "But I can guarantee someone in this family will go down regardless."

Now it was Charles who was confused.

"What do *you* mean?" he asked.

"You don't know your Aunt Leigh, but the rest of us do. She's a Wayne first, and she's the only one of us who ever defied our father. And she succeeded beyond any of our expectations, then went on to live a happily married life to spite him. She has five sons who, I suspect, would walk through fire for her, because that's the kind of loyalty she inspires. If the police can't determine what happened, she'll take us all down."

Charles was startled. He'd never heard his father talk like this before. He almost sounded uncertain, which was not how the Wayne family conducted business.

"Maybe it won't come to that," Charles muttered, and left the mansion, glad he'd had the foresight to park beneath the portico, because the thunderstorm was blowing the rain sideways.

He got into his car and headed up the driveway with his windshield wipers on high. By the time he got out to the street he'd already forgotten the family drama and was thinking about his night's entertainment.

Andrew was glad he wasn't going to have to put up with Nita tonight. She was fun and generous, but sometimes she was also too damn demanding. He knew why she liked him. It was the same reason everyone liked him. Because he was really good at what he did.

And he was simply following in the family footsteps.

In his day, they'd called his grandfather a ladies' man. In his father's time, the term was gigolo. Andrew had no qualms about his status and didn't care if people thought of him as cougar prey for middle-aged women. He happily accommodated the people who could afford him.

He walked barefoot through the house with a plate of fruit and cheese as he headed to the liquor cabinet. After a quick decision, he poured himself a glass of wine from one of the better reds, plugged his iPod into his docking system and smiled when his favorite music began to play. He popped a piece of cheese into his mouth, dimmed the lights throughout the house and then strode to a window to watch the lightning flashes from the storm.

He liked storms, and the wilder the better. Thunder rumbled. It was so loud it felt like it was on top of him. Lightning cracked and flashed as it struck the dark surface of the lake before him.

Just as the flash faded, he saw car lights. His pulse kicked. It was about time. He turned to face the front door and waited for it to open. When it did, his guest blew in with the wind and rain.

"It's about time you got here," Andrew said. "I've started without you." He held up his wineglass.

Charles Wayne began shedding his clothes. By the time he reached Andrew, he was naked. He took the wine out of Andrew's hand and downed it, then set it aside and challenged him with an in-your-face smile.

Andrew threw his head back and laughed.

Leigh sat on the side of her bed, looking around the shadowed bedroom she'd shared with Stanton for more than thirty years. It still smelled like his aftershave. His clothes were still in the closet, and a pair of his shoes was beside the chair where he'd left them when he had changed into his walking boots.

Wind blew rain against the windows and hammered on the roof above her head. She kept thinking of it as a cleansing. There wouldn't be a trace of Stanton's blood left after this, but there was no way to hide his presence here. She kept expecting him to walk in at any moment. Twice today she'd thought she'd seen him from the corner of her eye, only to realize it was Bowie. It broke her heart to be so conflicted about her son's presence. She needed him here. He was the last link to complete their family circle, and yet, because his resemblance to his father was so strong, he was also a painful and tangible reminder of what she'd lost.

Her eyes were burning from lack of sleep, but it wasn't going to happen in here, so she gathered up her pillow and a blanket and went into the living room to bed down on the sofa. The storm was still raging, and she was so sleep-deprived she felt faint, but there was no way in hell she could lie down in their bed without Stanton. Not yet. Maybe never.

She stretched out on the sofa, then rolled over on to her side and pulled the blanket up over her shoulders. Even with the curtains pulled over the windows and her eyes closed, she still saw the lightning flashes. She took a deep breath and then exhaled slowly, and as she did, tears pooled and fell.

"Oh, Stanton, I never saw this coming. I thought we would grow old together. I don't know how to do this yet, but I will."

Thunder rumbled again. She tensed, hoping it wouldn't wake Jesse. Then she heard footsteps in the hall and heard Bowie's voice.

"I'm here, Jesse. It's just a thunderstorm. You're okay."

She rose up on one elbow to look down the hall. Jesse must have called out. Thank God for Bowie. He wouldn't be here forever, but this respite from Jesse's every need was a blessing. She lay back down, settled into her pillow and cried herself to sleep.

It took Bowie a few minutes to get Jesse settled, and then he went back into his bedroom, but he left the door ajar in case Jesse called out again.

He knew his mother was in the living room on the sofa. He'd heard her leave her room, and when she didn't come back he'd checked on her and had seen her stretched out on the sofa, then quietly returned to his bed.

He hadn't gotten much of a chance to talk to Samuel before he'd left to take Aunt Polly home, but he and his brothers were meeting in Eden tomorrow morning around nine. There would be plenty of time to talk then while they were waiting to see if the law ever showed.

He glanced at the time. It was almost midnight—too late to text Talia. She didn't look like she'd had enough sleep in years, so no way was he taking a chance on waking her up, but he couldn't sleep. He moved to the window and pushed aside the curtain to stare out into the night.

Rain, blown by the storm, hit the glass with such force it made Bowie flinch. A shaft of lightning struck in the forest beyond the backyard. It was like watching fire explode. The tree caught fire, even in the rain, but the flames quickly died out.

He kept thinking of what he'd learned about the Wayne family's rumored involvement in the resort project. After giving Riordan that information earlier in the evening, he hoped it might point a finger at who had the most to lose, which could easily put a name to the killer. Either way, he wasn't leaving his mother until the murderer was behind bars.

Thunder rumbled across the sky as he dropped the curtain and moved back to the bed. He was tired and needed to rest, but as he stretched out on the mattress, all he could think of was his father in the morgue and his mother on the living room sofa, crying herself to sleep. It was the sound of the rain on the roof that lulled him, and the next time he woke his alarm was going off.

He rolled over to shut it off as the scent of fresh coffee drifted down the hall. Guessing his mother was already in the kitchen, he headed for the bathroom while it was empty. There was no time to waste this morning. This was Constable Riordan's chance to do the right thing, and he and his brothers intended to make sure the man was there to do it.

Bowie was in and out of the shower in record time, and dressed before Jesse woke. Leigh was at the stove frying bacon as he entered the kitchen. He paused to kiss her on the cheek.

"Morning, Mama."

Leigh's eyes were red-rimmed and swollen, but she had a smile for him.

"Good morning, son. I'm making pancakes shortly, and the coffee's done. Pour yourself a cup and sit with me while I finish up."

"Does Jesse need help dressing?" he asked.

Leigh shook her head.

"Not really. It's strange what he's still capable of doing. It's like his view of the world and his vocabulary are childlike, but his technical and motor skills are still there."

"How do you mean?" Bowie asked.

"For instance, he's still every bit as good a shot as he was in the army. And he can break a rifle down and put it back together better than Stanton could."

"Really? That's actually amazing. I didn't know that."

"Yes, and he's retained his tracking skills. Remember when he went through his Daniel Boone phase in grade school and pestered Dad to teach him the different kinds of animal tracks, and how to track people, too?"

Bowie smiled, thinking of the story he'd read to Jesse.

"Yes, I remember."

"He was a crack shot in the military, and still is," Leigh said.

"Translate that to sniper in the war and, yes, I knew that, too."

Leigh shrugged.

"War is war, and I'm at war right now with my blood kin."

"I know, Mama, and if Riordan knows what's good for him, he'll be at the Wayne estate today."

She sighed and wiped her hands on the front of her apron.

"I'm starting the pancakes now. If Jesse's not awake already, just tell him what I'm making."

Bowie grinned. "And then stand back?"

Leigh chuckled.

"Yes. It's proceed at your own risk, if you get between Jesse and his food."

Bowie left the kitchen in a hurry. He wasn't going to admit it, but he felt like Jesse when it came to Mama's cooking.

Constable Riordan left the precinct just after eight-thirty with Brady Griffin, the head of his crime scene team, riding shotgun. Two deputies escorted them in a second car. They were on their way to Eden.

Riordan had called Chief Clayton that morning and asked him to send an officer to meet them at the Wayne residence at nine, and then Riordan had called the Wayne estate. When the maid answered the phone, he identified himself and asked to speak to Jackson Wayne. He heard her gasp, and then she asked him to wait. Moments later he heard someone pick up on an extension, and then Mad Jack's voice was blasting in his ear.

"Do you know what time it is? I do *not* take calls before breakfast!"

Riordan held firm to his intent. He wasn't going to be bulldozed by the Wayne family or anyone else when he had a murder to solve.

"I called early to tell you that I'm on my way over. Please, inform the rest of your family that I expect them all to be there to discuss Stanton Youngblood's murder. If they are not, I will be visiting them at their places of business."

Jack Wayne cursed. "You do not threaten me or mine!" he shouted.

"No, Mr. Wayne, you do not threaten *me* or *my authority*. I am investigating a murder in which someone from your family was named as the killer. The fact that one of you was involved in the death of a good man is not my problem. It's *yours*. Do we understand each other?"

"I have connections and will not allow—"

"If you're referring to our illustrious governor, know that I have already replied to his request regarding you, and once it was pointed out to his office that he might want to distance himself from protecting a murderer, he understood the situation so much better. We will be there around 9:00 a.m."

"Our lawyer will be here," Jack fired back.

"This is strictly an interview to get everyone's statement regarding the day of the murder, but maybe you know something I don't. So am I to take your insistence on legal representation as an admission of your family's guilt?" Riordan asked.

Silence.

Riordan guessed Jack was thinking that over.

"No, of course not," Jack finally said.

"Then we will see you soon."

"We? Who's 'we'?"

"My team and I," Riordan said, and hung up.

It wasn't that Riordan was afraid of the Wayne family, but he *was* afraid of what they might do, and the more witnesses he had to their behavior, the better this interrogation would go.

What he regretted was that he'd hesitated to do the right thing, and if it hadn't been for Bowie Youngblood's angry call, he probably still wouldn't be doing this, which was his fault. If he'd done this to begin with, he wouldn't be starting on the wrong foot.

But after Bowie's second call and the news that Stanton had paid off the loans belonging to his brother and sister, meaning that the land the developers needed for the resort was no longer available, Clayton's call about the picketers had suddenly made a lot more sense.

At that point Riordan had called the bank to confirm the information with the president of the bank in Eden, who'd told him that, yes, they'd sold the loans to East Coast Lenders, Inc. He said when they began foreclosures on some of the notes, he was surprised, but had no say in the matter. He'd also confirmed that Stanton Youngblood had paid off his siblings' loans on several pieces of property, which he only knew because Stanton had mentioned it to him when he cashed in some IRAs to cover the loans. Those properties were in the same area as the planned resort. Riordan knew if that had delayed or even stopped the developers from building, then he had the motive that he'd been missing.

At that point he'd called in and had one of his officers research the ownership of East Coast Lenders, Inc., as well as the names of the investors on the property at the lake. When he got the call back with information, he wasn't surprised to learn Wayne Industries was an investor in the resort development and also owned East Coast Lenders.

The ride to Eden was mostly silent, with both men lost in thought. The magnitude of what they were about to do wasn't lost on either one of them, because they both knew the Wayne family had the power and pull to make their lives miserable as hell if they so chose.

By the time they reached the city limits, Riordan's gut was in a knot. CSI Griffin had been reading over his notes from the crime scene, so that it was all firmly in his mind. If anyone said anything incriminating, Griffin would know.

When Jack realized Riordan had just hung up on him, he was livid. Furious, he left the library, yelling loudly for everyone to get the hell out there and listen to him. One by one, the family emerged from their rooms to rush to the head of the stairs.

Blake was only half-dressed as he ran out, and when he saw his uncle at the bottom of the staircase, he called down, "What's going on?"

"Where's Charles?" Jack shouted.

Charles came out of his bedroom wearing nothing but a big bath towel wrapped around his waist.

"I'm here! I was just getting out of the shower. Is something on fire?"

"Nobody leaves the house this morning," Jack announced.

Justin frowned. "But I was supposed to—"

Nita shrugged and cut him off. "I wasn't going anywhere anyway."

"What the hell is going on?" Blake asked again.

"Constable Riordan is on his way here with 'his team.' He's coming to take our statements about the day of Youngblood's murder."

Blake's eyes narrowed angrily. "I thought you said you spoke to the governor about this?"

"It appears the governor has decided to distance himself from our unsavory situation. So one of you has put all the future of this family in jeopardy! The constable will be here around nine. Make sure you are all available, and don't confront him in any way or do anything to make yourself look guilty. I'm going in to breakfast. Feel free to join me."

He turned and strode into the dining room, leaving the rest of them staring at each other.

Blake threw up his arms and went back to his room. The others quickly followed suit, leaving Charles at the top of the stairs alone. His eyes narrowed thoughtfully as he, too, went back to get dressed. This had certainly put a damper on the good mood he'd been in from last night.

Bowie drove into Eden just before nine with his brothers in their separate vehicles right behind him. The convoy of Stanton Youngblood's sons was duly noted by the citizens of Eden, and when all four vehicles headed for the Wayne estate, curiosity grew. Then news began to spread that the Youngblood brothers were parked outside the gate to the estate. Before long, a small crowd began to gather a short distance away.

Aidan glanced over his shoulder as he joined his brothers beneath the shade of a large elm near the sidewalk.

"We're drawing a crowd," he said.

The others turned to look.

Bowie's eyes narrowed. "I hope the sight of those people ticks every one of them off," he said.

"So do I. I hope they get as hot as this day is getting," Michael said, and pulled a band from the pocket of his pants and tied his hair back in a long ponytail at the nape of his neck.

Aidan's hair was already in a ponytail, and Samuel's was in a long loose braid.

Only Bowie's was still loose. His hair was so straight and so black that from a distance he could have passed for Native American, but his tan was from countless hours outside on the oil platforms, rather than genetic. He'd taken after his mother's people. Scottish to the core. And now those people had become the enemy.

"It's nine fifteen," Aidan said.

Then Samuel pointed up the street. "And here they come," he said.

The brothers turned and watched the duo of county police cars as they neared the gate. They saw the startled expression on the constable's face as he recognized them, and then he quickly looked away.

"I guess he didn't think you were serious, because he looks shocked that we're here," Michael said. "Oh, here comes one of Eden's officers, too."

Bowie didn't say anything. He just kept watching as the police cars drove past them, then down the driveway, finally pulling up at the main house.

"Since it took him 'til the third day after Daddy's murder to get here, I'll be curious to see how long it takes to get everybody's statements," Bowie said, and proceeded to make himself comfortable on a bench beneath the tree.

His brothers joined him, and for a few moments

they were silent, each man lost in his own thoughts about the tragedy. Then Bowie spoke.

"Tell me about what went down after the police arrived on the scene. Did any of you hear them talking about any evidence they found?"

"Well, it was Samuel who found the shell casing from the shooter's rifle," Aidan said.

Samuel nodded, then added, "I also found footprints. Mama asked me to trail them, which I did. They ended almost a mile down the mountain where he got on a motorcycle and rode off." He leaned forward, his elbows resting on his knees as he stared down at an ant carrying a leaf across the grass at his feet. "Can we assume Mama isn't in danger, too?"

The shock on his brothers' faces was sudden.

"That never crossed my mind," Aidan said. "Now there's just her and Jesse at the house."

"We need to make sure she doesn't go rambling off in the woods until this is over," Michael said.

"I'll mention it to her when I get home," Bowie said.

"It's gonna make her mad," Aidan said.

Bowie shrugged. "Mad is good if it keeps her safe."

After that, conversation ended, but the crowd at the end of the street continued to grow.

While the people in the crowd were all curious to see if the constable left with a suspect in custody, the Youngblood brothers weren't nearly that optimistic. For all they knew, the constable was letting the Wayne family run the show.

# *Nine*

As ordered, the Waynes were present and seated in the library. Except for the ice tinkling in Fiona's bourbon and Coke, the room was completely silent. The fact that Fiona was already drinking spoke to her anxiety.

Mad Jack sat in the chair behind the grand desk, wearing a gray Gucci suit and a pink shirt. With the shock of white hair combed into a semblance of order, he posed like a king on his throne, glaring at his subjects.

The others were all seated in separate chairs, as if no one wanted to be too close to anyone else, afraid of guilt by association.

Blake's frown contradicted the casual style of his dark slacks and white shirt. The sleeves were rolled up a couple of turns past his wrist, and he'd left two buttons open at the collar. He had his laptop balanced on his knees, hoping he looked more at ease than he felt. His belly was churning with every keystroke as he ran through the latest figures from the New York Stock Exchange.

Justin had come down in a navy and silver robe over white silk pajamas—his silent rebellion against Mad Jack's earlier demand to get dressed—and was pretending to read the *New York Times* on his iPad. He couldn't help thinking that Leigh had orchestrated this inquisition, and he resented the hell out of his twin for that.

Charles was wearing designer sweats in a startling cardinal red, his head down, his entire attention seemingly focused on his phone and the text he was composing.

Nita was in white slacks and braless under a nearly sheer summer blouse that was bordering on indecent. At first glance she appeared to be reading a book, although she hadn't turned a page in almost fifteen minutes. She was daydreaming about sex with Andrew, and the excitement from the daydream had translated into a high pink flush on her cheeks.

Fiona had chosen a demure sundress with huge white lilies on black, a walking homage to Georgia O'Keeffe. She had bypassed breakfast for the bourbon and Coke, and was about to refresh it when they heard footsteps in the hall.

They all looked up as Frances, the maid, walked in.

"Constable Riordan to see you," Frances said, and made a quick exit as Riordan and his team entered the room.

Blake closed his laptop and stood, as if to initiate the conversation.

The action irked Jack, who quickly took charge. Last time he'd looked, he was still the head of this household.

"Well, we're here, Riordan. Feel free to begin at any time," Jack said.

Riordan eyed the assortment of family members and handed Jack a search warrant.

Forgetting his own warning to play it cool, Jack bellowed, "What the hell is this for?"

"We're confiscating all rifles registered to anyone in the family and taking possession of the motorcycle registered, as well."

"Well, you can look until hell freezes over, but you won't find any guns here. Guns have never been allowed in this house. And I don't know anything about a motorcycle, but I do know there's not one on these premises, so knock yourself out."

Riordan ignored him and nodded at the two officers he'd brought with him.

"Proceed," he said, then turned to the family. "Until this case is solved, you are not to leave the area. You may not travel out of the country, so I'll need your passports before I leave. I will speak to you one at a time, and when I am finished, you are not to return to this room. At my request, Chief Clayton sent one of his officers to assist me. He will stay here in the library to carry out my orders. I want no communication between any of you until my men and I have left the house, and I want all of your cell phones left on the desk when you exit the room. Is there another room I can use to take your statements?"

Jack's nostrils flared, but he didn't argue.

"Blake, he can begin with you. Show him to the game room. There are plenty of tables and chairs in there for him to choose from."

Blake left his phone on the desk and led Riordan and Griffin out of the library without comment, then down the hall about thirty feet to a doorway on the right. He turned on the light as he entered, revealing a room papered in red-and-gold stripes, with gold draperies and a fleur-de-lis pattern in the matching red-and-gold carpet. All the furniture, from the chairs at the poker table to the theater seating in front of the giant-screen television at the end of the room, was black.

"This will do fine," Riordan said. "Mr. Griffin, if you will set up the video equipment and prepare for fingerprinting, we'll get started."

CSI Griffin quickly unpacked the case he'd been carrying and within a few minutes had the digital recorder ready to go, then set up what he needed to fingerprint the suspects, as well.

"Ready when you are, sir."

Blake moved to the fingerprint setup, struggling with the fact that he was being fingerprinted like any common criminal, and when they were finished he sullenly took a seat. He took a deep breath and tried not to look as antsy as he felt with a video camera aimed at his face.

Riordan began with a request to have him state his name, age, place of residence and occupation.

Blake's defiance was obvious as he answered the questions with his chin up and his eyes fixed on Riordan's face.

"Do you know why we're here?" Riordan asked.

Blake nodded.

"Please, state your answers aloud," Riordan said.

"Yes, you're here to question us about the death of Stanton Youngblood," Blake said.

"No, I'm here to question you about the murder of Stanton Youngblood," Riordan countered.

Blake flushed as Riordan continued.

"What relation was Stanton Youngblood to you?"

"Legally, my brother-in-law," Blake said.

The questioning continued, with Riordan asking Blake to explain the ill will between the Waynes and their sister's family, asking if there had ever been a threat made against the victim's life.

"Yes, there was a threat, but that was over thirty years ago, when she married against our father's wishes, but we haven't had any contact with her or her husband since."

Riordan went through another list of questions, tailoring them to match the way Blake answered, until he got down to the murder weapon.

"Who owns a 30-30 hunting rifle?"

Blake's heart skipped a beat as he realized they'd already identified the weapon, but he shrugged.

"I'm sure the family owns guns, but as Uncle Jack already stated, there are no guns under this roof, nor have there ever been. Mother wouldn't have it, and our father always catered to her wishes."

Riordan caught a hint of a smirk in Blake's quick response, as if he was all too willing to share that information.

"Then where does the family store their weapons? Because our research shows that there are quite a few registered to the family corporation."

"I'm not sure. Hunting isn't my thing."

"Can you shoot?" Riordan asked.

Blake hesitated a moment too long before he answered.

"Well, yes, but I don't care for the sport."

"Where is the motorcycle that belongs to the family?"

"I remember there once was one, but I don't ride, so I have no idea."

"Just a few more questions, Mr. Wayne, and we'll be done. Where were you between 9:00 a.m. and 11:00 a.m. this past Tuesday?"

Blake kept his expression blank, despite the kick in his pulse.

"For most of that time I was at the job site for the new resort being built up by the lake."

"What was your purpose for being there?"

"We're investors in the project, and part of my job is to monitor the progress of our investments."

"What time were you there?" Riordan asked.

"I believe I arrived around ten o'clock, give or take a few minutes, and was there until almost one."

"Do you have any witnesses to your whereabouts that morning before your arrival at the site?"

Blake sighed. "No. I drove myself out."

"What does your family have to lose if the resort does not get built?"

Blake blinked. "What makes you think it's not going to be built?"

"I've been told that part of the land needed to move forward with the project is no longer for sale."

Blake stiffened visibly. "What does that—"

"Just answer the question," Riordan snapped.

Blake glared. His answer was mostly bluster, and he was afraid it showed. "We're merely investors. I don't know what the developers' plans are. I'm sure they'll figure something out."

Riordan watched Blake Wayne turning redder by the moment and knew he'd hit a nerve.

"You're not merely investors. The lending company that foreclosed on the properties around the lake belongs to Wayne Industries, so you all own the land the investment company will be using to build on. I'm not sure how many laws were broken there."

Blake paled, but said nothing.

"That will be all for now," Riordan said. "You're free to leave, just don't go back to the library. You'll all get your phones back when we're gone."

Blake left the game room with long, angry strides.

Riordan glanced at his CSI. "Call Jack Wayne in next."

"Yes, sir," Griffin said, and left the room.

A minute later Griffin was back with the patriarch of Wayne Industries. Jack entered in Mad Jack form, with long strides and a superior air that ended when he, too, was fingerprinted.

"Have a seat," Riordan said, pointing to the chair Blake had used.

Jack saw the video camera and tried not to react, but he was already regretting the fact that he hadn't called their lawyer.

Riordan went through the same set of questions with Jack. Jack showed no reaction whatsoever to any of them, which told Riordan that either Jack Wayne was ignorant of who'd committed the murder or he was a damn good poker player. He claimed no direct knowledge of where the guns were, nor did he know anything about a motorcycle, and he added their company owned many vehicles of all different kinds. His whereabouts during the time of the murder were vague. He'd been out for a while but had come home soon after, then played tennis with the pro until Nita and Fiona showed up with the news of Stanton's murder. And when questioned about the lake project and the lending company, he simply shrugged and said investments were under Blake's division.

Justin was called in next and fingerprinted, and despite his Uncle Jack's caution not to antagonize the police, he made no attempt to hide his disgust at being treated like a common criminal.

Riordan wasn't impressed with Justin Wayne's robe and pajamas or with his attitude.

He ran through the same questions with Justin

until things took a slight turn when he brought up the fact that Justin and Leigh were twins. Justin's cold reaction to his sister's grief seemed odd, and Riordan ran with it.

"How many years has it been since you spoke to your sister?" Riordan asked.

"More than thirty, I guess."

"Really? I thought twins had a special bond."

"The only thing our family shares is blood," Justin said shortly.

"So you're saying you have no empathy for the fact that Leigh just lost her husband?"

"She became a nonissue when she quit our family," Justin said. "We don't cry over spilled milk."

"Or blood?"

Justin's cheeks reddened slightly. He'd led with his anger, not his brain, but he managed to control himself now and didn't respond.

Riordan moved to the next question.

"Do you have a personal interest in the resort that's being built on the north side of the lake?"

"We all do. Wayne Industries is a family-owned corporation. Whatever investments the company makes are made with family money."

"And you all share equally in the profits?" Riordan asked.

Justin shifted slightly in his chair.

"Not exactly. Uncle Jack has controlling interest. Then the four of us have equal shares."

"Does your sister Leigh benefit in any way?"

"Oh, hell, no," Justin said, and then smirked. "Our

father wrote her out of the will when she ran away. It's what she gets for choosing to live below her social status."

Riordan frowned. "What do you know about your nephews?"

"I have one nephew. His name is Charles."

Riordan leaned forward just enough to invade Justin's personal space.

"But you just told me that the only thing the Waynes share is blood, and like it or not, Leigh's five sons share your blood."

Justin slapped the table with the flat of his hand so fast it startled Riordan.

"Her sons have been harassing our family ever since this began, and I'm sick of it. One even stood outside the gate yesterday, just staring and gesturing," he snapped.

"Well, there are four of them outside your gates right now, along with a gathering crowd of citizens of this fine town, and if someone in your family hadn't shot their father, I doubt we'd be having this conversation," Riordan drawled.

Justin's face went from an angry red to white so fast Riordan thought the man was going to pass out.

"It wasn't me," Justin said.

"Where were you that morning?" Riordan asked.

"I took a day off," Justin said, and met the constable's gaze without blinking.

"That doesn't tell me where you were," Riordan said.

Justin shrugged.

"I slept in. I went for a run. I took a shower and then went for a drive. It's how I deal with stress."

"Why are you stressed?" Riordan asked.

Justin smirked. "Everyone is stressed. I'd guess you're dealing with a little stress of your own right now."

"Do you have a witness to any of your activities?" Riordan asked.

"I don't know. I wasn't looking for witnesses, because I wasn't on the mountain chasing a man to kill him."

Riordan's heart skipped a beat.

"How did you know someone chased Stanton Youngblood? I never said he was chased. Leigh Youngblood never said he was chased. She said he was shot in the back."

The smile slid off Justin's face.

"I guess I heard it, okay? Don't twist my words trying to pin this on me."

"I don't have to try and do anything. Stanton Youngblood did the pinning before he died. All I have to do is sort through the basket of bad apples and pick the rottenest one."

Justin's fingers curled into fists.

Riordan pointed at them.

"You have some anger issues, boy. I'm done with you for now."

Justin stood abruptly, and then turned on one heel and stormed out of the room.

"He's a lit powder keg, isn't he?" Riordan said.

Griffin nodded. "Yes, sir. Who do you want to see next?"

Riordan thought for a moment.

"I think we'll leave the youngest Wayne for last. I'd like to talk to Fiona next."

"Yes, sir. Be right back," Griffin said.

Fiona entered carrying her second drink, which was a bad idea considering she hadn't had breakfast. But she felt confident that the constable would only be going through the motions interviewing her and Nita. They had the only really good alibis. Half the town of Eden could verify where they'd been.

She smiled at Constable Riordan, placed her drink on the table in front of her and started to sit down, then realized she was going to be fingerprinted first.

That rattled her enough that when she finally took a seat she kept her liquor in her hand.

Riordan eyed the glass, smelled the liquor on her breath and frowned. He didn't want it to come back on him that her statement wouldn't stand up because she was intoxicated.

"Officer Griffin, I would appreciate it if you'd set the lady's drink aside until we've finished."

Fiona was a bit taken aback, but she didn't argue as CSI Griffin put the glass on another table.

Satisfied, Riordan began again, starting by asking her to identify herself and her position in the family.

Fiona answered, and then continued to answer all his questions calmly. Finally she leaned back in the chair and crossed her legs in a casual manner.

"I'm happy to cooperate, but you need to know I

have an unimpeachable alibi, and so does my sister, Nita. We spent the morning in Eden shopping, and then went to a spa, and we were on our way to lunch when Leigh and her sons came racing into Eden."

"That doesn't relieve you of guilt. You could have hired someone. You could have conspired with one or more of your siblings. Right now, none of you are cleared of anything."

Fiona paled, then tucked a strand of hair behind her ear and frowned.

Riordan continued. "What is your interest in the resort being built out by the lake?"

She shrugged. "I know the family corporation made an investment in it. That's all."

"How much does the family stand to lose if it doesn't get built?"

She shrugged. "Blake handles the investments. Ask him."

Riordan watched the woman's gaze sliding toward her drink and wondered what he might learn if he kept her waiting long enough.

"What did you think of Leigh's decision to marry against the wishes of the family?"

"We all thought she was mad. Why would anyone give up all this to go live in poverty?"

"But they aren't poor," Riordan said. "In fact, just the opposite. The family thrived, and they're all quite successful."

Fiona shrugged. "Whatever spell Stanton held over her is certainly over now, isn't it?"

"Were you envious of her?" Riordan asked.

Fiona gasped. "No! Why would I be?"

"Your comments are less than kind toward a sibling who's just been widowed."

"I'm a widow, too, and no one is fussing over me," she snapped.

"Did someone in your family murder *your* husband?"

"Of course not!"

"Then you cannot compare your situation to hers. I think I've heard enough for the time being. You may leave now," he said.

Fiona stood abruptly, grabbed her drink and strode out.

"Wow," Griffin said.

Riordan grimaced.

"They *are* a coldhearted bunch," he said, and then sent Griffin back for the other sister, leaving Charles for last.

Back in the library, Charles watched his Aunt Nita leaving and then glanced at the officer standing at the door. They'd all heard the two officers going through the house looking for weapons. It made him uneasy, thinking about strangers touching their things. He wondered what was going on and kept trying to think if there was anything in his room that might make him look bad. He hated that he was going to be last. He didn't know how to read that. Was it because he was the youngest and had no personal ties to his aunt or her family, or because of something else? He supposed he would soon find out.

Meanwhile, Nita followed Officer Griffin into the

game room, almost burst into tears when she was fingerprinted, then again as she took a seat, looking everywhere but at the constable.

He frowned. She was the first one who'd come in behaving as if she had something to hide. He moved her quickly through the first part of the interrogation and then started on the specifics.

"Do you know how to ride a motorcycle?"

"I suppose, but I haven't in years."

"There's one registered to the family corporation. Where is it kept?"

"I'm sure I don't know," she muttered.

Riordan quickly changed the subject.

"Do you know how to shoot a gun?"

"Yes, as a matter of fact, I do. However, I haven't fired a weapon in several years."

Riordan glanced down at his notes, then back up at her. There were tiny beads of sweat on her upper lip.

"There are several guns registered to this family. Where are they kept?" he asked.

"Not in this house. Mother never allowed it," she said, verifying what Blake said and the same answer he'd gotten from all of them.

"Then where are they?"

She shrugged.

"I really don't know. I don't live here year-round. Fiona and I both have apartments in New York City, so we don't keep up with the family stuff like we used to."

"Where were you on the morning of the murder?"

"Fee and I had been shopping, and then we were in the day spa on Fifth Street. We were going to lunch when Leigh and her sons drove into town. It was the first time I'd seen her since she left home."

"Really? Not even at the supermarket?"

Nita smirked. "We have people who do all that," she said. "So, can I go now? Any number of people in Eden can verify my alibi."

"If you're that comfortable hiring everything done in your life, who did you hire to kill Stanton Young-blood?"

Nita gasped, choked and then began coughing.

He waited for her answer.

"How dare you insinuate I would do such a—"

"I didn't insinuate anything. I asked a question. The murdered man already named the family. As far as I'm concerned, none of you are innocent. You could all be in this together, thinking if no single person is named, you'll all be in the clear. But you're wrong. Abetting is against the law. Collusion is against the law. Whatever you know and aren't telling will send you to prison right along with the person who shot Stanton Youngblood in the back."

"But I didn't. I don't…"

"Then where are the family weapons kept?"

She was beginning to shake.

"Last I knew, they were at the lake house."

Riordan grunted. It seemed he was going to need another search warrant. This was the first any of them had mentioned the lake house.

"And what is the address of this lake house?"

"It's on Pine Road, about two miles past the cross-road of Pine Road and Boone's Way."

"Does anyone live there?"

She shook her head.

"No. It's just part of the family holdings. We used to host parties there when my father was still alive. Uncle Jack doesn't like it. I haven't been there in years."

"I think that will be all for now. You may leave."

"When can I have my phone back?" Nita asked.

"When we're gone and not before."

She left in haste, anxious to be gone before she dissolved into tears. She hadn't expected the intensity of the questioning, and it scared her.

Riordan glanced at Griffin.

"Call the office and tell Joyce to get a search warrant for that lake house. She can research the address and the other particulars the judge will need."

"Yes, sir," Griffin said.

"Go get Charles before you call. Thank God he's the last member of this damn family."

"There's actually one more, but she's the victim's wife," Griffin reminded him, and left the room.

Riordan knew that, and he wasn't looking forward to the visit. Moments later, Charles Wayne came in unescorted.

"We'll be waiting for Officer Griffin to fingerprint you," Riordan said.

Charles sat and then folded his hands in his lap. When he noticed they were videoing the interviews, he wondered how his family had fared. Aunt Fee was close to drunk. Uncle Justin had become, ever since this all began, a raging bull, and Aunt Nita was an airhead. The only two people in the family with common sense were his father and Uncle Jack. And him, of course, but he wasn't afraid to answer any questions, because he had nothing to hide regarding the murder of a man he'd never heard of, who'd been married to a woman he'd never met.

Riordan pretended to be checking his texts while surreptitiously eyeing the youngest Wayne. He looked nothing like the others, and Riordan wondered what his status was within the family. Did he actually participate in the family business, or was he just coasting through life on the family name and money?

At that moment Griffin entered and gave Riordan a slight nod to let him know the search warrant for the lake house was in the works.

"This way, please," Griffin said to Charles, then fingerprinted him.

As soon as Charles sat down again, Griffin adjusted the camera, then nodded.

"Ready when you are, sir," Griffin said.

"Then let's do it," Riordan said. "Mr. Wayne, please, state your name, your place in the family and how long you've lived in Eden."

Charles was calm, and stayed calm as the questioning went on. The tone of his voice was polite and properly respectful of an officer of the law. He answered with, a "no, sir" or a "yes, sir" and was more forthcoming than he had to be.

"Does your family own any weapons?" Riordan asked.

Charles nodded. "Yes, sir, but I'm not sure how many or exactly what kinds."

"Do you know where they're kept?"

"I know some of them are at the lake house, but I don't know if that's all of them."

Riordan paused. If the family never gathered there anymore, and if this kid had been away at college all those years, what did the lake house represent to him?

"I've been told your family doesn't use the lake house anymore," he said.

Charles shrugged.

"I don't think that's entirely true. I think Dad let some of the resort people stay there once or twice, and I believe someone in the family had a New Year's Eve party there my senior year of college. I remember wishing I was here to attend, because I was finally of legal age to drink."

Riordan began tapping his pen against his notebook.

"Do you know how to shoot a gun?"

"Oh, yes, sir. I'm actually quite a good shot, although I confess the only thing I've shot at are clay pigeons."

"Do you know how to ride a motorcycle?"

"Sure do. I had one when I was away at boarding school in DC. It was a lot easier to get around all the traffic and find a place to park, although I did use my car during inclement weather."

"Do you ride here?"

Charles shook his head.

"No, I sold the bike after I graduated college, before I came home."

"What about the motorcycle here?"

Charles frowned. "I didn't know there was one until you mentioned it this morning."

"There's one registered to the family corporation," Riordan said.

Charles shrugged.

"I'll have to ask Dad. I might like to ride here, too. The mountains around Eden are beautiful this time of year, don't you think?"

Riordan thought of the families who'd been displaced by the resort. He doubted there was much of anything beautiful about their lives right now. He glanced up. "How often do you go out to the lake house?"

Charles's gaze shifted momentarily, as if he hadn't seen that question coming, and Riordan knew immediately there was something he wasn't telling.

And then Charles grinned.

"As often as I can get a girl to go out there with me," he said.

Riordan's expectations took a nosedive. So the kid used it for a place to hook up. That wasn't what he was looking for.

"Does the family know?" Riordan asked.

Charles rolled his eyes.

"Lord, I hope not, and I would consider it a huge favor if you didn't mention it. It's hard enough living under this roof without anyone even close to my age. If my social activities away from home were curtailed, it would make my life so much less interesting."

"But you have five cousins somewhat close to your age."

Charles frowned.

"No, sir, I'm the only—" And then he stopped. "Ah...sorry, I didn't get what you meant. However, I didn't even know they existed until three days ago, so..."

Riordan closed his notebook and signaled for Griffin to turn off the video.

"That's all. You may go," he said.

"Yes, sir," Charles said, and left the room.

Griffin began packing up his video equipment. "At least one of them is normal," he said.

Riordan frowned. "Seemingly," he drawled.

Within a few minutes they were gone.

The family came scrambling out of their rooms, heading toward the library.

Justin was finally dressed, Fiona was carrying a cup of coffee and Blake seemed preoccupied. They headed for the desk to get their phones, but Jack got there ahead of them and pulled them all toward him in a pile.

"Not yet," he said. "I want to know what he asked you and what you said."

"Oh, hell, no!" Justin said, and grabbed his phone and put it in his pocket. "It's bad enough we had to put up with the goddamned cops. I'm not putting up with crap from you, too…sir."

Jack knew he'd only added that so he could claim he wasn't being disrespectful, even though he was. The others knew that, too, and one by one they followed suit, taking their phones and leaving Jack Wayne on his own.

Jack swiveled his chair around and glared at his brother's portrait hanging on the wall above him.

"They're just like you, so don't blame me if we all go down in flames."

Then he dropped his phone in his pocket and went to work.

# *Ten*

Bowie and his brothers were still at the gate when Riordan and his crew emerged from the house. It had been a little over three hours since they'd gone inside, and now the sun was directly overhead. The day was heating up, and distant clouds were already building over the mountain to the west. Likely another night of thunderstorms.

Bowie pointed. "They're coming out."

The brothers cast a short shadow as they stood together, but their message was unmistakable as the cars approached the gates. Riordan ignored their presence, but Bowie could tell by the set of his jaw that the constable was aggravated they were still there.

"I wonder what happened?" Aidan said, as the county cop cars drove toward the city limits and the Eden police cruiser headed uptown.

"We'll know in time," Samuel said.

"I need to get home," Michael said. "I work this afternoon until 6:00 p.m."

"I'm going to check on Talia and her dad before I leave Eden," Bowie said.

"Give her our sympathies," Samuel said.

"I will," Bowie said, and one by one they returned to their vehicles.

Once the brothers were gone, the crowd began to disperse. By the time Blake headed to the office, the street in front of the estate was empty. He was trying not to panic, but the constable's appearance had changed the way he viewed his life. He had thought their world impervious and their family above the law. Money had always made the difference, but not in this case. Damn Leigh for ever bringing Stanton Youngblood into their world, and damn Stanton's soul to hell for bringing it down.

Bowie called Talia on his way downtown, but the phone rang so many times he thought it was going to voice mail. When she finally answered, he heard exhaustion in her voice.

"Hello."

"Hello, honey, it's me. Is it still okay to stop by your house?"

Talia sighed. Just the sound of his voice eased the knot in her stomach.

"Yes, of course."

"Have you eaten anything?" he asked.

"Not yet."

"I'll bring food if you'll tell me what sounds good to you."

The offer momentarily stumped her. She hadn't had the luxury of being picky about food, but there was one thing she never turned down.

"A vanilla malt. I haven't had one in ages."

He chuckled. "If I'd thought about it, I would already have known that. I'll be there shortly."

She closed her eyes as they spoke, concentrating solely on that deep voice rumbling in her ear.

"I can't wait to see you. Last night I dreamed you weren't really here," she said.

"I'm real, and I'll bring a malt and a kiss just to prove it."

"Thank you, Bowie. See you soon."

He laid the phone in the console, took a right turn and headed for Larry's Drive-In to get their food. He added two burgers, fries and a chocolate malt to go with the vanilla malt he ordered for Talia. Maybe he could tempt her to eat something, too.

While she was waiting for Bowie, Talia went to change her shirt and brush her hair. It had been so long since she cared what she looked like that it almost felt foreign to feel that way now.

She glanced in the mirror as she put her hair back into a quick ponytail, and then stopped and looked— really looked—at what caring for her father had done to her.

She was at least twenty pounds underweight. She looked as tired as she felt, and she could see the faint tic of a muscle near her left eye. She laid down the hairbrush and walked out of the bathroom straight to her father's bedside.

Marshall Champion used to stand six feet tall in his bare feet, with a head of thick, curly brown hair he kept short. His body had been strong and muscular from all his years working on the railroad. But that was then, and this was now, and Talia could no longer see her father in the man lying in this bed. He was a shell of who he'd been, and she was so grateful for him that this hell was finally coming to an end.

"Hey, Dad, Bowie is coming to see us," she said, as she patted his arm, then straightened the edge of his covers and smoothed back the tiny wisps of the hair he had left.

Suddenly he exhaled so loudly that it startled her. She stood stock-still for a few moments, her heart pounding as she waited for him to take that next breath. Just when she thought it wasn't going to happen, she saw his eyelids flutter, and then she heard him inhale.

She sighed. He was still fighting the good fight.

"I'm here, Dad. For as long as you need me, I'm here," she whispered, then kissed his forehead and eased down in the chair beside his bed.

She didn't mean to fall asleep, but she did. The next thing she knew, someone was knocking at the door. She stood abruptly, checked on her father and then headed for the door.

Bowie's hands were full as he leaned in and kissed her instead of saying hello. He handed her the malt and carried the rest inside, smiling to himself when she closed her eyes at that first sip. Then he glanced toward the bed.

"How's it going today?"

"He's still here," she said softly.

"Where do you want to eat?" he asked. "I'm good with in here if you want to stay close."

She nodded, and pointed to the sofa.

"You can use the coffee table."

He put down the food and waited for her to settle, then sat beside her and began unwrapping the burgers. He laid the fries out close to her, then put one in her mouth before he took a bite of his burger.

They ate without talking.

Bowie could tell by her red-rimmed eyes that if she had to talk she was going to cry, and he wanted to get as much sustenance in her as he could beforehand.

For Talia, it had been so long since she'd allowed herself to feel that now it was all overwhelming her. Bowie had brought her back to life when he'd forgiven her for the lie. The fact that he still wanted her hadn't really sunk in. Everything she was feeling now felt new: the cold, sweet taste of ice cream on her tongue, and the savory bite of salt on the fries. She could feel the warmth of Bowie's body as she leaned against it and absorbed the gentleness of his presence as proof she wasn't dreaming. When he coaxed her to eat a few more fries, she did so to please him, and all the while she could hear her father's unsteady breathing and the occasional rattle in his chest.

"You eat the other burger, too," she said.

He frowned. "Are you sure you don't want at least a few bites?"

"I'm sure," she said, then pushed the food aside and allowed herself to look, really look, at Bowie. He was still so beautiful in her eyes. She remembered how much she loved making love with him. One day it would happen again. The thought was a promise to hold on to.

"The malt was so good. Thank you."

"You're welcome." But when he saw tears pooling in her eyes, he opened his arms. "Come here to me," he said gently.

Talia swallowed past the knot in her throat and wrapped her arms around his neck. When she did, he pulled her into his lap. She laid her head against his shoulder, then flattened her hand over the strong steady beat of his heart. His strength was what was pulling her back into the land of the living.

"He's worse, isn't he?" Bowie asked.

She nodded.

He held her just a little bit tighter. "Is your hospice nurse coming today?"

"Yes. I called her."

"Because...?"

She lowered her voice to a whisper so her father couldn't possibly hear.

"Because I think today he will die."

Bowie felt her shaking.

"Are you not ready to lose him? Is that why you're trembling?"

"No, God, no," she said. "I wish for all this to be

over for him. But I also want it to be over for me, too. I don't have another week of this left in me. I'm not even sure I have another day, and I feel guilty for thinking that with every breath I take."

Then she started to cry, and Bowie pulled her close.

"I won't leave you alone, okay? I'll be right here with you until it's over. Don't cry, please don't cry."

As he held her, he wondered how many times she'd cried like this alone, and why life was so damn hard to get through. His parents had been the happiest two people he'd ever known, and look what had happened to them.

He and Talia had been so ready to begin a life together when another man's fate ended their dreams. When she buried her father, the sacrifice she'd made for him would be a thing of the past, but his mother was still waiting for justice. Life sure wasn't fair.

A few moments later Marshall gasped. Talia flew out of Bowie's arms and ran to her father's bedside just as someone knocked at the front door.

"That's probably Erin," she said, and quickly let her in. "Dad's really struggling," she told Erin abruptly, and ran back to the bed.

Erin saw Bowie cleaning up the remnants of a meal, and since they'd already met, she nodded a quick hello.

Bowie headed for the kitchen with the trash and then walked out onto the back porch to call home. Even though he'd told Talia he would stay, he was torn about where he belonged. He needed to make sure all was well back home.

He made the call and then, as he was waiting for his mother to answer, noticed the helipad was easily visible from here and wondered if Talia had seen him arriving.

"Hello?" his mother said.

"Mama, it's me. I'm at Talia's."

"How is she? How is Marshall?"

"That's part of why I'm calling. She thinks it's just a matter of hours."

"Oh, bless her heart. Who's there with her?"

"The hospice nurse just got here…and me."

"Don't they have any family in the area? Isn't there someone from the church? She shouldn't face this alone. You should stay."

"I wanted to, but I had to make sure you would—"

"Oh, good Lord, Bowie! We're fine. Polly is here right now, and Samuel already called to let me know he'd do the evening chores. We're all in a state of wait-and-see, and you know it. You've lit a fire under the authorities. Now we have to wait for them to do their job."

He breathed a quiet sigh of relief.

"Thank you for understanding. I'll call or text you later."

"I love you, Bowie. Be happy with her, and tell her we love her and are sending her our prayers."

"Yes, ma'am, and I love you, too," Bowie said, and then went back inside.

Erin was at Marshall's bedside assessing his vitals while Talia stood at the foot of the bed, watching. Bowie walked up behind her and wrapped her in his arms. She curled her fingers around his wrists and leaned against him, grateful for his strength.

"Was I right?" Talia asked.

Erin looked up and nodded.

Talia's shoulders slumped, and then she stepped out of Bowie's arms and moved to her father's side. She touched his arm, his cheek, leaned over and kissed his forehead, then whispered in his ear, "It's okay now, Daddy. It's time to go home."

Bowie couldn't hear what she said, but he knew she'd just let her father go. He took a deep breath and focused on a picture on the wall above the bed to keep from crying. He knew what she was feeling. Even if the circumstance were vastly different, the loss was still the same.

Erin McClune was filled with empathy for Talia and what was happening. She'd been in this place so many times before, and it never changed. The medical staff who helped bring babies into the world always had their moments of elation, while Erin and others like her had their own sense of quiet accomplishment knowing they were helping families as their loved ones passed on.

For all three of them standing watch, time seemed to stop. It was as if the only sound in the little house was the faint, intermittent inhale and exhale of Marshall Champion's breath.

Bowie wondered if Marshall was in pain, and wondered if, in his father's last seconds, the pain had faded for him. God, he hoped so. His father had died alone.

Marshall would not, and yet neither man would have ever imagined the way he would exit this world.

Talia had always heard that when someone died, their life flashed before their eyes. She didn't know what her father was experiencing, but she was being bombarded with precious memories of their life together.

Once she glanced up at the clock. It was almost three in the afternoon. They'd been standing there waiting for more than two hours, and in that time Bowie had not budged from the foot of the bed. She hurt for the tears on his cheeks. This had to remind him of losing his dad, and yet he'd stayed.

She looked back at her father just as he exhaled again, and waited for him to take the next breath. When he didn't, the hair stood up on the back of her neck.

Erin already had her stethoscope on his chest, listening for a heartbeat.

Talia's fingers tightened around the bed rail as they waited. Bowie walked up behind her, then put a hand on one shoulder, just so she wouldn't feel alone.

Erin glanced at her watch and called it.

"Time of death, 3:15 p.m."

Talia took that deep breath her father had not needed as she laid her hand on the crown of his head.

"Rest in peace, Dad. You have so earned it."

She was crying again, but Bowie didn't think she knew it.

"What happens now, Erin? Is there anything I can do?" he asked.

Erin glanced at Talia.

"Maybe you could take her outside on the back porch for a bit. I'll need some warm water, and a towel and washcloth. I'll notify the funeral home. Talia already gave me all the necessary information. This much I can do for her."

Talia realized this was where her path with her father ended. Wherever Marshall went from here, she could not follow.

"I'll get the bath stuff for you," Talia said.

"I'll help," Bowie said. As soon as they had everything Erin needed, Bowie took her hand. "Let's go sit in your porch swing, okay?"

She glanced at her dad and then nodded.

Bowie grabbed a cold bottle of Pepsi from the refrigerator as they passed through the kitchen.

Talia settled in the porch swing, and Bowie slid onto the seat beside her. He unscrewed the lid on the pop and handed it to her. She took a drink, and then handed the bottle back to him and leaned against his shoulder.

"Oh, Bowie," she said softly, and then let go of everything she'd been trying to hide.

It was over, and she didn't know how to feel, only that she couldn't hold back the tears. They marked her relief. They stood for the joy that her father was no longer suffering, and at the same time, they were mute reminders of the years she would never get back.

Bowie set the Pepsi aside and held her. By the time the hearse from the funeral home arrived, she'd cried herself out. When they went back inside, once again Talia had to watch others take charge of her father's body.

Mr. Monroe, the funeral director, was talking to her, but they were moving her father's body to a gurney, and she felt like she should tell him good-bye. Instead, she got the garment bag from her father's bedroom that held the clothing they would need to ready him for burial. She handed it over and then tuned everything out. She didn't know how long she'd been standing there when she realized Mr. Monroe was repeating her name. She flinched. When she did, Bowie gently squeezed her shoulder.

"I'm sorry," she said. "I wasn't…"

"It's okay, honey. I'll fill you in later," Bowie said.

"We're going to leave now," Mr. Monroe said. "You and I have already talked about your father's wishes. We'll do this right for you."

"Thank you, but remember it's a closed casket for visitation," Talia said.

"Yes, ma'am. We understand," Monroe said.

Bowie heard a quiet anger in her voice as she kept talking.

"No one came to see him before. I'm not putting him on view for the curious to remark upon now."

"Of course. I'll call and let you know when we have him ready. You can say your goodbyes before we seal the casket."

She swallowed past the lump in her throat.

"Yes. Thank you."

And then they were gone, and Erin was waiting with papers for Talia to sign.

"I'll have the company call you before they come to pick up the hospital bed. It will likely take two or three days for them to get here," Erin said.

"Thank you," Talia said, and threw her arms around Erin's neck. "I couldn't have done this without you. I will hold you in my heart forever for this."

Now Erin was tearing up.

"It was my honor to help your father and you," she said; then she looked at Bowie. "My sympathies to your family, but I hope you and Talia will be very happy. You both deserve to know joy."

And then she, too, was gone.

Talia turned around. Bowie was standing between her and that empty bed. When he opened his arms, she walked into them.

Neither one of them spoke. He just held her, but he could feel her shaking.

"Do you think you could sleep? You're still trembling," he said.

Talia shuddered.

"I can't quit shaking, and I don't know why. I feel cold inside, but the room isn't cold."

"That's shock. You need to get off your feet and into bed. Even if you can't sleep, you need to rest, okay?"

She was shivering harder now.

"I feel like I could sleep for a week, but I don't know if I can relax."

"Let's try," he said, then picked her up in his arms and carried her into her bedroom. He set her down by the bed and pulled back the covers.

Talia couldn't think what to do next.

"Take off your shoes and jeans, honey. You'll rest better," Bowie said, but when she tried to unbutton the waistband of her jeans her hands were shaking too much to grip.

"Here, let me help," he said, and had her barefoot and her jeans off in moments.

She crawled in between the sheets, and when her head hit the pillow, she sighed. She closed her eyes as Bowie drew up the covers to warm her, then pulled the shades and curtains to darken the room. She needed to thank him, but she could barely focus.

"Bowie?"

"Yes?"

"Thank you for coming back. Thank you for forgiving me. Thank you for—"

Bowie sighed. She'd fallen asleep in midsentence. He glanced around the room to the easy chair near her desk, pulled it close to her bed and settled in. He sent a text to his mother, telling her Marshall was gone, and that Talia was in shock and he couldn't get her warm. He said that he'd put her to bed and wouldn't leave until he was sure she was okay.

Within seconds he got a text back.

Stay with her. Samuel and Bella are spending the night. They send their love and so do I.

Bowie pinched the bridge of his nose to keep from crying as he laid his phone aside. There was a knot in his belly. The past few days had, without doubt, been the worst days of their lives. Things had to start getting better.

He heard Talia crying, but she was asleep and so fragile he couldn't bear to see her lying there alone. He kicked off his boots and eased down on top of the covers beside her. He put one arm over her waist, and stretched the other on to the pillow above her head and just held her.

Slowly her shaking began to ease until she was finally still.

And they slept.

# *Eleven*

Constable Riordan and a search team rolled up to the Wayne lake house at mid-afternoon. Riordan had asked Chief Clayton of the Eden PD to deliver the second search warrant to Jack Wayne as he and his men were on their way to the property. He intended to be there before the family got word of the search to make sure no one had time to remove any incriminating evidence.

Riordan had just dispatched part of the team to the large outbuilding west of the house when two vehicles suddenly appeared on the road leading down to the house, driving at a high rate of speed.

"It appears the search warrant has been served," he said, and then headed for the house with the rest of his team behind him.

Blake Wayne was in the car behind his Uncle Jack without knowing exactly why. He'd received a brief text from Jack that he couldn't ignore.

Get to the lake house now.

He'd reacted without question, but now that he saw the contingent of police vans and vehicles on the property, his gut knotted.

"What the hell?" he muttered, as he came to a sliding halt beside Jack's car.

Jack had pulled up practically to the front door and was already out of his car and heading for the house, bellowing at the top of his voice, when Blake caught up with him.

"Stop them!" Jack yelled, pointing at the police, who were about to break in the door.

Riordan heard Jack shout and stopped his men in the act of forcing the door.

"It appears the man with the key just arrived," he drawled.

Jack waded through the officers surrounding Riordan, resisting the urge to push and shove.

"If you wanted to search this property, you should have asked," Jack blustered, as he fished the door key from his pocket.

Riordan resented the man's attitude and didn't bother to hide it.

"No, sir, I don't have to ask you for anything," Riordan said. "Your legal notification was served, and that's all the warning you get when you are a suspect in a murder investigation."

Jack sputtered and muttered beneath his breath as he unlocked the door, but it was hard to argue with the truth. The door swung inward, and Jack started to lead the way inside, when Riordan stopped him.

"No, sir. You will be staying outside."

"But I can help—"

Riordan's eyes narrowed angrily.

"You didn't even mention this place existed when we asked where the guns might be, so your assistance is not only unnecessary, it is unwanted. It's a trust issue. I'm sure you understand."

Blake made his way through the crowd in time to hear Riordan ordering Jack to stay out of the house, and when Riordan saw him, he waved Blake away, too, designating a young officer to stay outside with both of them, under orders not to let them out of his sight.

Jack threw his arms up in a gesture of exasperation. "I resent the hell out of you continually treating us like criminals." But the moment he said it, he realized how ridiculous it sounded. In the eyes of the law, they were all murder suspects. "Whatever," he muttered, and strode back toward his car.

Blake followed, saying nothing. When he saw a half-dozen other officers milling around the garage, he started toward them when their guard stopped him.

"No, sir. You stay here."

"Oh. Right," Blake said, and walked back to his uncle.

"Hell of a mess," Jack said.

Blake nodded.

Jack glared at him.

"When I find out which one of you brought this down on our family, he or she will be on their own. I won't waste a penny on legal services for any of you."

Blake glared back.

"Well, hell, Uncle Jack, I hate to break this to you when you're so out of sorts, but you don't have the legal power to do that. Every one of us, including my son, is part of Wayne Industries, and we can and will, at any time we choose, avail ourselves of all that entails." Blake glanced at the guard and lowered his voice. "I don't know who did it, but I can understand what triggered the impulse."

Jack's eyes widened as his lips parted in sudden shock.

"Really? You understand a killer's thoughts so well you can make an excuse for the deed?"

Blake reacted before he thought, getting in his uncle's face to challenge his sudden do-gooder attitude.

"Oh, hell, no! You don't pretend with me. You and Justin and I all know what a big knot Stanton Young-blood tied in the resort plans when his siblings' properties were no longer eligible for foreclosure."

Jack shrugged. "So we'll buy them out."

Blake rolled his eyes.

"Why do you think Stanton paid off their loans?"

Jack shrugged. "I don't know. Because he was trying to stop something we—"

Blake sighed.

"No! Hell, no! We weren't even on his radar. He was keeping his brother and sister from losing their homes—homes that had been in both families for a good three generations. They won't take your money. They don't give a shit about that resort as long as it doesn't displace them. I told the investors when they set out to accumulate property that it might be an issue. Now the central part of the land they need is no longer available, nor will it be, which means plans for the resort are now at a standstill. And there better not be any discussion of so-called accidents to either family now, or the cops will blame the whole damn lot of us and we'll all wind up in prison."

Jack glanced at the guard and then lowered *his* voice, too.

"So when did you know Youngblood was the one who paid off those loans?"

Blake shrugged. "I guess as soon as the other investors knew. We were all notified there was a hitch."

"Why wasn't *I* notified?" Jack asked.

"Because investments are my job, that's why. I didn't need your advice or permission."

Jack stopped and then stared at Blake as if he'd never seen him before.

"You didn't need my permission to do *what*?"

Blake looked a little taken aback and flushed.

"To do my job," Blake sputtered.

"Indeed," Jack muttered, and then noticed the officers coming out of the garage pushing a motorcycle.

Blake sighed. "Should have figured they would find that," he said.

"Who owns that?" Jack asked.

"The company," Blake said.

"Who rides it?"

"I guess everyone but you and Fiona has been on it at one time or another," Blake said.

They watched without further comment as the officers loaded the motorcycle into the back of one of the county vans and then headed into the house to join the others.

Moments later, other officers began coming out carrying rifles.

Jack flinched. "Did you know these were out here?" he asked.

"Yes," Blake said.

"Did you tell Riordan?"

"No."

"I wonder who did?" Jack said.

"It doesn't matter," Blake said. "They knew we had them. They're all registered."

"Do we know what kind of weapon killed Young-blood?" Jack asked.

"Riordan didn't mention a particular model. He just asked the location of any rifles that were registered to the family. I said I wasn't sure anymore. I obviously lied," Blake muttered.

Jack shook his head, handed Blake the door key, then got back in his car and drove away.

Blake leaned against his car with his arms crossed, watching the uniformed officers continuing to emerge with still more rifles.

The wind was beginning to quicken. He glanced up at the sky and then frowned. It appeared they were in for another thunderstorm, which seemed fitting. Their whole way of life was in turmoil.

Finally the cops finished their search and exited the house. Riordan was the last to emerge.

Blake approached with the key in hand.

Riordan looked around for Jack. "Where's your uncle?" he asked.

"He left. I waited to lock up."

Riordan gave Blake a studied look. "So you didn't know where the guns were?"

"I haven't been out here in years," Blake said.

"That's not what I was told," Riordan said, and then got in his car and led the way off the property.

Blake's gut was in a knot as he went inside to see what damage they'd done. Cabinet doors and drawers were open, room doors were ajar. And the gun cabinet was empty. He went through the house closing doors and drawers, putting things back to rights as best he could, and then locked the front door on the way out.

He drove back to Eden with one thought on his mind. Which member of his family had blabbed about the location of the rifles? And why? What did they know? Were they trying to point a finger at someone else by being too forthcoming? He couldn't imagine which one of them would do it, but he was going to find out.

Bowie was dreaming of his father. He could see him standing in the tree line just beyond the garden, talking and waving, but he couldn't hear what he was saying. Thinking he needed to get closer, he started forward just as a loud explosion erupted behind him. Before he could turn around to see what had happened, his father's image began to fade. Then he heard another sound, like the crack of a gunshot, and his father was gone.

He woke abruptly, only to realize the explosion he'd heard was thunder, and the gunshot, a bolt of lightning. And he was in Talia's bedroom, but she was gone.

He rolled out of bed and headed toward the front of the house, following the scent of fresh-brewed coffee. Talia was standing at the kitchen sink, looking through the window and watching it rain.

He walked up behind her and slid a hand around her waist. It bothered him that he could so readily feel her ribs, and he didn't know where to start to help her heal. "Are you okay?"

She nodded as she leaned back against him.

"I woke up, thinking I needed to check on Dad. It will take a while for me to get out of that habit, I guess."

"Is there anything you need to do? I'll do it for you if I can, or take you to do it," Bowie said.

"No, there's nothing. I prepared for this day a long time ago, but I forgot to plan for what I would do without him."

Bowie kissed the back of her neck.

She turned to face him.

"You're sure you still want to resurrect this relationship?" she asked.

He heard the uncertainty in her voice and frowned.

"Yes. I want to grow old with you, Talia. All I ever wanted from you was for you to love me."

She traced the curve of his jaw, brushed a thumb over his lower lip, then reached behind his neck and pulled the band from his hair. The long dark strands fell over her hands and down on to his shoulders.

"I've been trying to tell myself that wanting to make love with you now is inappropriate so soon after my father's death, but when I woke up and saw you lying beside me, I was reminded that I had given up enough. It's time to live for me. I'm not pretty anymore, but my heart still beats the same for you. Will you make love to me, Bowie?"

It was, to Bowie, tragic that she thought she had to ask when the sight of her still made his heart race.

"You will always be beautiful to me," he said, and swung her up into his arms.

He carried her back through the house and into her room, kicking the door shut behind him. The moment he put her down she began to strip.

He came out of his clothes erect and aching, and took a condom out of his wallet. The last thing she needed was to get pregnant before she got well. Wind was blowing rain against the windows as he slid into bed beside her. He heard her sigh as she put her arms around his neck.

"Oh, Bowie, please, tell me I'm not dreaming."

He brushed a kiss across her lips, then ran the back of his finger against her cheek.

"Not a dream. Just a beautiful reality for both

of us, and I am so damned scared I'm going to hurt you, I can't think."

"The pain of the last seven years nearly killed me. I want to feel whole again. I want to remember what it's like to feel joy."

He groaned beneath his breath as he took her in his arms. This he could give her, knowing full well it would be just as healing for him.

Thunder rolled above them as he centered his mouth on her lips. Holding her in his arms like this wiped out the pain of believing she didn't love him, easing the loneliness of the past seven years and giving him something he'd thought he would never have: a family with the only woman he had ever loved.

Their kisses quickly awakened an urgent need for more. Her skin was so smooth and soft, just as he remembered, and when he cupped her breast, the moan that came up her throat vibrated within him.

It was joy.

Talia couldn't contain her elation. She kept stroking his face, then his arms, across the back of his shoulders, marveling at how wide they'd become. He'd left her as a teenage boy and come back a man. When he slid a knee between her legs, she shifted to let him in, then exhaled slowly as the hard length of him filled her.

Bowie's blood was racing. He wanted her, all of her—and now—but he paused, giving her time to adjust.

Then she wrapped her legs around his waist and

whispered in his ear, "Love me, Bowie. Love me like you used to."

And so he did.

All the emotional pain they had been suffering slowly turned into passion. The more time that passed, the hotter the heat grew within them. The act became a desperate chase for the climax that stayed just out of reach.

Talia had lost all consciousness of self and was focused on that blood rush with every sense she possessed. When the climax happened, it came between one breath and the next, rolling through her in waves, and leaving her weak and spent for the aftershocks that followed.

The moment Bowie felt her muscles contracting around him, he let go, riding out the shattering spasms of release that followed. Just before he lost the ability to think, he rolled onto his back to keep from crushing her and took her with him. They savored the aftermath in silence, with Talia stretched out on Bowie's chest and his arms holding her gently in place.

Finally, she rose up enough to look at him and smiled. This was just as she had remembered him. Dark hair framing that strong, beautiful face and a look of love in his eyes.

"Are you okay, baby?" Bowie asked.

"So happy," she said softly, then frowned as her cell phone rang. She checked the caller ID and rolled off him to answer.

He could tell by her one-sided conversation that

she was setting up a time for the hospital bed to be removed from her house. Life had intruded.

He rolled out of bed and went across the hall to the bathroom. When he came out she was already getting dressed. He grabbed his clothes and started putting them back on.

"They're going to pick the bed up in the morning, around ten," she said, and then glanced toward the window. Even though the shades and curtains were pulled, she could hear the rain still blowing against the house.

"I told Mama I was staying with you tonight," Bowie said.

Talia's heart skipped. It was wonderful news, but she felt guilty for keeping him away from his family in the midst of all their troubles.

"Is it okay? I mean, don't they need you?"

Bowie smiled, and combed the unruly strands of her hair away from her face,

"My three able brothers and their wives and a bunch of relatives are on hand. Mama said Samuel and Bella are spending the night, so, no, she doesn't need me tonight. And even in the middle of her grief, like me, she was worried about you. I'll go home in the morning. I would ask you to go with me, but I know you have things to do here, funeral arrangements to make."

"Don't worry about me," Talia said. "Everything was decided months ago, but I still need to stay here, and your mother doesn't need guests when she's grieving."

"The offer stays open," Bowie said, as he finger-combed his hair and fastened it back at the nape of his neck. "I'm getting hungry. How about you?" he asked.

"A little," she said. "I don't have a lot of groceries in the house, but we could make omelets."

"Sounds perfect," he said, then leaned down and kissed the smile on her face. "You're perfect, too."

Talia was still smiling as she led the way to the kitchen.

Dinner at the mansion alternated between sardonic discourse and silence. The storm was making more noise than they were. When a nearby flash of lightning made their lights flicker, Justin cursed.

"Oh, hell, yes. Let's add to the mood by winding up in total darkness."

Nita glanced at her younger brother.

"Who tied your tail in a knot today?"

Justin looked up and then at the family seated around the table—everyone except Jack. Acknowledging his presence, even for propriety's sake, wasn't happening. He wasn't going to let go of being bitch-slapped.

"All of you. None of you. One of you. I am so weary of having the police on our ass from sunup to sundown that I can't think. If my sister wasn't such a royal bitch, this wouldn't be happening."

"No, if your sister's husband hadn't lived long enough to point a finger at his killer, this wouldn't be happening," Nita snapped. "And that means the killer is the one who fucked up, and I'm tired of hearing you whine. Someone at this table caused this. Not Leigh. Not Stanton. Not the cops. One of *us*," Nita said, and then picked up her spoon and tapped it against her water glass until the maid came in. "We're ready for the dessert course," she said.

"Yes, ma'am," the maid said, and hurried out of the dining room.

The whole family stared as one at Nita.

"What?" she asked.

"Do you ever have serious thoughts?" Jack asked.

"I'm serious about dessert," Nita snapped, and then clinked her spoon against the water glass one more time purely for the sake of aggravating him.

Fiona rolled her eyes.

Blake ignored her.

The lights flickered.

Justin glared up at the chandelier.

The maid returned with the pastry cart.

"Pecan pie with bourbon-infused chantilly cream, sir," she said, and served Jack first.

Jack nodded.

"Looks good. My compliments to the chef tonight."

"Yes, sir," she said, then moved around the table, serving the others. She followed up the pie with a carafe of freshly brewed coffee and filled their cups before leaving the room.

"This is really good," Charles said, as he dug in with enjoyment.

"Indeed," Jack said, eyeing their youngest family

member. "So how did you feel being questioned by the police this morning?"

Charles glanced up from his pie. "Who? Me?"

Jack nodded.

"It was strange, for sure," Charles said.

"Did any of the questions upset you?" Jack asked.

Charles chewed and swallowed. "No, sir."

Justin slapped the table. "Why don't you just spit it out, Uncle Jack? You want to know what each of us said, because you're mad that the cops showed up at the lake house, right?"

Jack glared. Justin was the nephew who always picked at the scabs this family had until they bled. Every damn time. But now that they knew what he was getting at, he asked point-blank, "So how *did* they know the guns and motorcycle were out there? I didn't even know we owned a motorcycle."

Blake sighed.

"They're the police. They research shit, Uncle Jack. Since nothing was here, they searched the next place we owned. It's simple."

Nita poured two scoops of sugar into her coffee and stirred with enough vigor that it sloshed on to her saucer.

Jack's eyes narrowed when he saw her fingers shaking.

"What did you tell them, Nita?"

She shrugged and took another bite of pie without looking at him.

Now Jack was the one slapping the table, hard

enough that the dishes rattled. "It *was* you who did it, wasn't it?" he shouted.

"Who did what?" Nita asked. "You told us to play it cool. You told us to comply without anger. I complied."

Charles was now completely silent, listening as his uncle began harassing his aunt. Finally he stood up and then clinked his spoon against his water glass.

"Excuse me," he said, as everyone turned to look at him.

"They interviewed me last. I don't know what everyone else said before they got to me. They already knew we owned them, remember? I assumed since the killer rode a motorcyle and the family owned one, and Youngblood wrote the name Wayne... Obviously the only thing the cops didn't know was where they were kept."

Jack's glare darkened, and the tone of his voice turned ugly, almost threatening, when he asked, "What did you tell them, boy?"

"That there were guns in a gun case at the lake house. I didn't know about any motorcycle or I would have been riding it."

Nita shoved her coffee aside and stood up, too.

"I told them about the motorcycle when I was asked where it was, because I don't want to be a part of this anymore. I am ashamed that Leigh's husband is dead because of us, and probably because we continue to feel the need to be richer than we already are. And don't treat me like this again, Mad Jack Wayne. You aren't lily-white, and we both know it."

She walked out of the dining room with her head up and her backside swinging.

Fiona sighed. "Excuse me," she said, and followed her sister.

Charles glanced at his dad.

"Sorry if I did something wrong. This is the first time I've gotten enough insight into this family to realize that I should always lie. I thought I was supposed to tell the truth."

"You didn't do anything wrong," Blake said. "Don't worry about it again, okay?"

Charles shrugged, then left, as well.

Justin picked up his fork and took another bite of dessert.

"Damn good pie," he said, chewing as he spoke.

Blake ignored his younger brother just as he'd done ever since Justin learned to walk.

"Uncle Jack, you're only making a bad situation worse. You're successfully dividing this family in a way no one has ever done before."

"Except Leigh," Justin said, and took another bite of pie.

"Shut up, Justin. As a favor to me," Blake muttered.

Jack glared at both of them.

"Which one of you did it?" he asked.

Blake shook his head and left the room.

Justin just kept eating pie.

Jack knew his nephew would probably never forgive him for the slap-down, and while a part of him didn't give a damn, he regretted it just the same.

"Look, Justin, we need—"

Justin dropped his fork and walked out, still chewing the last bite of his dessert.

Jack was, for one of the few times in his life, speechless.

An hour had passed since the dessert fiasco. The killer was tired of the turmoil within the family, but staying under the radar was simple. Just act indignant along with everyone else.

So the cops had the rifle. So they had the motorcycle. So what. No matter what fingerprints or DNA they found, it would never be conclusive evidence against one person. Not when there were multiple owners and easy access.

Nita was in her favorite pink silk pajamas. Her makeup was off, and she'd already pinned her hair up for the night when her phone rang. She glanced at caller ID and then grabbed it.

"Hello, my darling. How sweet of you to call," she cooed.

Andrew fell right into his "adoration of Nita" tone.

"I've been missing my girl," he said. "I kind of thought *you* would call *me*. Have I hurt your feelings in any way?"

Nita wiggled with delight. Finally someone focusing on her in a special way, and even if it was bought and paid for, he was good at it.

"You have not, you silly thing. It's just been a day of hell. The county constable was here this morn-

ing, interviewing everyone about that nasty murder thing."

"I can only imagine," Andrew said. "What you
need is a little loving from a good man. I'd readily
volunteer—unless you have a better one waiting in
the wings?"

Nita moaned beneath her breath.

"No, no, there's no one in my life but you, and I
do need you. I would thoroughly love a session with
you and your big, hard dick."

Andrew chuckled. He did enjoy a satisfied customer.

"Do you want me to pick you up?" he asked.

Nita sighed. "I'm already undressed and in bed,"
she said.

Andrew growled softly in her ear.

"Then you're ready. Turn out the lights and lock
your door. I'll talk you through the biggest orgasm
you've ever had."

Nita moaned.

Andrew smiled.

Success, and he didn't even have to break a sweat.

# *Twelve*

The thunderstorm passed before morning, and Bowie slept all the way through it with Talia in his arms. Although the passion between them had him longing to make love all night, she was fragile in so many ways that all he could bring himself to do was hold her.

Waking up beside her was a wonderful glimpse of their future. He was already planning how to change his job for the oil company so he didn't have to work the offshore platforms anymore. No way could he stand being on-site for weeks at a time. Whatever it took to be able to go home to her each night would be worth it. They'd lost time, but thank God they hadn't lost each other.

After a quick breakfast together, he was already regretting he couldn't stay, but he had to go home and help there, too. Talia followed him out onto the front porch and then shamelessly threw herself into his arms to say goodbye.

Bowie laughed as she wrapped her arms around his neck.

"You're not going to make this easy, are you, sweetheart?"

She shook her head.

"Once I let you leave my life without a word. That will never happen again. Come back to me, love, when you can."

He cupped her cheeks as he brushed a kiss across her lips.

"Oh, I have to come back. I'm leaving my heart with you." Then gave her one last hug before leaving.

Talia watched him back out of the drive, then went inside to wait for the people to come pick up the hospital bed. While she was waiting, the funeral home called to tell her that her father's body was ready for a last viewing. Too many things happening at once.

Justin Wayne was on his way to the helipad, thinking about what Blake had asked him to do. The investors were going to fly over the area one last time to see if they could find a suitable substitute for the resort location. If they couldn't settle on anything here, they would scrap the resort altogether and take their project to the state that had been their second choice. Justin knew what that would mean to the family. If the developers took the resort out of state, the Waynes would be the proud owners of a whole lot of useless land on a mountain and nothing more.

His mind was on the job until he turned down the street that would take him to the helipad. He noticed a couple kissing on a front porch. When it dawned on him that the man was the same one who'd stood outside their gates challenging him, he nearly hit the brakes. What stopped him was the realization that the man was even bigger than he'd thought. He was suddenly glad Fiona and Nita had stopped him from making a fool of himself. Still, the urge to take the man down was strong, and ways to make that happen floated through the back of his mind all day.

Once Bowie got home, his job became keeping Jesse busy so that Leigh could work in peace in the garden.

She'd been hoeing these green beans when Stanton was murdered, and now it was time to pick them again. Later they would all sit out on the porch and break the beans so she could can them. Stanton was gone, but they were not, and life's needs went on. She finished about an hour before noon and left the green beans inside the utility room when she went inside to start the midday meal. It passed in relative quiet once Jesse settled down to eat. They were just finishing when they heard a car coming up the driveway.

"Someone's here!" Jesse cried, and bolted from the table.

Leigh sighed.

"Go run him down for me, will you, son? I want to gather up the dirty dishes."

"Yes, ma'am," Bowie said, and left the kitchen.

Jesse was already outside on the porch, but when Bowie came out, Jesse backed up against him.

"I don't know this man," Jesse said.

"It's okay. I do," Bowie said. "Go tell Mama the constable is here."

"Yeah, the constable," Jesse said, and headed into the house as Riordan approached.

"Afternoon, Constable. Did you come to tell us you have the killer under arrest?" Bowie asked.

Riordan sighed.

"Not yet. I need to talk to your mother. I'm hoping she might have some insight into her family that would help us."

The screen door opened behind Bowie.

"Come in, Constable Riordan, and take a seat," Leigh said.

Bowie stepped aside as Riordan followed Leigh into the house.

Jesse was sitting in Stanton's chair, ready to visit.

Leigh glanced at him. "Jesse, would you like to take the peelings out and feed them to the chickens? Remember to close the gate behind you when you go in *and* when you come out."

Jesse beamed. "Yes, ma'am. I like to feed the chickens."

"I know you do. The peelings are in the blue tin bowl on the cabinet. When you're done, come right back, okay?"

"Yes, ma'am. Close the gate in and close the gate out."

Leigh ran a hand over Jesse's head to smooth back a strand of hair. As she did, she felt the ridges of scar tissue beneath.

"Run along now," she said.

"Do you want me to go with him?" Bowie asked.

"No. I want you to stay with me," Leigh said, and sat down on the couch opposite the chair where Riordan was sitting.

Bowie sat beside her.

"I'll make this brief," Riordan said. "First of all, I want to tell you again how sorry I am for your loss. The reason I'm here is that I'm hoping you can shine some light on your family for me."

"I haven't talked to any of them in over thirty years," Leigh said.

"How did you keep from running into them in Eden?" Riordan asked.

"Because they don't lower themselves to shopping where people like us would go. They have people to handle the mundane things in life," she said.

"Your children never ran into Charles while they were in school?"

"I don't know who Charles is," Leigh said.

Riordan didn't bother to hide his shock.

"He's Blake's son."

She shrugged. "I homeschooled my boys."

"You must be a very intelligent woman, Mrs. Youngblood."

She shrugged. The fact that she'd graduated college by the time she was seventeen was immaterial. Being the brain of the family had gotten her nothing but disdain. She'd had it drummed into her from her youth that her smarts were wasted on a girl.

"Stanton helped tremendously. He already had his

college degree in business and economics before we married. He was an online broker and licensed for quite a few years. He had his own clients."

"What will happen to them now?" Riordan asked.

Bowie touched his mother's arm and answered for her, because he knew she wouldn't.

"Mama took over the investment part of Daddy's business years ago. She and Daddy's clients will all be fine."

Riordan eyed Leigh with renewed respect.

"That's good to know. Meanwhile, as to why I came... Now that I understand the distance you kept between you and your family a little better, I want to know if you suspect any one sibling in particular. Is there anyone you think is capable of murder?"

She rolled her eyes. "Any of them. All of them."

Riordan grunted softly. "Seriously?"

Leigh sighed. "Our father was a hard taskmaster. He never liked to fail, and he drilled that same fear into all of us. I guess if I had to pick one, I'd pick Justin."

Bowie was surprised and let it show. "Your twin brother?"

Riordan frowned. "He's your twin?"

"I'm older by a minute and a half," Leigh said.

"Why Justin?" Riordan asked.

"He holds grudges, and he's mean like our father was," Leigh said. "Do you have any evidence against him?"

Riordan sighed.

"The evidence I have doesn't point to anyone in

particular, or I wouldn't be here. Telling you that is highly irregular, as I'm sure you know. Normally we don't admit there isn't much of a lead to follow."

Leigh's hands curled into fists.

"You aren't telling me they're going to get away with this, are you?" she asked.

"Not if I have anything to do with it," Riordan said. "I'm hoping someone panics and gives up the guilty party, or the killer panics and makes a mistake."

Leigh frowned.

"The only one who might panic is Nita, but unless it's common knowledge among them as to who did it, the guilty one will never tell."

"Why not?" Riordan asked.

"Because the others would turn him or her in just to get the monkey off their backs," she said.

Bowie was stunned. He couldn't imagine having that kind of relationship with family.

Riordan made a couple of notes and then moved to another topic.

"I need to ask you about paying off the loans on the property belonging to Stanton's brother, and also his sister's property."

Leigh nodded, then glanced over her shoulder, a little concerned Jesse wasn't back.

"Bowie, would you make sure Jesse is okay?"

"Yes, ma'am," Bowie said, and left the room.

Riordan could only imagine what it cost her emotionally to take care of a grown man with a child's mind. Her situation strengthened his determination to solve this crime as soon as possible.

"Did you and Stanton know when you decided to pay off those loans that your estranged family was heavily invested in the resort, and did you know they owned the lending institution that bought up the loans from the local bank?"

"No, of course not. Like I said, I know nothing about them now. Nothing. We did it because Polly and Carl are living on the Cyrus home place, and because Thomas and Beth are living on the Youngblood home place. Stuff like that matters to us. People hit hard times. It's not the first time the homesteads were ever mortgaged, but it was the first time the loans were called in. It was the abruptness of it that caused the hardship, and the new owner of the loans wasn't giving anyone a break."

The moment Leigh said that, her eyes welled with tears. She'd forgotten for a moment that there was no more "us." She took a slow, shaky breath and looked away.

Bowie came back at a lope.

"I had to take a picture," Bowie said. "You need to see what Jesse's doing." He was smiling when he sat down beside Leigh and handed her the phone.

The sight of her son happily sitting in the middle of the chicken yard hand-feeding peelings to the hens all bunched around him was exactly what she needed to see. She laughed.

"Oh my goodness, I've never seen him do that before," she said. Then she leaned forward to show the picture to Riordan. "He's going to be my saving grace in this heartbreak."

Riordan grinned. "If you could bottle up that joy and sell it, you'd be a rich woman," he said.

Leigh sighed. "I already am rich…in love and family."

"Yes, ma'am," Riordan said, as he handed the phone back to Bowie.

"Is there anything we can do?" Leigh asked. "I'll do anything to get justice for Stanton."

Riordan frowned. "No, ma'am. You do not put yourself in harm's way. You have a family who loves you and a son who needs you."

At that moment the back door banged, and then they heard footsteps.

"Speaking of that son," Leigh said, as she got up and caught Jesse on the run long enough to pick a little chicken feather from his hair, then check the back of his jeans to make sure he hadn't sat in chicken poop. "Go wash your hands, Jesse, then Bowie will get you a root beer."

"Root beer!" Jesse cried, and loped toward the hall.

Riordan's admiration for Leigh Youngblood rose even more as she sat back down.

"I'm sorry I wasn't more help," she said. "Maybe Polly or Thomas could tell you more, only they aren't at home today. One of Thomas's grandchildren is having surgery to fix a broken arm. They're all at the hospital."

Riordan nodded.

"No matter. Again, sorry to have bothered you, and thank you for your information."

"It wasn't nearly enough," Leigh said, and then got up to see the constable to the door.

She stood in the doorway until he was gone, then turned around and went to check on Jesse.

Even though she'd maintained her emotions, Bowie could tell she was upset. He heard her calling Michael and leaving a message, asking him to find out who now owned all the foreclosed property around the lake.

A short while later Michael returned her call. Bowie didn't know what was said between them, but whatever it was, she was quiet all afternoon as they sat out on the porch breaking beans. When they had finished, she carried them straight into the kitchen, ran some water into the huge basins of beans waiting to be canned and once again headed for her phone.

Bowie knew something was brewing when she called Samuel to ask if he was free to go to Eden with her now, and apparently he said yes, because she asked him to wear good clothes and bring Bella to stay with Jesse. Then she called Aidan and Michael and asked them the same thing, to which they, too, apparently agreed.

When Leigh turned around and saw Bowie looking at her, she lifted her chin.

"I'm going to change clothes. Did you bring any dress clothes?"

"Yes, ma'am. What I was going to wear to Daddy's funeral."

"Well, I need you to change into that for me, son."

"Where are we going, Mama?"

"To visit my family. They're not going to break ranks unless I rattle them, and I know just how to do that. I think it's time I introduced my sons to the enemy, and then I'm going to scare them so bad they'll uncover the guilty party and turn him or her in on their own."

Bowie's eyes widened. "Can you do that?"

She sighed.

"I vowed when I left that I'd never set foot in that hellhole again, but this situation calls for desperate measures. They value money and power, and I am their threat to all of that. Yes, I can make them very afraid."

"Where's Jesse?" Bowie asked.

"In his room, watching cartoons."

"Then I'll go change," he said.

As it turned out, all three of her daughters-in-law came, too. They settled in with Jesse, who was delighted his nephew, Johnny, was there to play with.

"We won't be long," Leigh said, as she thanked them for coming to help, and then gave her sons' appearances the once-over, just as she used to do when they were young.

They were all dressed in suits, or sports coats and slacks. Samuel's hair was in a braid. Aidan and Michael had pulled theirs back at their napes. Bowie had left his down in honor of his father. She seemed satisfied with how they looked.

"You look pretty, Mama," Samuel said.

Leigh smoothed a hand down the back of her hair and picked a tiny piece of lint from the front of the little black dress she was wearing.

"I know you're wondering why I asked you to do this. We're going to pay an unannounced visit to the Wayne family. Partly, I want them to see the beautiful sons Stanton and I made. I want them to know they did not beat us down, do you understand?"

"Yes, ma'am, but what are you going to do?" Samuel asked.

"I am going to put the fear of God in every one of them."

Samuel nodded.

"Good. I'm happy to do my part to make that happen," Michael added.

"Let me know if I need to growl at them, Mama," Aidan added.

There was a moment of confusion among the brothers until Leigh suddenly threw back her head and laughed.

"I'd almost forgotten about that," she said. "The year you were a dog. I didn't think you'd ever quit that."

Bowie grinned.

The other brothers laughed, too, now that she'd reminded them.

"You were four. I thought something was wrong with you, but your daddy just laughed and said you were being a boy, and he was right," Leigh said, and then the smile slid off her face as she drew a quick, shaky breath. "Damn them for taking him away from us. Let's go while I've still got my wits about me."

Moments later they were loading up in two vehicles, and then they were gone.


Because of the hot phone sex she and Andrew had shared last night, Nita woke up in a mood of euphoria. It lasted most of the day, until the family began coming home for dinner. At that point the mood in the house quickly darkened.

Blake and Justin were arguing when they entered the mansion. It escalated to a shouting match, which Jack brought to an abrupt end.

"What the hell is wrong with you two?" Jack asked.

When they both started to talk at once, he stopped them again. "Justin, what is your problem?"

"Your golden boy sent me to do a job this morning, which I did. I turned in my report, and he doesn't like what I had to say, which is stupid as hell, because I only did what he wanted."

Jack shifted focus to Blake. "Did you send Justin on a job?"

"Yes, but—"

"Did he do it to your satisfaction?"

Blake shoved a hand through his hair in frustration.

"I guess, but when the investors asked him if we'd be interested in buying into the resort at a different site, he told them he doubted it, but that he'd run it by the family."

Jack frowned at Justin.

"Why would you give them such a negative impression?"

Justin threw up his hands.

"Oh, hell...I don't know...maybe because of all the money we pumped into the project in the first place to make sure they could proceed on the first site."

Blake frowned.

"But you already know we don't have what we promised them. Keeping an interest in the project is the only way we'll ever recoup what we're going to lose when they officially call a halt to their plans here."

"Exactly how much *did* we spend accumulating the land they wanted?"

Blake shrugged. "I don't have the exact figure."

"I do," Justin said. "Wayne Industries, through the lending institution we own, is the proud owner of millions of dollars worth of mountain, part of which we bought up without issue, and the other part we got when we bought up the loans from the bank and foreclosed on the owners. An investment in a resort of that quality would have been worth it. But the land we own is no longer suitable because the *only* place the investors are willing to build the actual resort is about five hundred yards from the Youngbloods' front door, and the facilities to house horses for trail rides and hold the gift shop selling local artisan crafts was at the back corner of the Cyrus property."

Jack frowned.

"And if we stay with the consortium and invest in another site, what are your plans for recouping our initial investment?" Jack asked.

Blake was backed into a corner, and he knew it.

"I guess we'd parcel up the land and sell it to people wanting to build homes on it."

"But we just bought it from people with homes that were torn down. They aren't going to buy back their own land, and well-to-do tourists aren't going to build their fine vacation homes on it if the resort and all its amenities are in another state," Justin said.

Jack sighed. "I never thought I'd say this, but Justin is right."

Justin glared at his uncle. He wasn't that much older than them, and yet he was still the boss. And now, even when he was right, the son of a bitch couldn't give him anything but a backhanded compliment.

Blake was now officially pissed. "So, Uncle Jack, what would you have us do?"

Jack frowned.

"I don't know, but I do know this witch hunt wouldn't be happening if whichever one of you shot Youngblood had just finished the job. Back-shooting and then walking away without confirming the kill is sloppy work."

They both glared at each other, then at Jack, then strode up the stairs side by side without speaking.

Jack headed to the kitchen to find out what Cook was making for dinner, then retired to the library for a stiff drink.

When dinner was finally announced, the argument between the brothers had been put on hold. The meal was served without incident. The conversation was purposefully polite and nonconfrontational. They were halfway through the main course when they heard the doorbell sound in the hall.

Jack glared at Nita. "Did you invite Andrew again?"

"No, we're going out dancing later, but if I had, I don't need to get your permission, you know."

He glanced around the table at the others.

"Are any of you expecting company, because if you are, I want you to know having them arrive at dinnertime is the epitome of rudeness."

Before they could answer they began hearing the sound of footsteps coming down the hall. All of a sudden Frances came flying into the dining room on the verge of tears.

"I tried to stop them, Mr. Wayne, I swear I did." Then she moved out of the doorway just as Leigh and her sons walked into the room.

The shock of her appearance was evident in the sudden silence, and before any of them could begin to raise hell, Leigh took the floor.

"I thought since you are all so comfortable with attacking when someone's back is turned, that it would only be fair if I arrived in the same fashion."

Blake started to get up, but Bowie stepped forward.

"Sit the hell down," he said softly.

Blake wasn't accustomed to threats, but he felt the power of this one in every word.

Leigh touched Bowie's arm, and he moved aside.

She lifted her chin, giving all of them a slow, studied look.

"I vowed never to set foot on this property again, but you made it impossible for me to keep that vow. I'm here now because I want my sons to know the faces of their enemies."

Jack slapped the flat of his hand on the table in his usual dictatorial manner and started to rise.

"Leigh! This is highly irregular and—"

Leigh moved so fast no one saw her coming. One moment she was standing beside Bowie and the next she had flung a piece of crystal stemware at the wall just above Jack Wayne's head.

"You heard my son. Sit the hell down! I have something to say to the lot of you, and then I will be gone, but for the time I am here, I don't want to hear another peep or the next glass I throw will be at your damn face!"

Her sisters' hands went straight to their cheeks, as if the need to protect them had already arrived.

Jack was stone-faced.

Blake was in shock.

Justin was so angry he was shaking.

Charles was almost mesmerized by the woman and the giants she called her sons.

"One of you murdered Stanton, but I don't know who. Constable Riordan paid me a visit today. He asked me if I was to guess which one of you would be capable of murder. I told him any of you...all of you."

Blake reached for his wineglass. Bowie pointed a finger. Blake put his hand back in his lap.

Leigh glanced at Blake.

"My dear older brother Blake hides his deceit behind fancy suits and a wad of money. My little brother Justin is just mean. He always was. He always will be. He's just like Father, and you all know it."

Justin reacted as if she'd slapped him when she called him her little brother. Samuel knew his mother was oldest by little more than a minute and grinned at Justin, which made him even angrier.

Leigh pointed at Nita and Fiona.

"Sisters are supposed to be close, someone you can share secrets with. Someone you can depend on. My sisters didn't like me, and I knew it by the time I was ten. Why? Because I was smarter than all of you. Taller than both of you, and I didn't cater to our father's demands just to stay on his good side. I can see by the age and anger on your faces that you're still mad, and I still know why. Because I escaped and you didn't. And you need to know that I don't think for a minute that either one of you is innocent. You'd just as soon hire a hit man as buy a new pair of shoes if the need arose."

Fiona gasped, and Nita started crying.

"Yes, cry, sister, cry, just like I cried when I found my husband lying in a pool of blood with a bullet hole in his back and his killer's name scratched in the dirt."

Jack Wayne inhaled slowly, mesmerized in spite of himself by the majestic anger in this woman he barely knew. He saw the way her four sons stood beside her in such tight formation, ready at a second's notice to back her and protect her. Then he thought of the childish behavior of Blake and Justin, fighting this evening like hateful children, and closed his eyes, for the first time wishing he'd retired to the south of France years ago instead of staying on as CEO.

Then Leigh looked at the youngest man at the table.

"I have been given to understand that you're Blake's son, Charles. I didn't know you existed until Constable Riordan told me about you today. I didn't know what I would think, seeing you for the first time, wondering if you were already too caught up in this family's sins, or if you were still young enough to escape with your soul."

She took a step closer to the table, and her sons moved with her.

She leaned forward, staring intently into Charles's eyes, and then abruptly straightened.

"This one has secrets. Big secrets."

Blake jerked, and when Charles flushed a dark, angry red, making him look guilty even though she hadn't specified a thing, everyone saw it.

"Just one more thing, and then we're gone. Your resort is never going to be built."

# *Thirteen*

Everyone reacted as if she'd thrown cold water in their faces.

"Not only have we kept you from getting the land you need, I will ruin you in this town. I'll make it my mission to remind people a man was murdered for the land you stole from good people."

The shock on their faces was obvious. They were clearly surprised she knew they'd initiated the fore-closures.

"The people of Eden don't like any of you. Yes, they're afraid of you, but they don't like you. And now that one of you has committed murder, they see weakness where once they saw power. The end of your reign hasn't happened yet, but it will. You are all finished here. You'll never recoup that money. No one here will buy your land, and it won't take long for word to spread that the land is cursed by the blood you shed to get it. So if you want to come off looking like you give a shit, then you will make it your business to turn in your killer or face the consequences. I can and I will take every one of you down, and you know it. I'm through here, and if you don't do the right thing, you're all through here, too."

Time had not faded the hate Justin felt for her. He wanted her to shut up. He wanted her gone. He was so angry he was shaking. He saw his steak knife, still greasy from the fat he'd cut away from his meat, and slid his fingers over the handle.

He waited until she was turning away before he leaped from his chair and snatched the knife from the table.

Bowie saw the knife just as Justin drew back to throw it. He reacted without thinking and snatched a bread plate from the table and flung it across the table like a Frisbee, hitting Justin squarely on the bridge of his nose.

"Son of a bitch!" Justin yelled as he dropped the knife, and grabbed at his face as blood spurted. The knife hit the floor as the plate shattered at his feet.

Samuel went one way around the table and Aidan the other, and they took Justin down. Bowie was now standing in front of Leigh, and Michael had her in his arms.

Justin was cursing and kicking, trying to reach for the knife.

Samuel had had enough.

"Hold him, Aidan," Samuel said. He grabbed the knife with one hand, then straightened and yanked Justin out of Aidan's grasp with the other. "Settle down!" Samuel said, and shook Justin by the collar to get his attention.

Justin had blood in his eyes and murder on his mind, but he had already accepted the fact that it wasn't going to happen today, so he quit fighting.

"Bowie! Catch!" Samuel said, and tossed the knife across the table to Bowie, hilt first.

Bowie caught it in midair as Aidan slammed Justin back into his chair.

Justin pointed across the table at Leigh, who had watched the takedown in total silence.

"I am going to make you sorry!" he screamed. "I'll make all of you sorry!"

Bowie palmed the knife from one hand to the other while watching Justin Wayne's face turn an ugly shade of purple.

"You had every intention of putting this knife in my mother's back, so you need to know that the urge to slit your throat is strong. But in *my* family, we don't kill our kin," Bowie said.

He circled the table and laid the steak knife across Jack Wayne's plate.

"Sir, I believe this belongs to you."

Leigh scanned the expressions of the people sitting at the table with a look of disgust on her face.

"You saw him, and none of you even seem bothered that he was about to kill me? None of you can bring yourselves to even look at me? Not even the mighty Jack Wayne?"

They still wouldn't look at her, and they didn't respond.

Leigh kept staring at Justin, trying to remember if there had ever been a time of peace between them and drawing a blank.

"So, little brother, you just proved yourself the bully and coward I always knew you to be. You waited until my back was turned. You seem to favor the coward's way. Did you shoot Stanton in the back, too?"

Justin growled at her from across the table, like an animal on a chain.

Blake reacted as if his brother had just bitten him and pushed his chair back from the table, literally distancing himself from Justin's madness.

Nita was openly crying, and Fiona kept making the sign of the cross over and over.

Jack Wayne was in shock. He didn't know what surprised him more, Justin's behavior or Fiona pretending to pray.

Leigh turned her back on them again, and this time it was in defiance.

Bowie frowned.

"Mama, I don't care if these people are your blood kin, you do not turn your back on them again. I hope you're done with what you came here to say, because we're taking you out of here right now."

He slid his arm around her shoulders and headed her toward the door, with his brothers right behind them.

Before anyone could react, they were gone.

"I am going to fucking kill him," Justin muttered, as he grabbed a napkin to stem the flow of blood.

"Like you killed her husband?" Jack asked.

Everyone turned to look at Justin.

And that was when it hit him that they were about to lay the guilt for the murder on him just to make all this go away.

"I will not take the blame for that!" he shouted.

The front door slammed, their signal that their uninvited guests were gone. At that point the room erupted in chaos.

Leigh was silent on the ride home until they started up the mountain.

"I don't know whether that was a good move or a mistake, but I'm still glad I did it," she said.

Bowie glanced at her briefly as he drove.

"I know one thing. Your twin brother is a mean son of a bitch."

She nodded. "We never had any pets when we were growing up because Justin always killed them."

The hair stood up on the back of Bowie's neck. "Really?"

She nodded.

"Do you think he killed Dad?"

"I think he's fully capable of it, but I have no idea who did it. It all depends on who had the most to lose when Stanton and I unknowingly stalled the resort project."

"Are you afraid they'll come after you, too?" Bowie asked.

"No. They won't come into my world. It frightens them, and now that they've seen my sons, you frighten them, too," she said.

"Because of our size?"

Leigh reached across the console and gave his arm a quick squeeze.

"No. You have something they'll never have. You have each other," Leigh said.

"I got the idea that the level of competition between them is high."

"And the bond a family should have is sadly lacking," she added. "By the way, thank you for making sure that knife didn't wind up in my back."

Bowie couldn't fathom a hate like that between siblings and was still a little shaky over how close she'd come to being hurt.

"You're my mother," he muttered. "You don't have to thank me for that."

She sighed, and then was quiet for another mile. Next time she spoke, her mind was on another subject.

"How is Talia?"

"She's going to be okay, but she's not there yet," he said.

"If she doesn't want to be alone right now, you know you can bring her home to us," Leigh said.

"Thank you for the offer, Mama. Maybe after she has a better handle on everything she has to do."

"I am happy for you, Bowie. You've lived alone long enough, and she's sacrificed enough. It's time for you both to know happiness."

Bowie couldn't bring himself to comment, because he knew she was thinking of Stanton with every beat of her heart.

The sun was setting as they pulled up to the house.

They went inside to find the women washing quart-size canning jars and filling them with the fresh green beans.

Leigh was grateful to see how far along they were in a job she'd dreaded facing.

"This is wonderful," she said. "As soon as I change my clothes I'll join you."

Leslie pointed a wooden spoon at her.

"We're almost done. You can sit here and play with your spoiled grandson to keep him out from under our feet."

Leigh laughed as she scooped him up into her arms and hugged him close.

"Where's Jesse? He's usually a pretty fair babysitter."

"In his room watching a movie about Daniel Boone."

"Ah…that explains it," Leigh said, then kissed the back of Johnny's neck. "You want to come help Nanny change her shoes?"

The baby immediately pointed to her feet.

Leslie laughed again.

"Yes, he does love shoes, doesn't he? We caught him trying to put on one of Aidan's boots the other day. He got so far into it that he was stuck, and then he got mad."

Bowie grinned and ruffled his little nephew's curls.

"Hey, little guy, they're telling tales on you," he said.

Johnny grabbed hold of Bowie's finger and tried to poke it in his mouth.

"He's teething again," Leslie said. "You've been warned now, so proceed at your own risk."

Leigh left the room smiling, with the baby on her hip. They smiled as they watched her go, but the smiles ended as soon as she was out of sight.

"Was it bad?" Bella asked, referring to the meeting with the Waynes.

"If it hadn't been for Bowie's quick reaction, Mama's twin brother would have put a knife in her back," Samuel said.

"Oh my God," Bella whispered. "What's wrong with those people?"

Bowie shrugged. "Who knows? Too greedy? Too rich? A sense of entitlement that's larger than their collective IQ?"

Aidan grinned.

Michael sighed. "Weird to think how closely we're related to those people. They're total freaks."

"You should have heard Mama break it down for them," Samuel said. "They were scared and mad, and I would be surprised if they don't sacrifice one of their own for the sake of the others, regardless of who's really guilty."

"She was awesome," Bowie said. "But we've seen that side of her before. Remember when we let Jesse play in the lake and he couldn't swim? I honestly thought she was going to give us all away."

Michael chuckled.

"Actually, I would have voted for that rather than face the spanking Daddy gave us for not minding her."

Aidan shrugged.

"I still say I should have gotten a break. I was only seven and had no vote in what we did."

"And Jesse was five. Lord, it's a wonder he's still here," Samuel said, and then realized what he'd said and wiped a shaky hand across his eyes. "If we'd known how his life would turn out, I wouldn't have teased him when he was little."

"Hey, he grew up tough. It's probably *why* he's still here," Bowie said. "We all did, and we're the better for it. And now I'm going to change clothes, then come back and help any way I can," he said.

"I won't say no to that," Bella said. "So let's get back to it, girls. We're almost finished."

As soon as Bowie changed, he sat down on the end of the bed to call Talia. After the chaos of this day he longed for the sound of her voice.

When she answered, she sounded exhausted. "Hello?"

"Hey, honey, it's me. Just calling to hear your voice. You sound beat. Are you okay?"

Talia rolled over to the side of the bed and sat up.

"Yes, I'm okay, Bowie, just tired. Honestly, I just showered and was thinking about going to bed early when you called. They came and got the hospital bed out of the living room this morning. I was so relieved to have it gone."

"I can only imagine," he said.

"The funeral home also called. I went to see Dad

today." Her voice broke, and it took her a moment to catch her breath.

"I'm sorry you had to go alone," Bowie said.

She sighed.

"No, no, it wasn't like that," Talia said. "In a way, it seemed fitting. We'd gone through the illness together. Paying him that last visit was mine to do alone."

Bowie hurt for her, but he understood all too well.

"Have you set a date for his service?"

"Yes. Day after tomorrow, graveside only. We don't have any relatives, so there's no need to wait for people who would be traveling. His service was paid for already, and he'll be buried beside Mom at Bluebird Cemetery on the hill outside town."

"I remember going with you to her grave," Bowie said.

Talia wiped a shaky hand over her face.

"Yes, you did, didn't you?"

"Every year on her birthday for four years straight."

Talia sighed. "I remember."

"I would be honored to accompany you to the ceremony."

"Yes, please," she said.

Bowie hesitated. Something had been on his mind ever since he'd come home and discovered her secret. Now felt like the time to say it.

"I have to tell you what a special woman I think you are. You gave up everything you wanted to care for and honor your father. I can't imagine how hard it was, and how lonely you must have felt, but I am so proud of you. I feel blessed that we get to pick up where we left off."

Talia shivered.

"Thank you. I love you, Bowie. So much." She scooted backward and then curled her legs up beneath her. "Is everything okay at your house? Do you know anything more about the case?"

"We don't know anything new, and today has been hectic but it's getting better. Everyone is in the kitchen canning green beans. It's noisy and chaotic and kind of wonderful at the same time."

Talia smiled, imagining the life she'd always dreamed of with his family.

"That sounds like fun," she said.

"Mama said to tell you that you're welcome to come here. She's worried about you being on your own."

"I'm not afraid to be alone," Talia said. "I'll be fine."

"Okay," Bowie said. "But promise you'll call me if you need me."

"I will. I promise."

Bowie wished he was curled up in bed beside her.

"Love you," he said.

"Love you, too," Talia said, then lay back down on top of the bed with her phone tucked under her chin and closed her eyes.

The green bean canning proceeded just as Bowie had predicted. Working together amid laughter and an occasional bout of tears was strengthening the incredible bond that already existed between them. Shared work, tears and laughter were always good for what ailed a broken heart.

Once the canning was over, they put together a quick supper. The baby had long since gotten enough of everything, and had been fussing and crying off and on for the past hour. Leslie and Aidan loaded up their stuff and took him home to put him to bed while the others finished cleaning up the kitchen.

The dark mood from Leigh's visit to her childhood home had long since lifted, and she was at peace, surrounded by family.

Justin Wayne was not nearly as Zen as his sister Leigh. Thanks to the plate that had hit him in the face, he had a wicked cut on the bridge of his nose, and both eyes were getting blacker by the hour. He'd left the house right on the heels of Leigh's departure and driven the back roads of the county with one purpose in mind. Payback. He wanted to take that oldest son of Leigh's down and make him hurt like Leigh was hurting, and after several hours of plotting, he knew just how to do it.

Go after his woman.

He drove into Eden and took the back streets to get to the house where he'd seen them kissing, then found a place to park unobserved.

There was no moon, and the stars were mostly hidden by slow-moving clouds. The street light near the woman's house was out, which made it that much better.

It was just after two in the morning, and he was about to get out of the car when he saw a police cruiser coming down the street, driving slowly. He sat motionless in the car and waited until it left the neighborhood. The moment the taillights disappeared, Justin bolted from his car and slipped through the alley, and then across the street. He didn't know this woman's name or anything about her, but it didn't matter. He no qualms about what he was going to do. She was a means to an end and had the misfortune to love the wrong man.

His heart was pounding as he moved across her backyard to the window where a night-light was glowing. There was a two-inch clearance beneath the Venetian blinds and the windowsill, enough to see the woman curled up asleep on top of the bedspread. She didn't look like much. Too skinny for his tastes, but he wasn't here for that.

He moved away from the window to the back porch. He got all the way up the steps and was about to pick the lock on the back door when he began hearing sirens, and then the sound of an incoming helicopter. All of a sudden the landing lights came on at the helipad behind the house, and when he turned to look, he realized he was easily visible from both the sky and the ground should anyone happen to be looking this way.

He leaped off the porch, then ran around the house and across the street to his car. Seconds later a police car came flying down the street in front of the woman's house with lights flashing, and for a moment he thought they were after him. When he realized they were going to meet the Life-Flight helicopter, he let out a shaky breath. His heart was pounding as he drove away, but it had calmed by the time he got home. He crawled into bed and closed his eyes, already thinking of a different and better way to take her out.

The day of Marshall Champion's service dawned on a clear and beautiful morning. It was, for Talia, a reminder from God that her father's suffering was over. Dressing for the service, she rejected tradition and pushed aside a little black dress. Black was for grief and sorrow. She dressed in yellow, rejoicing that her father's spirit was finally free from the disease that had ended his life.

She glanced at the clock. It was almost nine thirty. Bowie would be there soon, and she still needed to finish her makeup. She'd left her hair loose, letting the soft curls fall on her shoulders. All she needed was a little mascara and some lipstick, and she would be ready.

She had just put the cap back on her lipstick when she heard footsteps on the front porch and then a knock. She hurried to let Bowie in.

The moment she opened the door and saw him, the anxiety of the day disappeared. The black pants he was wearing made his long legs look longer. The white shirt against his dark tan was stunning.

"Come in, come in. The car from the funeral

home should be here shortly. I just need to get a light jacket and I'll be ready."

Bowie couldn't quit staring.

"You look beautiful," he said, and gave her a quick kiss on the cheek.

"I wore yellow to match this glorious day. Dad always loved this dress, so I'm wearing it for him."

"It's perfect, and so are you," Bowie said.

Talia was still smiling as she hurried to get the white jacket she always wore with the dress. By the time she was back, the car had arrived to pick them up. She grabbed her purse on the way out the door.

Bowie took her hand as he walked her to the shiny black Lincoln. Even though they were going to a funeral, a part of Talia felt like she was walking away from the past and into a future with Bowie.

She shivered as she settled into the seat, and he saw it and took her hand.

"Look at me," he said softly.

She turned.

"You're not alone. Lean on me when you feel the need. I'm here for *you*."

Her eyes welled, but she didn't cry.

"It's just harder than I expected it to be," she said.

Bowie squeezed her hand.

"Together, Talia. Remember that."

Justin Wayne was leaving the bank and on the way to his car when he paused at the crosswalk. He adjusted the sunglasses he was wearing to hide his black eyes and, as he did, recognized the big black

Lincoln passing in front of him as the one from the funeral home. The back window was down, and as they passed he saw the passengers and smiled.

Bowie Youngblood and Talia Champion.

After what had happened between him and his sister's sons, he'd made it his business to learn the name of the woman who lived in the white frame house. At the same time, he'd also learned her father had recently died, which explained the car. They were on the way to the funeral, which meant she was out of the house and not due back for quite a while. It was the chance for which he'd been waiting.

He crossed the street at a lope, got in his car and headed to the residential area where she lived; then, when he got there, he made one pass through the neighborhood to check out the other houses on the block. He saw a pickup parked behind her car and recognized it as the one he'd seen Youngblood driving. Except for those two vehicles, there was only one other car parked on the street, and it was at the end of the block. None of the houses had garages, so if there wasn't a car in plain sight, he took a chance and assumed the people who lived in those houses were either at church or had jobs that took them away during the day or they were at their neighbor's funeral.

He made a second pass to check for traffic, but when there was nothing in sight, he wheeled into her driveway and pulled up behind Youngblood's truck.

His pocket knife was open as he jumped out on the run. He went to her car first. When he realized it was unlocked, he quickly popped the hood, located the brake line and made a small cut in the hose, then dropped the hood, wincing at the noise. He glanced around once more to make sure no one was watching, then moved to the truck. The driver's-side door was locked, so he dropped down, slid beneath the engine and then had to search to find the brake line before he cut it, too.

In only minutes he'd set up a scenario for disaster. The pissed-off feeling he'd had toward Bowie Youngblood was now a burgeoning sense of satisfaction. The cut on his nose was healing, and his black eyes would fade. Now the unknowns in this scenario were if they would be together or apart when their brakes failed.

Talia hadn't expected many people to be at her father's service and was surprised at the number already waiting at the gravesite when the driver pulled up behind the hearse.

"I didn't expect this," she whispered.

"The obituary was in yesterday's paper," Bowie said.

"I know, but I guess Dad and I were alone for so long that I thought people had forgotten him."

"More likely they knew he had forgotten them and didn't want to cause you trouble."

"I never thought of it like that," she said.

As soon as the casket was carried beneath the canopy, the driver opened the door for them to get out.

Bowie slid out first, then took Talia's hand to steady her as she stepped out.

"This way, please," the driver said, and led them to a pair of chairs.

People reached toward her as she passed, some whispering "God bless you," and others expressing a word or two of sympathy. Their compassion undid her. She was in tears by the time Bowie got her seated.

When the minister began to speak, she reached for Bowie's hand and held on tight, wishing she was anywhere else. She heard the eulogy and the first few words of the minister's message, then everything around her began to fade.

*The sun was shining.*

*The crowd around the open gravesite was silent as the minister began to speak.*

*Her father's eyes were red from crying, but he was holding her so close against him that they were almost sitting on the same chair.*

*She knew her mother was dead but had yet to fully grasp that also meant she was never coming back. All she knew was that her stomach hurt and she wanted to go home.*

*She was looking down at the ground instead of at the casket in front of them, desperate to find something new on which to focus, when something rather wonderful happened. A robin flew beneath the canopy under which they were sitting and landed on the top of the casket.*

*The crowd gasped.*

*It was a sign, they said.*

*Faith Champion was letting her family know she was with the Lord, they said.*

*Talia looked up at her father. Tears were running down his cheeks.*

*She watched the bird as it hopped across the flower-draped casket and flew away. She wanted to chase after it, just in case it really had been Mama, but Daddy was holding on to her so tight she couldn't move, and then it was too late.*

*The bird was gone.*

"Amen," the minister said, and Talia jumped, only this time it wasn't her father holding her close, it was Bowie, and the service was already over.

Before she could compose herself, people began filing past where they were seated. Most of them came just to say hello, to tell her they were sorry, to excuse themselves for never calling, to ask if there was anything they could do.

It was their last chance to do the right thing, so they'd come to the burying partly "to see how hard she took it" and partly to pay their respects to the man Marshall Champion had been. To say they were surprised to see Bowie Youngblood at her side was putting it mildly. Few of them knew they'd ever been a couple, but all of them knew Youngblood had just lost his father, too, and in a tragic way.

Talia was shaking by the time the last of the mourners had passed beneath the canopy. Bowie took it upon himself to end things.

He stood up to see where their driver had gone

and saw him standing beside the Lincoln, so he helped her up and quickly moved her through the lingering guests and into the car.

"Miss Champion needs to leave now," he said.

"Yes, sir," the driver said, and took them back into Eden, then to her house.

Just as they were about to go inside, Bowie's phone rang. He frowned when he saw who it was, knowing that, because of the funeral, she wouldn't have called unless something was wrong.

"It's Mama," he said, then answered, "Hello?"

"Bowie, I'm sorry to bother you. Is the service over?"

"Yes. What's wrong?"

"Oh, Jesse got it into his head to go hunting and I told him no, but now I can't find him, and his hunting rifle is gone. Samuel is out of town. Michael is working, and Aidan is on his way here. Could you—"

"I'm on my way," he said. "Be there as soon as I can. Don't worry. We'll find him."

"I'm so sorry. I don't want Talia left on her own today, but this is how our life goes with Jesse. Bring her with you, why don't you?"

"I'll see," he said, and disconnected.

"What's wrong?" Talia asked.

"Jesse went hunting without permission, and Mama can't find him. I've got to get home and help search. I meant to stay here with you, but—"

Talia brushed a kiss across his mouth.

"I'm fine. Go home and help your mother."

Bowie didn't like to just walk off and leave her on her own like this. It wasn't right.

"Go change clothes and come with me," he said. "I don't want to leave you here alone, and Mama is going to skin me if I come back without you."

"Really?" Talia said.

"Yes, really."

Talia hesitated.

"Okay, but you need to get home now, and I want to take a few minutes and pull myself together. I'll drive myself. I promise I'll be right behind you, okay?"

"Yes, okay. Be careful, and i'll see you soon," he said, then gave her a quick goodbye kiss and jumped in the truck.

She waved as he drove away and went into the house to change.

# *Fourteen*

Bowie accelerated once he passed the city limits. There was no telling how long his mother had searched before giving up and calling for help, and he was worried. He was trying to remember all the hunting places his dad would have taken Jesse when his cell rang again. This time it was Aidan.

"Bowie, are you on your way home?"

"Yes. Are you already there?"

"No, I'm probably behind you now. I got held up at home. Johnny fell and cut his lip. He's okay, but I couldn't leave until I made sure he didn't need stitches."

"Oh, man. Sorry about the little guy."

"Yes, me, too. Being a father is the best and the scariest thing that can ever happen to you. Anyway, I'll see you at Mama's."

"Right," Bowie said, and disconnected.

It was nearing noon. The shadows were short, and the sky was clear. Jesse knew the woods too well to be really lost, and as much as Jesse liked to eat, he would surely take himself home soon. But Bowie knew what was worrying their mom most. She was afraid Jesse had hurt himself. Bowie's urge to go faster was strong, but the road had too many curves, so he stuck to a safe speed.

He was about three miles from home and beginning to steer into a curve when he tapped the brakes to slow down. But instead of slowing the car, the brake pedal went all the way to the floor without anything happening. He had a moment of panic, then downshifted to a lower gear and steered the truck off the road and down into the ditch, which slowed it down even more before he purposefully steered it into the trees. He was jolted hard on impact, but he'd gotten the vehicle off the road, which was what mattered most.

"Just when I need not to be late," he muttered, as he got out and popped the hood.

He leaned in to check the brake fluid and was shocked to find that there wasn't enough there to measure. Now he was stuck waiting for Aidan. He tried to call his mother, but he didn't have a good signal, so he dropped the hood and walked a short distance up the road until the signal was strong enough for him to make the call.

Leigh answered on the second ring.

"Hello? Bowie? Are you on the way?"

"Yes, ma'am, but I had to pull off the road. I was driving into a curve when the brakes went out. I had to drive the truck down a ditch and into some trees to get it stopped. I just checked, and there was no brake fluid."

"Oh, no," she muttered. "I'm sorry. Stanton never mentioned anything to me about the brakes being bad. Want me to come get you?"

"No, I just talked to Aidan. He's coming up behind me. I'll ride with him. I'm sure sorry. Don't worry. We'll find Jesse."

"He's not far from the house, because I heard a couple of gunshots after I called you. I keep hoping he'll walk out of the woods any minute now."

"Don't worry. We'll be there soon." Then Bowie heard a vehicle coming up behind him and turned around. "Hey, Mama, Aidan just got here. We're less than three miles from home."

"Oh, thank goodness. I'll see you soon."

Aidan braked as Bowie came running toward him.

"What happened?" Aidan asked, as Bowie slid into the seat beside him.

"No brakes. The brake fluid leaked out. It was lucky this curve had trees. Most of the curves don't have anything but that wire cable to keep someone from driving straight off the side of the mountain."

"Yes, and the cable is barely four feet off the ground. I don't know how the county thinks that's protecting anyone. I know Dad has brake fluid in the shop because I've seen it. He probably knew the truck had a leak. We'll get you fixed up after we find Jesse."

"I just talked to Mama. She said she heard a couple of shots not too far away from the house."

Aidan shook his head.

"Leslie and I talk about this all the time. I don't know how Mama is going to cope with him on her own."

"No, don't worry about that," Bowie said. "She told me the other day that taking care of Jesse was going to be what saves her."

"Really?" Aidan said.

Bowie nodded. "She's one strong woman, brother, and you know it. She'll find a way, and for the times like this, there are three of you within driving distance."

"You're right. Dad would have said we're just borrowing trouble, thinking like that," Aidan said.

A couple of minutes later Aidan took the turn off the blacktop onto the long graveled driveway leading up to the house.

Leigh was waiting for them on the porch, and she frowned when she saw Bowie was alone.

"Where's Talia?"

"She wanted to change clothes. She's probably already on her way here."

"You need to change out of your good clothes, too," Leigh said.

"Yeah, all right. Give me a couple of minutes and I'll be right back," Bowie said, and hurried into the house.

"I'm sorry I was late," Aidan said. "Johnny fell and cut his lip. I had to make sure he didn't need stitches before I left."

"Oh, no!" Leigh said. "Poor baby. I shouldn't have called. You need to be home with your family."

Aidan frowned.

"Mama, stop! This is what family does for each other. We worry as much about Jesse as you do. We would be hurt, even angry, if you didn't include us in your lives."

Leigh hugged him. "You're all such good sons."

"We had good parents to raise us," Aidan said, as Bowie came running back out of the house.

He'd changed from the dark pants and white shirt to jeans and a blue denim work shirt. He had on his old boots and had pulled his hair back in a ponytail.

"I'm ready," he said.

"Okay then," Leigh said, and pointed into the woods behind the garden. "He went in back there. You can see his tracks until they disappear farther up into the woods. I heard shots down that way about a half hour ago. I'm going to lock up every gun in the house when I get him back home."

Bowie grinned.

"We'll find him, Mama. Just remember what you told me. He's still a crack shot, and if he's still good at tracking, too, he's not going to get lost."

Leigh sighed.

"I know that. I guess it's just knowing I don't have your daddy for backup that's making me so anxious."

Bowie gave her a quick kiss on the cheek.

"We'll see you soon, and if we need any help, we'll call."

She patted her pocket to feel for her cell phone, and then watched them jogging across the backyard and into the trees.

\* \* \*

By the time Talia had changed clothes and pulled her hair up and away from her face, she was feeling grateful for the invitation to the Youngblood house. Staying here alone right after the service would have been difficult, and there was no longer a reason not to leave the house. She'd always loved Leigh and for years had assumed one day she would belong to her family. Getting this second chance with Bowie meant getting his family back, too—except for Stanton. She still couldn't believe he was gone.

She left the house through the utility room, exiting into the carport. She slid into the car and tossed her purse into the passenger seat, then buckled up before backing out of the drive. There was a part of her that felt guilty for being happy. Her father was gone, and Bowie's father had been murdered. Tragedies, and yet she'd been given this wonderful second chance.

She drove toward Main Street, and she was thinking about the visit ahead when she slowed down for the stop sign at the end of the block. Within seconds a robin flew across her line of sight. It was summer in Eden, and robins were everywhere, so it wasn't all that unusual. Except that wasn't how she took it.

There had been a robin at her mother's funeral, then today she'd buried her father and here was another one. She took a quick shaky breath as her eyes welled with tears. No matter what anyone else might think, it felt like a message from her dad, giving his approval that she was right to be moving on with her life.

"Thank you, Dad. Say hello to Mama for me."

A little tearful, she drove through the intersection and then eventually out of town. She couldn't remember the last time she'd gone anywhere without a need to hurry home. By the time she reached the road that would take her up the mountain, she was smiling. The windows were down, the radio was on. Bowie Youngblood was on her mind. Even though it had been years since she'd driven this road, it was as familiar to her as the man she loved. She knew exactly how much to accelerate as the incline grew steeper, and she knew where the easy curves were, and where the sharp ones appeared with little warning.

When she reached the first hard curve her fingers automatically tightened on the steering wheel. She tapped the brakes as she took the turn and frowned when they felt soft.

"What on earth?" she mumbled, and glanced down at the dashboard, looking for some kind of warning light, but she saw nothing.

A couple of minutes later she came up on Bowie's truck parked off the side of the road and frowned. It looked like he'd had engine trouble, and she wondered if she would catch up to him walking home. She thought about calling him, but when she picked up her phone and saw there was no signal, she tossed it aside and kept driving.

She was still keeping an eye out for Bowie as she approached another curve. Once again she tapped the brakes, then felt sheer terror when the pedal went all the way to the floor.

"No, no, no! Oh my God!" she cried, still stomping the brakes and thinking this couldn't be happening. She was holding on to the steering wheel with every ounce of her strength, trying to pull the car into the curve, but she was going too fast. There was a huge jolt when she hit the cable, and just when she thought it would save her, it popped. The cable was suddenly in the air, coiling and recoiling like a dying snake. From the corner of her eye she saw it flying backward into the trees and had no more than a split second to realize what was happening before everything turned into a nightmare. She was in the air and screaming, dropping, down, down, down toward the trees growing out of the side of the mountain.

She threw her arms up in front of her face just as she hit the first tree, snapping it off at the point of impact. Then the car nosed downward, sliding almost perpendicular to the slope until it caught between the trunks of three tall pines and stopped. The engine was smoking. The door on the passenger side had popped open. Except for the repetitive *ding ding ding* from the open door, there was nothing to be heard but wind through the trees.

Bowie and Aidan were less than a hundred yards from the house when they heard another rifle shot off to their left.

"That was a rifle," Aidan said. "Has to be Jesse."

Bowie nodded. "I think we need to start shouting his name to let him know we're in the area."

"Good idea," Aidan said. "I'll head for the creek, then walk north, and you head for the spring above it and walk south. I think he's somewhere in between."

"Agreed," Bowie said, and took off at a lope, calling Jesse's name every few yards.

At first he could hear Aidan doing the same, and then his brother's voice got fainter and fainter, until Bowie could no longer hear him.

The pine trees on this part of their land were thick and straight, like toothpicks in a shot glass. Bowie moved as quickly as he could through them, knowing Jesse wouldn't be hunting in here and was more likely closer to the water.

He thought of Talia as he searched, wondering if she was already at the house with his mother and imagining what their first conversation would be like after so many years.

He paused to get his bearings and called again, "Jesse! Jesse! Where are you?" then waited without an answer. "Dang it, Jesse, where are you?" he said, and kept moving until he finally reached the spring.

Within seconds of his arrival he saw footprints and breathed a sigh of relief. Jesse had been here.

"Jesse!" he shouted again.

And then he heard something faint in the distance, and ran another couple of hundred yards before he stopped and shouted again. "Jesse! Where are you?"

He heard a faint voice and the words, "I'm here!"

"Stay there! I'm coming toward you!" he shouted, and began following the flow of water downhill.

He was still going downhill when he heard another voice. It was Aidan.

"I found him!" Aidan yelled. "We're here!"

Bowie lengthened his stride and soon came up on Aidan and Jesse cleaning squirrels.

"Look at all my squirrels," Jesse said proudly.

Aidan looked up. "He nailed five…all clean head shots. I can't do that."

"I'm a good shot," Jesse said. "Just like Daniel Boone."

"I see that," Bowie said, and then gave Jesse a big hug of relief. "You know, Mama is worried about you."

Jesse frowned. "I know how to take care of myself," he muttered.

"Did you tell her you were leaving to hunt?" Aidan asked.

Jesse frowned but didn't answer.

Bowie took out his phone to check for a signal, then made a call to Leigh. Her voice was shaky when she answered, "Hello?"

"Mama, it's me. Aidan and I found him. He's fine. We're cleaning squirrels, and then we'll be home."

"Thank goodness," she said. "I'll see you soon."

"Okay. Hey, Mama, is Talia there yet?"

"No."

Bowie frowned. "Okay. I'll give her a call."

He disconnected and then made a quick call to Talia.

The phone rang and rang until it went to voice mail. He left a brief message for her to call and hung up.

It took another fifteen minutes to clean the last two squirrels. They washed the blood off their hands in the creek and headed home.

Jesse's stride was long and sure. His head was up, and there was an expression of satisfaction on his face that Bowie hadn't seen in a long time. He wondered what it felt like to be Jesse now, a grown man and yet a boy again.

Leigh was standing on the back porch watching for her sons to come out of the woods, and when they finally appeared she said a quick prayer of thanksgiving, then went back into the house and cried.

By the time they all came in the back door, she was sitting at the kitchen table with a cup of coffee between her hands.

Jesse looked at her, and then ducked his head and plopped the field-dressed squirrels into the sink, got out a big dishpan and ran it full of water to clean them again.

"Thank you, Bowie. Thank you, Aidan," Leigh said, and got up and hugged them both.

"You're welcome, Mama," they echoed.

"Do you need us to stay?" Bowie asked, wondering what was keeping Talia.

"No, and I'm sorry I called you away from what you were doing."

Jesse's shoulders slumped. He might have lost some of his acumen, but he still knew enough to know he was in trouble. And when Leigh turned around and took the gun he'd left in the corner and headed out of the room, he was instantly wild-eyed and worried.

"What's Mama doin' with my rifle?"

His brothers shrugged.

"You need to be asking her that," Bowie said. "I told you she was upset that you left without telling her. That's called running away, Jesse, and Young-bloods don't run away from home."

Jesse's eyes welled.

"I didn't run away. I wouldn't ever leave Mama."

"Well, she didn't know that, buddy," Aidan said.

Jesse took a shaky breath.

"I gotta go say I'm sorry, don't I?"

"That's what a man would do," Bowie said.

Jesse straightened his shoulders and dried his hands. "I am a man," he said, and left the kitchen.

"Lord," Bowie said.

"Glad you were here to help," Aidan said.

"I need to check on Talia," Bowie said. "She should have been here by now."

"I'll run out and get the brake fluid," Aidan said. "Meet you out front."

Bowie called Talia again and got her voice mail again, and now he was worried. She'd said she was coming. If something had changed that plan, she would have let him know. He went through the house to find his mother. She was sitting on the bed with Jesse, letting him apologize because it was impor-tant for him to acknowledge he was wrong. Bowie hated to interrupt, but he didn't want to leave without telling her goodbye.

"We're leaving now, Mama. I've got to go get the truck, but I'll be back. And I'm worried about Talia. She should have been here by now."

Jesse stood abruptly.

"I'm a good tracker. If she's lost, I can find her," he said.

Bowie smiled. "I know you are, Jesse. I don't think she's lost, but she might have had some kind of trouble."

"Uh... Bowie..." Leigh hesitated, as if debating with herself about what she was about to say, and then she blurted it out anyway. "Like the trouble you had coming here?"

The idea startled him. "What made you say that?"

"There wasn't anything wrong with Stanton's pickup before. If it had been leaking fluid for a while, we would have seen it on the ground where he parked. There's nothing there, and there's nothing where you've been parking. I went to look after you called."

"Why would you do that?" Bowie asked.

"Because Justin threatened to get even with us. Once you make an enemy of that family, you always have to watch your back."

"Well, hell," Bowie muttered. "But when could he possibly have done that?"

"Where did you park when you went into Eden?"

"At Talia's house. In her driveway."

And then he panicked. She was late. She wasn't answering her phone.

"You don't think—"

Leigh stood up.

"I don't know what to think. I keep going over and over in my mind that decision Stanton and I made to help his sister and his brother to keep their homes. If we hadn't, Stanton would still be alive."

"You can't second-guess yourself on that," Bowie said. "That was nothing but pure love, helping them keep their homes, and everything that happened after that is all on the Wayne family. I love you, Mama, but I have to go. I need to find Talia."

Jesse stood up.

"I will go with Bowie. I have sharp eyes."

Leigh was getting ready to say no, and Bowie could plainly see her eyes were red from crying. Between the murder, her grief, and the stress of how the investigation was playing out, he guessed she was nearing her breaking point.

"It's okay, Mama. Let him come with me. I'll get the truck and refill the brake fluid. It'll be enough to get us back into Eden, and if the brakes were tampered with I'll get them fixed. And on the way we'll look for Talia. We'll be coming back this way later, so it's no big deal."

Leigh frowned. "Are you sure?"

"Yes, ma'am, I'm sure. Jesse does have sharp eyes. He shot five squirrels right through their heads."

Leigh relented.

"Okay, Jesse, you can go. But you have to promise

to do everything Bowie tells you to. He's the oldest brother, remember?"

"Yes, ma'am. He's in charge," Jesse said. "Like my lieutenant in our unit. He gives the orders, and I say 'yes, sir' and 'no, sir' and I do my job right."

Aidan honked.

"There's our ride, Jesse. We need to go now, Mama. We shouldn't be long, but if we get held up I'll give you a call."

Leigh nodded, then followed them to the door, but there was a knot in her belly as she watched them leave.

Jesse was sitting in the backseat of Aidan's car, and true to his word he rolled down the window and set up watch as if he was on patrol. He scanned the trees as they drove down the drive, and when they reached the blacktop, they had to caution him to not hang his head out the window.

He quickly obliged, but he sat as close to the door as he could get to watch the cliff side of the road as they started down the mountain.

Bowie glanced back and smiled at how seriously Jesse was taking his job.

"What are you looking for, Jesse?"

"Looking for your girl," he said.

"Do you remember what she looks like?"

Jesse shrugged. "Kind of, but I'm not really looking for her. I'm looking for what's not right."

Bowie frowned. "What do you mean, little brother?"

Jesse just shrugged and leaned his head a little

farther out the window to look at the road as they passed a big curve.

"The truck is just a little bit farther," Bowie said.

All of a sudden Jesse shouted, "Stop the car! Stop the car!"

Aidan slammed on the brakes, making the car fishtail before coming to a stop. Before Bowie and Aidan knew what was happening, Jesse was out of the car and running.

They got out and followed him, grabbing him before he got too close to the edge of the cliff.

"Jesse! What the hell's wrong with you?" Aidan shouted.

"It's gone!" Jesse cried.

"What's gone, Jesse?" Bowie asked.

"Can't look. Can't look," Jesse muttered.

"Can't look at what?" Bowie asked.

Jesse pointed over toward the cliff side of the road.

"The fence is gone. It was there, and now it's not. Someone's dead like Daddy. Can't look."

Bowie stared, unable to believe they hadn't noticed, and then he saw the broken cable in a tangle off in the trees.

Even though he understood the ramifications of the broken cable, he wouldn't let himself believe it had been Talia who'd broken it.

His heart was pounding as he ran to the cliff's edge and looked down. When he saw the back end of a blue car plainly visible among the trees below, he had a brief understanding of how his mother must have felt finding Stanton.

"Oh my God! Aidan! It's Talia. Call 911. Get an ambulance. Get a wrecker. She went over the cliff."

Without waiting for Aidan to answer and without thinking about the danger, Bowie stepped off the edge of the mountain and took the fast way down in a running, stumbling slide.

Talia couldn't be dead. God wouldn't let that happen.

Aidan grabbed his phone to make the calls, and while he wasn't looking, Jesse took one giant step out into space and followed Bowie down the side of the mountain.

Bowie couldn't focus on anything but getting to the car.

He lost his footing countless times and started sliding down on his back. Then he dug in his heels and began grabbing at saplings to slow his descent until he could regain his footing.

As he neared the car, he kept hearing a strange dinging sound. By the time he got close enough to see, there was no movement inside the vehicle and no one shouting for help. He was almost on top of the car before he realized the dinging sound was because the car door was ajar on the passenger side and the keys were still in the ignition.

He scooted sideways until he reached the car. Seconds later rocks began rolling down at his feet, and he looked up to see Jesse less than ten feet away with an intent expression on his face, waiting for orders.

Bowie was stunned that his brother had made it in one piece. He didn't know whether to be glad

Jesse had followed him or worried that he was going to have two people to get back up the mountain instead of one.

"Grab a tree," Bowie said, and Jesse did. "Just stay there a minute and let me see if I can get to her."

"Staying here," Jesse said.

Bowie gave him a thumbs-up and began inching his way from the back end of the car to the driver's-side door. His first sight of her was heart-stopping. She was slumped over the steering wheel, unconscious, and bleeding from the nose and from a cut he could see above her forehead. There was no way to tell what kind of internal injuries or broken bones she might have, and he was just praying for a pulse when he leaned in and felt her carotid artery. To his everlasting relief, it was strong.

"She's alive!" he yelled.

Jesse raised his arms in jubilation.

"Alive! Alive!" he yelled, and waved at Aidan, who was staring down at them in disbelief.

Bowie tried to open the door, but it was jammed. He thought about circling the car to the open door and getting inside, but he was afraid his added weight would cause the car to start sliding again. And he hesitated to move her for fear he would make bad things worse. All he could think to do was pray the rescue units would get there soon and make those decisions for him.

"Talia, can you hear me?" he asked, and put a hand on the back of her neck. "Talia, baby, it's me, Bowie. Can you move? Can you feel your arms?"

She moaned, and the sound was such a relief he almost cried.

"Baby, I need for you to wake up and talk to me," he said.

She moaned again, then moved one hand toward the steering wheel.

Seeing that much motion was a relief of sorts. At least now he knew her neck wasn't broken or she wouldn't have been able to move her arm. She could, however, have a spinal fracture, and a wrong move there could cause permanent damage.

He was debating with himself about what to do when the car slid a few feet forward, followed by a sudden explosion. Bowie fell backward, and Jesse jumped a good foot in the air and then hit the ground looking for cover.

Within moments Bowie saw that when the car slid forward it had rammed into a broken-off sapling, which had pierced the tire like a knife. He got to his feet shouting, "Jesse, it's okay! It's not a gunshot. The tire blew out. It's just a flat tire."

Jesse rolled over and sat up. There was a frantic expression in his eyes.

"You're okay," Bowie said. "It was just a tire going flat."

But Talia's situation was no longer okay. The blowout had caused the car to shift position. Bowie could see it beginning to move, and waiting to get her out from the other side was no longer an option.

He made a split-second decision. It was this or risk losing her for good.

He grabbed his pocket knife, slashed the seat belt holding her in place, then leaned in the window and slid his hands beneath her shoulders.

The moment he shifted her weight the car moved some more.

*Please, God, no.*

He planted the heel of his boot on the slope to keep from going with the car and began to pull.

All of a sudden there was a loud thud. The car vibrated, rocked once, and then the slide suddenly stalled.

Bowie looked up to see Jesse spread-eagled on the trunk of the car, putting all his weight on the back end to steady it.

"Hurry, Bowie!" Jesse yelled.

Bowie took him at his word and pulled her free. He fell backward with her in his arms just as the car began to slide again.

"Jump, Jesse!" Bowie yelled.

Jesse pushed himself backward as the car slid out from under him. He grabbed on to a tree as the car continued to slide before catching in more trees farther down.

Jesse crawled over to where Bowie was lying with Talia in his arms and threw his arms around his brother's neck.

"You're okay, Bowie. You're okay," Jesse said, then looked at Talia and gently patted her on the arm.

Bowie held on to Talia with one arm and grabbed his brother with the other.

"Jesse Youngblood, you are one awesome dude," he said softly, hugging him tight.

"I have sharp eyes," Jesse said.

Bowie started crying and hugged him again.

"You sure as hell do, little brother. You helped me save Talia's life."

Aidan was shouting at them from above, but Bowie couldn't hear what he was saying. Moments later he heard a siren in the distance. And then another, and another.

Bowie looked at Jesse. "Help is coming," he said. "Do you hear the sirens?"

Jesse nodded, then looked down at the knees of his jeans, and frowned at the dirt and tears.

"Mama's gonna be mad I tore my jeans," he muttered.

"No, she won't. Not this time," Bowie said. "I promise you, she won't be mad."

Leigh was pacing the floor. She had a bad feeling about what might have happened to Talia, and when she began to hear sirens, she ran outside.

The sirens were close, which wasn't good, considering the short time her boys had been gone. She grabbed her cell phone from the hip pocket and was about to make a call when it rang in her hand. She jumped, saw it was from Aidan and was officially scared. She didn't bother with hello.

"What's wrong?" she cried.

"We found Talia. Her car went over the side of the

cliff. Bowie went down to the wreck site, and before I could stop him, Jesse went, too."

"Oh my God!" Leigh groaned. "Is Talia alive? Are the boys okay?"

"Talia is alive, but I don't know how badly she's hurt. Her car was partway down, hung up in some trees. While Bowie was pulling her out the window the car began to slide again. Jesse threw himself on top of the trunk to slow it down so Bowie had time to pull her free. I never saw anything like it, Mama. He may be slow, but in times of danger, his soldier instincts kick in. They're still down there waiting for rescue to get to them."

Leigh could hardly believe what she was hearing.

"I'm coming down. I won't get in the way, but those are my children hanging on to the side of the mountain, and I need to be there."

"Yes, ma'am," Aidan said, and then saw the first rescue truck appear around the curve. "Oh, thank God. The first rescue unit is here. Gotta go."

Leigh ran inside the house for her purse, tossed in the phone and pulled out her car keys. Moments later she was in her Jeep and heading for the main road. Never had she felt Stanton's absence as strongly as she was feeling it now. They were all under attack, and it was turning into a blood feud.

"Oh, Stanton, this is just more of the madness related to your murder. I don't know how this is going to turn out, but I'll go down fighting for you and our children," she said, and kept driving until she came up on the rescue vehicles blocking the road.

She got out, trying not to be overwhelmed by the panic she was feeling, and began moving through the crowd of men and vehicles looking for Aidan. When she saw him talking to Constable Riordan she headed straight toward them.

Aidan saw her coming.

"Mama's here. You can ask her about all this."

Riordan saw the look on her face as he turned around. She looked upset, bordering on enraged. Just as he thought she would stop to talk, she walked right past him and all the way to the edge of the road.

Aidan ran to catch up with her.

"Mama?"

She pointed at the men rappelling down the mountainside just below where they were standing.

"I can't see Jesse or Bowie."

"They're lying down. See the top of Bowie's head there, between that stump and that scrub brush?"

She looked again, then put a hand to her heart, as if to steady the beat.

"My God, yes, I see. Where's Jesse?"

Aidan pulled her a few feet to the right and pointed again.

"See him there? Bowie has one arm around him and the other holding Talia."

"Do you know how badly she's hurt?"

"No, only that Bowie yelled that she was alive before he pulled her out."

Leigh shoved her hands through her hair.

"I can't believe this happened. Are they going to be able to recover Talia's car?"

"Yes, ma'am. The wrecker crew is waiting until they have Talia in the ambulance before they get to work."

Leigh looked out across the mountains to the valley below. Eden was down there somewhere beyond the trees, harboring a den of vipers. It was time to run the snakes out of Eden.

"I need to speak to Constable Riordan again."

"He's waiting to talk to you, too," Aidan said. "Want me to go with you?"

"No, you stay here and watch out for Talia and your brothers."

"Okay," he said.

He'd seen that look on her face before. He recognized that take-charge attitude. Shit was about to hit the fan.

Leigh looked for the constable, then ran over to where he was standing.

"I need to talk to you," she said.

"Yes, ma'am. Let's step over here so we're out of the way."

She followed him a few yards uphill and then stopped.

"You saw Bowie's pickup down the hill?"

"Yes, on the way up. Aidan said Bowie's brakes went out."

"I think they were tampered with, and the fact that Talia's car went off the side of the mountain leads me to believe *it* was tampered with, too."

"That's a pretty far stretch, saying someone got access to both their vehicles and then they just happened to be driving up the mountain on the same day," Riordan said.

"It's not a stretch at all. Circumstance put both cars right beside each other today, and I'd bet money that's where and when it happened. Talia buried her father this morning. Bowie went into Eden to be with her. Both cars must have been parked at her house, because the funeral home would have picked them up there to take them to the service."

"Why do you automatically assume it was tampering?"

"Because a couple of days ago I had a run-in with my family. It wasn't pretty. The bottom line is, when we went to leave, if it hadn't been for Bowie's quick thinking, Justin would have put a knife in my back. My boys took him down and took the knife away from him. He threatened to get even. He told all of us we would be sorry. And now this? There is no such thing as coincidence when it comes to those people."

Riordan frowned. "Did you report the assault to Chief Clayton?"

"No."

"Why not?"

"They committed murder and are still living their privileged lives. With the incident being their word against ours? Why bother?"

Riordan frowned.

"I understand how you feel, and I hear your theory. But we still don't know why Miss Champion's car went over the cliff."

"You don't know yet, but you *will* find out. But

by the time you do, something else will have happened. If anyone else in my family is harmed, or even threatened in any way, and the law still has done nothing, I will go to war with them. Do you understand what I'm saying?"

The hair rose on the back of Riordan's neck. Leigh Youngblood had just given him fair warning.

"Okay, I hear you," Riordan said. "I'll have both vehicles towed into the county impound and get my crime scene team to check them out ASAP. And I'll have Chief Clayton start investigating your accusation today."

"Thank you," Leigh said, and then heard a commotion and saw a lot of people beginning to gather at the edge of the road. "What's happening?"

Riordan glanced over his shoulder.

"I'd say they were bringing up the injured woman. Excuse me. I need to be there," he said, and hurried away.

Leigh followed, praying Talia's injuries weren't life-threatening. It would kill Bowie if anything happened to her now.

While all the confusion was happening up on the road, Bowie and Jesse were waiting for help to get down to them.

Initially, when the car had rolled away, leaving Talia in Bowie's arms, he was more or less perpendicular to the slope. Desperate not to move Talia any more than he'd already been forced to, he dug in his heels to keep from sliding and dropped the rest of the way to the ground. His arms were beneath Talia's breasts, and he had her head immobilized between his chin and his chest to brace her. He hadn't moved since, except once to grab Jesse, and now they were stranded, waiting for someone to get Talia before they dared to move.

The sun was directly overhead and brutal. There was a bit of a breeze that high up, but not nearly enough. He needed to shade her face, but didn't have anything.

"Hey, Jesse, do you have a handkerchief or a bandana in your pocket?"

"Got a yellow bandana."

"Can you get to it without sliding away from me?"

Jesse moved enough to pull it out of his back pocket.

"Here it is!"

"Would you please unfold it all the way and then lay it over Talia's face so she won't get sunburned?"

"Yes, yes, I can do that," Jesse said.

Still holding on to Bowie, he opened the bandana, then gently covered her face with it.

"That's great," Bowie said. "Thank you, brother. You're really doing a good job."

Jesse smiled. It was a smile of innocence that touched Bowie's heart.

Bowie was relieved the sun was off her face, but he was concerned about her breathing, which didn't sound good. There was a slight rattle to her breath every time she exhaled. He feared everything from internal bleeding to a deflated lung, and he was hanging on to each breath she took as his lifeline. He'd turned himself into a backboard to keep her as immobile as possible and just needed this hell to be over with. Sweat was burning his eyes, but he didn't dare move.

Then he began to feel a change in her breathing and tried not to panic.

"Jesse, I think my girl is waking up, and we don't want her to move until doctors can check her out, right?"

"Yes, sir. What do you want me to do?"

"I need you to scoot down beside me and just hug her legs a little so she can't move around. Do you understand?"

"Yes, sir. I'm gonna hug your legs and hers, but not too tight."

Bowie sighed in relief.

"Yes. Exactly. Go ahead now and scoot, but don't ever turn loose of me, okay? I don't want you to accidentally fall farther. Mama would be really angry with me if I brought you home hurt."

"Won't turn loose. Gonna hug your legs now," Jesse said, and did just that.

Bowie breathed a sigh of relief when he felt the weight of Jesse's arms across their legs, and it was none too soon. Within seconds Talia stiffened and let out a moan that tore through him. She began mumbling, but he didn't understand until he listened closer.

"No brakes...no brakes...no brakes."

Bowie groaned. His mother had been right.

"Talia, can you hear me, baby? You're alive. I'm holding you in my arms."

She moaned.

"Don't move. You're hurt, but help is on the way."

She moaned again, then he heard her whisper, "Hurt…"

"I'm so sorry. Stay strong. Don't die, baby, please don't die. I love you so much."

"Brakes," she said again.

"I heard you. I'll tell them. No brakes."

She sighed.

He felt her body go limp again, and it scared him until he realized she had just passed out. He could also feel Jesse patting them. If love could heal, she would already be well.

"Thank you, Jesse. Thank you. You're my hero, do you know that?"

"No more war. No more medals," Jesse muttered.

"No. No more war. Just you and Mama on the mountain. How's that for a good life?"

"Yes," Jesse said. "Gotta take care of Mama."

Bowie was struggling to wrap his head around the complexity of this whole damn mess as he looked up at the cloudless blue of the sky. He saw an eagle soaring high over the mountains and heard a faint screech before it flew out of sight, and he wished he could fly. They would already be off this mountain if he could.

When he began to hear voices, he knew the rescue unit was close.

"Are you okay, Jesse?" Bowie asked.

"I'm okay," Jesse said, still following orders.

Still holding on.

Then all of a sudden rescuers were swarming the area. They put a cervical collar on Talia to keep her neck immobile, checked her vitals and then moved her to a backboard. As soon as she was in their hands, Bowie rolled over onto his knees to help them steady her. They put her and the backboard into a caged lift basket and signaled the rescuers above that she was good to go.

Jesse was strangely silent, which worried Bowie, but it was too late to change what had happened. All he could do was pray the incident didn't throw his brother into an episode of PTSD. He needed to get Jesse home safely, and he also needed to be at the hospital with Talia. Once again, he was torn between his heart and his responsibilities.

Once Talia was on the way up they strapped Jesse and Bowie into rappelling gear to steady them should they slip and began pulling them up, too. Bowie couldn't climb up fast enough, but he wouldn't go ahead of his little brother.

When they finally reached the top, it was with a huge sigh of relief. The ambulance was already on the way to the hospital with Talia onboard, and Leigh was waiting for them with open arms. She had Jesse in a fierce embrace when Bowie reached the top. The minute she saw him, she hugged him, too, pulling her oldest and her youngest as close as she could get them.

Her voice was shaking when she said, "You two scared me, but I'm very proud of you."

"Is Aidan still here?" Bowie asked.

"No. Leslie called while they were loading Talia into the ambulance. She was on her way to the ER with Johnny. She said his lip wouldn't stop bleeding and probably needed stitches after all. Aidan left to meet them there."

"Poor little guy," Bowie said.

"Johnny will cry," Jesse said, and frowned.

"Yes, but his mommy and daddy will make him better," Leigh said.

Jesse put his arms around Leigh.

"Like you make us better. I am a man, Mama. I won't scare you again."

Leigh just shook her head and hugged both of them again as Riordan approached.

Bowie gave his mom a quick pat and shifted his attention to Riordan. "Was Talia okay when they got her topside?"

"Yes. They had her stabilized before transport," Riordan said.

"You need to know that she said her brakes went out," Bowie said.

Leigh moaned, thinking how close she'd come to losing both Bowie and Talia.

"That does it," she said.

Riordan glanced at Leigh. The calm tone of her voice was deceiving, because the look in her eyes was frightening. It was the first time he saw the resemblance between her and her twin, Justin.

"I told you," Leigh muttered, then handed Bowie her keys. "Jesse and I will walk home. It's not far, and you need to be with Talia. You're all the family she has now. Be careful today, and know that this won't happen to any of my family again."

Riordan flinched. "Now, Mrs. Youngblood… Leigh…don't do anything you'll regret. Jesse needs you with him, not behind bars."

She ignored him and spoke to Bowie again.

"Call me as soon as you know something. We'll say prayers. She *will* be well. I believe that for you."

"Will I be able to take the truck and get it fixed?" Bowie asked.

Riordan shook his head.

"No, I'm going to have both vehicles towed so my crime scene team can look for signs of tampering. I know what's been said, but you know where I stand. I have to go by the letter of the law, and facts are what will stand up in court."

"What about Chief Clayton?" Leigh asked.

"I'm going to call him right now and have him interview the other residents on Ms. Champion's block. Maybe we'll get lucky and find a witness."

Bowie looked down at his clothes.

"Mama, you and Jesse get in the car. I can't go to the ER with all this blood on me, and I'm not driving off and leaving the both of you to walk home. I'll get to the hospital soon enough. Jesse and I did all we could for her. It's up to God and the doctors now."

Riordan walked away to call Henry Clayton as Bowie took his family home.

\* \* \*

Chief Clayton was coming out of the courthouse when his cell phone rang. He glanced at the caller ID and frowned.

"Hello, Constable, what can I do for you?" Clayton asked.

Riordan didn't waste time getting to the point.

"We've had an incident up on the mountain near Stanton Youngblood's home. The brakes on Bowie's truck went out. He managed to stop it before it wrecked. Talia Champion was about a half hour behind him when her brakes went out, too. She went over the cliff. She's alive, but that's all I know."

The hair stood up on the back of Clayton's neck. He knew without Riordan saying anything that the Wayne family was somehow involved.

"That's terrible. I'm assuming you called to do more than fill me in."

"Leigh Youngblood had another run-in with her twin. He was about to put a knife in her back when her boys stopped him. According to her, he threatened all of them and told her he'd get even. She swears he's responsible."

"But—"

"Hear me out. You know where Miss Champion lives?"

"Yes."

"Both vehicles were parked at her house this morning while she and Bowie were at her father's funeral. I need you to do a door to door down that block and see if you can get me an eyewitness to someone messing around her house."

"Will do. I'll start first thing tomorrow morn—"

"No. Today. Please. No more delays. We could have another body next time instead of a hospital patient."

Clayton's shoulders slumped. Shit. He was about to wind up in Mad Jack Wayne's crosshairs again. "I'll give you a call if I find out anything."

"I appreciate it," Riordan said, and disconnected.

He was still at the site of the wreck when the tow company began pulling Talia Champion's car up the mountain. Behind him, Bowie was in his mother's Jeep, weaving his way past the rescue units on his way into Eden.

# *Fifteen*

The ambulance sped through Eden with its lights flashing and siren screaming, putting everyone who saw it on alert and feeding the gossip mill's curiosity to find out who was inside.

That information began to spread quickly after they wheeled Talia Champion into the ER and began to assess her injuries. The EMTs were explaining her condition, where they'd found her, and what her stats had been when they'd loaded her for transport up on the mountain.

Someone overheard "car wreck."

Someone else overheard "off the side of the mountain," and by the time Bowie got to the hospital the news was spreading throughout Eden.

When he asked where she had been taken, he was directed through a set of double doors to room A3. There were people all around her when he walked in. She had an IV, which they'd probably started in the ambulance, and a heart monitor and a blood pressure machine were hooked up to her fragile body. What he saw was enough to make him sick.

This had happened to her because of him.

"How is she?" Bowie asked.

The doctor paused and looked up. "Are you Bowie?"

"Yes, sir."

"She was asking for you."

Bowie frowned. *Damn it. I should have come straight from the mountain, even with the blood and dirt.* "I got here as fast as I could. Is she going to be okay?"

"She has two broken ribs, a concussion, and I'm putting staples in the cut on her head. Her knees have serious contusions, and she had a dislocated shoulder, but it's already back in place."

Bowie winced with every injury the doctor mentioned. He wanted to break Justin Wayne's damn neck.

"Is she going to need surgery?"

"X-rays didn't indicate the need at this point. It's a miracle, considering what happened to her."

"I know. My brother and I were the ones who pulled her out of the wreck."

The doctor looked shocked. "You went down the side of a mountain?"

"I love her, so, yes, I—*we*—did that. You *are* admitting her, right?" Bowie asked.

"Yes. They're getting a room ready for her now."

"Am I allowed to stay with her?" Bowie asked.

"Yes. One more staple and we'll move you both upstairs."

\* \* \*

While Bowie was waiting for Talia to be taken to her room, Chief Clayton was beginning his investigation in her neighborhood. He took the east side of the block. His deputy took the west.

It was nearing four in the afternoon. The sun was hot, and the breeze was pretty much nonexistent. The beauty in this part of Eden came from the old growth elms and oaks lining both sides of the streets and the welcome shade they provided. He parked against the curb in the shade of a majestic elm and headed for the first house. A couple of sharp knocks at the door made a small dog inside begin yapping.

He frowned. A damn ankle-biter. Man, he did not like those little yapping dogs.

As soon as the door opened he recognized John Bailey, a fifty-something man who owned a local auto parts store.

"Mr. Bailey, I wonder if I might have a few words with you?"

"Well, sure, Chief. What can I do for you?" John asked.

"By any chance were you home this morning?"

"No, sorry. I didn't get home until a few minutes ago, but Patsy was here."

"May I speak to her?"

"Sure, I'll go get her," John said, and a few moments later his wife, Patsy, came to the door, wiping her hands on a kitchen towel as she approached. She stepped out onto the porch to talk.

"I'm here. What's up?" she asked as John came out with her.

"By any chance did you notice someone loitering in the neighborhood this morning? Specifically, around the Champion property?"

Patsy thought back.

"No, I can't say that I did, but I wasn't here all morning. I went to Marshall Champion's funeral. It was graveside only, so I was out at the cemetery for about an hour, and then I went straight from there to the supermarket before I came home. Why do you ask?"

"Just checking some facts."

"Is Talia okay? I mean, I did notice her car is gone. It was there this morning, along with a pickup truck."

"She had an accident but I don't have any information on her status."

"Oh, no! Bless her heart. She just buried her daddy today, and now this happened to her? Sometimes life can be so unfair!"

"Yes, ma'am," Clayton said. "Thank you for your help, and sorry to have bothered you."

"No bother," Patsy said.

Chief Clayton walked down the shade-covered sidewalk to the next house, but no one was home.

He walked to the third house, a small red brick with a white picket fence, and as he rang the doorbell, he noticed a big black-and-white cat inside the house, sitting on the windowsill to the right of the door. The cat blinked big yellow eyes and proceeded to stare him down.

Clayton was frowning at the cat when the door finally opened. He recognized a retired teacher named Edith Fairview, who looked a bit startled when she saw him.

"Chief Clayton?"

"Yes, ma'am. I wonder if I might have a word with you?"

Just like Patsy Bailey, Mrs. Fairview had been at the funeral service, and when she came home, she'd lain down and taken a nap. Another dead end.

He bypassed the next house because it was Talia Champion's and headed for the one beyond. As he was walking, he saw Deputy Wells leaving one residence on his way to the next. When he saw Chief Clayton, he shook his head no to indicate he'd found no leads as of yet.

Clayton interviewed a retiree named Mr. Burns, who had also been at the funeral. After learning why the chief was there, Burns informed him that the people who lived in the next two houses down worked at the hospital and wouldn't be home until after dark.

The last house on his side of the block belonged to a woman named Mayrene Potter. She didn't have anything helpful to say but did offer him cookies. He was walking back up the street to his cruiser when he heard Deputy Wells shout out his name. He looked up, and Wells waved him over.

He stepped off the curb and then winced at a sharp pain in his foot. That damn ingrown toenail was still giving him fits. He was going to have to take time and go to the doctor before he got some vile infection and lost his damn toe.

"What's up?" he asked, as Wells came running to meet him.

"Chief! You have to come see this."

"See what? Do we have a witness or not?"

"We have security footage from the house directly across the street from Miss Champion's."

"What's the resident's name?" Clayton asked.

"Silas Ballard."

Clayton frowned.

"Isn't he the man who keeps reporting someone stealing roses from his prize bushes?"

"Yes. So he set up a security camera to catch his rose thief and caught what looks like someone vandalizing vehicles at the Champion residence, instead."

"Do we have an ID?"

The deputy rolled his eyes. "I'm not saying the name aloud. You come look for yourself."

Clayton's gut knotted. "Fine, just lead the way."

Silas Ballard was standing in the doorway waiting for them to come in.

"Afternoon, Mr. Ballard," Clayton said.

"Afternoon, Chief."

"So, where's this security footage?" Clayton asked.

"Follow me," the old man said, and led the way through the house to a small room off the utility room. "This used to be the wife's sewing room, but since her passing it's just a catch-all. I set up my security camera out front a few days ago. You can see today's footage here. I got it ready for you," he said.

Clayton sat down in the old office chair in front of the viewing screen and leaned forward as the footage began to play.

Within moments a black car appeared, driving slowly through the neighborhood.

Clayton saw the Champion house in the background, and he saw a pickup parked behind Talia Champion's car in the carport. He watched as the dark car drove out of camera range.

"Keep watching," the deputy said. "He's coming back."

And sure enough, there it was again, only this time it stopped right behind the pickup. Unable to get a good view of the license plate, they were focused on the unfolding scene. Within seconds a man jumped out, and even though he was a bit out of focus because of the distance and the quality of the camera, his identity was immediately visible.

"Oh, sweet hell. It's Justin Wayne, just as his sister predicted," Clayton muttered.

The three of them continued to watch as Justin popped the hood, then ducked down behind it. A couple of minutes later he shut the hood and moved to the truck. They watched as he unsuccessfully attempted to open the pickup doors, then actually lay down and scooted himself beneath the engine. At that point Clayton's ears began to roar.

*This is my worst fucking nightmare.*

"Mr. Ballard, I'm going to need to take this into evidence. Can you get the disc for me, please?"

"Sure thing. Won't take but a minute," Silas said.

Clayton sent the deputy across the street to his car to get an evidence bag, and then proceeded to bag, sign and date the disc before leaving the premises.

He and his deputy paused on the street.

"Good job, Wells. Head on back to the office, write up your report and enter this into evidence. Whatever you do, don't talk about this, understand?"

Wells was a bit wild-eyed and nervous just talking about it with his boss.

"Yes, sir, I sure do. Mum's the word," he said, then took the evidence bag and headed to his cruiser as Clayton pulled out his phone and called Constable Riordan. His ingrown toenail wasn't going to catch a break tonight.

Riordan answered quickly. "Chief! Do you have any news for me?"

"Yes, sir."

"Do we have a witness?"

"We have something better," Clayton said. "We have security camera footage showing Justin Wayne in the act of vandalizing both vehicles."

"You're not serious?"

"Oh, yes, sir, I am. I took the footage into evidence. My deputy is on his way back to the precinct to log it in. So how do you want to handle this? You worked the wreck, so technically this belongs to your case, not to mention it's connected to the murder case you're still working. Am I right?"

"Yes, but I want you there when I arrest him, because you discovered the evidence. I want the Waynes to know they're not above the law anywhere—especially not in the town they think they own."

Clayton sighed. "Yes, sir. When do you want to do this?"

"As soon as I can get an arrest warrant. Your day's not over yet. I'll let you know when I head your way. In the meantime, no talking about this, okay? And say nothing about this to Leigh Youngblood. I want Justin Wayne behind bars before she finds out her suspicions were true."

"I already issued the no-talking order to my deputy, so you have no worries there."

Clayton ended the call and headed back to the office. He could at least get off his feet for a bit before the arrest.

As soon as Bowie left the house, Leigh sat Jesse down at the kitchen table and fed him the lunch he'd missed.

While he was having a bowl of stew and corn bread, Leigh walked all the way back to Stanton's office. She hadn't been in there since before he was murdered and guessed there would be emails galore from clients. But first things, first. She sat down at the desk, then booted up the computer and retrieved the contact information for William Frazier. He was one of their clients, but he was also a rather well-known journalist out of Chicago. She gave him a call, then sat back with her eyes closed, listening to the phone ring. Just when she thought it was going to go to voice mail, he picked up.

"Hello!" he answered, sounding out of breath.

Leigh took a deep breath herself.

"Hello, Mr. Frazier, this is Leigh Youngblood."

"Oh, hello, Leigh. What's up?"

"I have something that I believe you would call a scoop."

"You're serious?"

"Yes, deadly serious. Feel free to record this if you want, or if you're going to take notes, I'll speak slowly."

"Oh my God…you *are* serious! Give me a second to get this recorder going and…uh…okay. It's on now. You may begin."

"My husband, Stanton Youngblood, was murdered. Before he died, he wrote the last name of his killer in the dirt."

And then she proceeded to give him the whole ugly story. By the time she was finished she was sick to her stomach. The only good thing about reliving the horror was knowing it was going to destroy the Waynes.

Frazier was stunned at the scope of what she'd told him. Through all the years he'd been the Youngbloods' client, he had never known the connection between Leigh and the Waynes. Although Wayne Industries was a private, closely held company, they had other holdings and had diversified off and on throughout the years. But the other investors in the resort were public and listed on the New York Stock

Exchange. Their shareholders, as well as government regulators, wouldn't be happy about their involvement in the Wayne family's problems. The ugliness of this story and the Waynes' manipulation of the banking industry, causing poor people to lose their ancestral homes, wouldn't play well in the press. As for East Coast Lending, which was owned by Wayne Industries and had cleared the way for them to buy up the land for a resort, this was enough to ruin both them and the Wayne family, and send people to jail for more than murder. He had a lot of investigating to do before he could break the story, but he sensed the need for haste.

"Thank you for this. I have a lot of calls to make for verification. If I can get what I need, I *will* run with it. I thought a lot of Stanton. I'm so sorry about what happened."

Leigh's eyes welled.

"Thank you," she said, and as soon as their connection ended, she laid her head down on the desk and cried.

It was a few minutes after four when Andrew arrived at the mansion. He had a date with Nita, which would involve a couple of hours upstairs complying with her endless need for sex and whatever sex toys she wanted to play with, then dinner with the family, after which he was meeting Charles at the lake house for dessert. It wasn't the first time he'd involved himself with more than one member of a family, but it was tricky.

He rang the doorbell and winked at Frances when she let him in. Nita met him at the foot of the staircase wearing white skinny jeans and a loose red blouse with a deep V in both the front and the back. She gave him a very brief kiss, and then led him to the library and the pitcher of margaritas she had waiting.

"I'm so glad you're here," Nita said. "This whole murder thing is getting tiresome. Everyone is mad at everyone else. Even Fee is behaving strangely. If we hadn't been instructed not to leave Eden I would already be back in New York City."

She pouted as she poured him a drink and scooted it across the wet bar.

"Thank you, my darling," Andrew said, then ran a fingertip from her chin to the vee between her breasts. "Did I tell you how much I love this blouse?"

She giggled as he took a sip from the salt-rimmed glass and then lifted his drink to her.

"This tastes marvelous. Kudos, my darling."

Nita smiled. "Nothing is too good for you, because you are so good to me," she said.

"Shall we take our drinks upstairs?" he asked.

"Yes, please."

He grabbed the pitcher in one hand and his drink in the other, and followed her out of the room.

The killer sat at his desk, his fingers on the keyboard, his gaze fixed on the computer screen before him. It hadn't been quite a week since the murder on the mountain, and in that short period of time their world had imploded.

If he was honest with himself, he would admit that killing Stanton Youngblood had been the single worst mistake of his life. Looking back, it had all been so random.

*The sky was cloudless, the breeze just enough to cool the sweat. He'd been concerned about the investors, after hearing nothing from them for days, so he'd come out to the job site to find it completely devoid of people and equipment.*

*And then his phone rang.*

*With an uneasy feeling, he answered. "Hello."*

*"Hello, Bryant Booker here. I need to give you a heads-up on the lake resort. The board has decided that since we will not be able to acquire the two key pieces of real estate we needed to follow through, we're putting the project on hold. We'll do a flyover in the area to search for another location, but right now it's a no-go. I'm sure you understand."*

*The uneasy feeling he'd had turned to panic.*

*"What about the land that was our part of the investment?" he'd asked.*

*"Oh, that will just revert back to Wayne Industries. You haven't lost a thing."*

*Even after the call had ended, he thought he'd taken the news rather well, considering the shock running through him. This explained why the site was vacant. What pissed him off the most was that they were the last ones to find out. Even lowly workers had been told the job was scrapped before Booker notified Wayne Industries. Furious, he picked up a rock and threw it as far across the water as it would go. He was looking around for another one to throw when he caught movement from the corner of his eye.*

*Looking back, if the workers had still been there, he would never have seen Stanton Youngblood leaving his sister's house, but he was alone and saw him walking confidently, that long hair swaying as he strode along the edge of the forest. In that moment he hated Youngblood all over again. When Stanton's route took a sharp turn uphill, he guessed he was heading home to Leigh. She was part of this—part of the reason everything was over. He thought of the vast amount of man hours they'd put into accumulating the land for the resort. All the money they'd spent. Money he'd taken from other investments because he'd been sure it would be repaid. Money he'd taken without board approval. From offshore bank accounts. From the company. All to acquire land that was now useless.*

*He hadn't looked at it as embezzling, because he was part of the family and he was taking it on behalf of the family, not to mention he fully intended to put it all back with interest. And now he was in big trouble, all because of that man disappearing through the trees.*

*Without thinking what he was going to do when he caught him, he ran for his car and drove to the lake house for one of the hunting rifles. Then he looked up at the trail behind the house, afraid he might never*

*find where Youngblood had gone. Then he remem-
bered the motorcycle and raced toward the garage.
Within minutes he was on his way.*

"Sir, there's a call for you on line four."

The killer blinked, startled that his secretary was
standing in the doorway and that he was at the office, then remembered the Sunday conference call
and nodded his thanks, glancing at the clock before
picking up the line.

Bowie couldn't sit still.

Talia had yet to wake up again, and he needed to
hear her voice and know she was going to be okay.

He'd called home earlier and relayed all the information he had on her condition, but his mother had
seemed out of it, as if bothered by something else.
He'd asked her if everything was okay and if Jesse
was causing problems, but she had reassured him all
was well, so he'd chalked it all up to this being a bad
day for everyone and let it go.

Aidan had stopped by Talia's hospital room not
long after her arrival. He was upset for Bowie, sorry
for Talia, and bothered that his baby boy now had
three stitches in his lip. After eliciting a promise
from Bowie to call if her condition changed, he'd
hurried back down to the lobby, where Leslie and
Johnny were waiting, and took his family home.

When Samuel came home and found out what had
happened in his absence, he'd called Bowie to check
on Talia's welfare. Within minutes of his call, Mi-

chael had called, too, upset that no one had let him know what was going on. After a quick explanation, Bowie had settled back into the chair by Talia's bedside and closed his eyes.

His heart hurt for her in a way he couldn't explain. The last seven years had been so hard for her, and just as the suffering was coming to an end he showed back up in her life wanting so desperately to be the good guy she needed, and instead this was what he'd brought to her.

The door to her room opened, and he refocused his thoughts.

It was a nurse coming to check Talia's IV. "Any activity?" she asked, as she adjusted the flow of the drip.

"No, ma'am," Bowie said.

She made a note, but when she'd finished what she'd come to do, she hesitated to leave.

"I'm Amber Stewart. I live at the end of Talia's block. I guess you don't remember me. I was in the class behind you and Talia in high school."

Bowie stood up. "Amber Hatfield?"

She smiled, pleased he had remembered.

"Yes, I was a Hatfield. I just wanted to say that I remember how close you two were back then, and while it's none of my business, I want you to know I'm so happy you're back in her life. She sacrificed everything for her father. She deserves to be loved."

"And I'm going to spend the rest of my life on that project," he said.

She grinned. "When you see Samuel and Bella,

tell them Amber said hello. Bella is my first cousin. Her mother and my mother are sisters."

Bowie reached across the bed and shook her hand.

"Well, then, in mountain terms, it appears we're family. Nice to see you again, and I'll pass your message along to Samuel and Bella for sure."

She smiled and then was out the door.

Bowie looked down, taking comfort in the faint blush of pink beneath Talia's skin, and brushed a strand of hair away from her face.

"That nurse is Amber Hatfield. She was a year behind us in school. She's taking good care of you, baby. She's helping you heal so you can wake up for me."

Then his voice broke. He looked up at the monitors registering the strength of her life force. The readouts on the machines were nothing but numbers. But they were talking to him when she could not.

*My heart still beats. I'm still here*, they were saying.

He leaned over the bed to kiss her forehead, leaving his tears on her face. When he reached down to wipe them away, her eyelids fluttered.

His pulse leaped.

"Talia? I'm here, baby. It's me, Bowie. I'm here."

Her lips parted ever so briefly as he heard her exhale.

When he reached for her hand, her fingers curled, holding him fast.

"She's coming back. She's coming back. Thank you, God," Bowie whispered.

# Sixteen

It had been a long and frustrating day for the Wayne family. People's behavior toward them was shifting.

That fear of lordly power was gone. The head-ducking unwillingness to make eye contact with the family who held the purse strings to the city was all but gone. Mad Jack had even noticed an outright glare from an employee in the restaurant at the golf course. By the time the day was winding down and the family was gathering for dinner, nerves were on edge.

Nita had already informed Jack that she had invited Andrew and notified Cook of the added guest. And because she was so mellow from a pitcher of margaritas and two straight hours of intermittent orgasms, she'd ordered Cook to prepare a rustic bruschetta to pair with the aperitif she'd chosen for the evening. The light wine was meant to spark an appetite. She could only hope that it might soothe ruffled feathers, as well.

Andrew was his usual urbane self, keeping her entertained and laughing as they waited, and she was congratulating herself on finding him. They'd been together now for almost six months, ever since she and Fiona had come back from New York City, and he was still holding true to his promise to be the best she'd ever had. He was pricey, but well worth it to her.

She'd heard the front door open and close several times in the past half hour, which meant more family members were home. Andrew had just moved to the wet bar to refill Nita's glass when Jack Wayne entered the library.

"Evening, Andrew. Good evening, Nita," Jack said, and then politely kissed Nita's cheek.

"Good evening, sir," Andrew said. "Would you care for an aperitif?"

"Yes, please," Jack said. His eyebrows arched as he scanned the delicate bite-size toasted baguette slices topped with a black olive and sun-dried tomato tapenade. "How inviting. Is this your doing, Nita?"

"Don't be so surprised. Mother had fifteen years of my childhood to induct me into the Emily Post way of life and learning what fork went with which course."

"Touché," Jack said, and tried one. "Mmm, quite tasty," he added, and chased it with a sip of the wine.

Blake entered with Charles on his heels.

Justin strode in with his usual "don't mess with

me" attitude and poured his own wine before claim-
ing his favorite chair.

Fiona straggled in last, muttering something about
the condition of her hair and how it needed a cut, and
the sacrifices that had to be made being stranded
in this town and left to the services of people who
barely knew how to wash and dry a client's hair.
After delivering that gripe, she went straight to the
bar and demanded a drink.

Nita frowned.

"Really, Fee. Andrew is our guest, not a servant."

"Sorry," Fiona said, and took her wine without
bothering to look at him, then sauntered toward Nita,
leaned down and whispered in her ear, "It was an innocent mistake, since I had two solid hours of hearing you being *serviced* by our guest."

"You should have joined us," Nita snapped, rel-
ishing the dull flush of red that moved up her sister's
neck and cheeks.

Fiona's eyes narrowed. "It is times like this when
I am grateful for the fact that we live our own lives
in New York."

Nita glared.

Fiona's lips pursed in disapproval as she headed
for the lavishly upholstered chair their mother used
to favor. The fabric, huge red poppies on a snow-
white background, was still as pristine as the day
the chair had been delivered to this house. Rarely
did anyone sit in it. It stood mostly as an homage to
the mother they'd lost so young, but Fiona felt a little

rebellion of her own was long past due and sat down with a defiant glare.

It was noticed by all but remarked upon by none, which made the gesture anticlimactic, so she settled for lowering the wine level in her glass instead.

The next thirty minutes spent in familial proximity and booze had the same effect as always. They were already poking at each other to see who would have the most drastic reaction to some snide remark, which was what passed for conversation between them, until Jack put a stop to it.

"I believe it's time we moved to the dining room," he said. He had turned to set his wineglass on the bar when the doorbell rang. "Are we expecting more company?"

When no one spoke up, he frowned. "I'm going to tell Frances to turn whoever it is away. This is the height of rudeness." Then he left the room in a huff.

Blake popped the last piece of bruschetta into his mouth and was still chewing when he heard shouting in the foyer. Everyone except Justin and Fiona ran out into the hall to see what was happening.

"I'm sick of all this," Fiona muttered.

Justin shrugged.

When the noise from the foyer began coming closer and Justin could hear Uncle Jack shouting at Blake to call their lawyer, he stood. It was a gut reaction, an attempt to avoid being in a vulnerable position should trouble come through the door. And come it did, in the guise of the county constable and the local chief of police, followed by a pair of deputies. He saw the looks on their faces and knew he had nowhere to run.

As he feared, the two deputies headed for him without hesitation.

"What the hell are you doing?" Justin yelled.

Riordan began reading him his Miranda Rights as the deputies cuffed him.

"Justin Wayne, you are under arrest for the attempted murders of Bowie Youngblood and Talia Champion. You have the right to an attorney. If you cannot afford one, one will be provided to you. You—"

Justin's ears began to roar. His family was looking at him as if they'd never seen him before, and he was wondering what the hell he'd missed this morning that had led to this happening.

In the middle of it all, Jack started shouting again.

"I demand to know what insanity prompted this!"

"He tampered with the brakes on vehicles belonging to both Bowie Youngblood and Talia Champion."

Jack threw up his arms in disgust.

"This is just a witch hunt, isn't it, Riordan? You don't have anyone to arrest for murder, so you cook up this pathetic charge to—"

"No!" Chief Clayton interrupted. He knew he was putting his own job in jeopardy, but he also knew this was one more nail in the incident that would eventually bury this family, and he wanted to disassociate himself from them before that happened. "This is not a trumped-up charge, and there's nothing 'pathetic' about attempted murder. It was only providence that kept Bowie's truck from going off the road and down a cliff as he drove home earlier today. Unfortunately, Miss Champion was not so lucky. Her brakes went out on that same mountain road about thirty minutes later, and she *did* go over the cliff. She's in the hospital as we speak, with an assortment of injuries. We recovered security footage from a neighbor that clearly showed Justin Wayne in the act of vandalizing both vehicles."

Jack's face paled.

"Oh my God," Nita muttered.

Blake recoiled as if he'd been slapped, and Charles staggered backward to the nearest chair.

Fiona gasped. "Beast!" she cried. "You killed Stanton Youngblood, too, didn't you?"

"I didn't have anything to do with that!" Justin shouted.

"I don't believe you," Fiona said.

In that moment Justin realized what he'd done. Thanks to his own rash behavior, his family had given him up as the scapegoat.

The authorities swept him out of the mansion as swiftly as they'd entered, leaving a stunned and silent family behind.

Finally it was Fiona who stood up, set her glass aside and announced she was going to dinner.

One by one, the others followed.

The killer ate with a sense of relief. The law wouldn't be after him anymore, but it was yet to be determined what his family would do to him once they found out what he'd done. And find out they would, because right now he had no earthly idea how to cover up the money he'd taken for the resort.

Two words.

Words Bowie had been waiting to hear.

"…love you," Talia said, before she fell back into a drug-induced sleep.

Now he was sitting at her bedside once again and watching her sleep, remembering a day from the time before, when they were young and full of love and lust.

*Watching the sunlight on the rippling lake water was like watching starlight at night, always the light against the darkness, the way life was supposed to be lived.*

*Bowie lay on his side watching Talia sleep while the afternoon wore its way toward evening. He would have to wake her up soon to take her home, but this day together at the lake had been magic. Today, their lovemaking had seemed like so much more than just mind-blowing sex. The laughter came easy. The fun in the water was something more than manic play. Sharing food had become a quiet moment of refueling more than their energy. Today felt like a rift in time where nothing could hurt them and everything was possible.*

*And now she slept beside him with utter abandon and implicit trust that she was safe and she was loved. It was the greatest gift she had ever given him, and in those moments when anything was possible,*

*the inherent consciousness of being alive had infused
itself into every cell in his body.*

*It was their heaven on earth.*

The memory of that day faded as Bowie's phone
signaled a text. He looked down, noticed it was from
Chief Clayton and pulled it up.

Justin Wayne arrested for attempted murder. Security footage from Talia's neighbor shows him vandalizing both vehicles. Your mother has been notified.

The shock of such a rapid response to today's accidents after the unforgivable delay in reacting to his
father's murder filled him. He was still absorbing the
facts when Talia's doctor walked in.

Bowie immediately stood. "Good evening, Doctor Rollins."

"Good evening, Bowie. Any noticeable changes
in your girl?"

"She woke briefly again and knew who I was."

Rollins nodded as he checked the log with her
readouts and numbers, then checked the wound on
her head. Only the slightest bit of blood was seep-
ing from beneath the staples. Luckily her broken
ribs hadn't punctured any internal organs. Her shoulder was almost as badly bruised as her knees, but
she would heal. Satisfied with what he saw, he gave
Bowie the news.

"I'm upgrading her status and pleased with her
progress."

"Thank you for the good news," Bowie said.

Rollins smiled. "I can't really take credit for any of that. She's the one making strong strides toward healing," he said, and then he was gone.

Once the room was theirs once more, Talia's silence no longer felt ominous to Bowie. In his heart, he'd asked God for her to be alive, and she was. He wouldn't ask for more. Not yet.

Talia was still sleeping when Amber Stewart returned, carrying a tray of food.

"This is for you," she said. "I'm going off duty, and I know you're not budging. Didn't want you to go hungry, although you may wish you had once you take a bite. It's cafeteria food, but it sustains us, so I think it will do the job for you, as well."

Bowie took the tray and set it aside.

"Thank you for being so thoughtful," he said. "I keep meaning to ask, if she wakes up again and asks for water, is she allowed anything…even ice chips?"

"She didn't have surgery, so I'll check the doctor's orders. If she can have anything, I'll ask one of the nurses on duty to bring it."

"Thank you so much," Bowie said, and then gave her a quick hug.

"You're more than welcome, cousin," she said, and waved as she went out the door.

Bowie eyed the food, took a bite of the sandwich, then dumped the chips out on the plate and ate until all of it was gone. The ice in the sweet tea was melted, but it was still cold, and he downed it, too. He used the small bathroom to wash up before returning to the seat beside the bed.

About a half hour later, a nurse came in with a cup of ice chips and a spoon, gave him directions as to how much and how often Talia could have them once she woke up, and took away the tray.

Bowie glanced at Talia again, wishing for another sign, then leaned down and whispered near her ear, "Hey, baby, this is Bowie, and I want you to know you aren't alone."

After a brief kiss on her forehead, he moved to the window. Night had come to Eden. Street lights were lit. The security lights in the hospital parking lot were burning. He could see a steady stream of headlights coming and going beyond these walls.

For the first time in his adult life, he was bothered that he didn't own a home or even rent an apartment. His way of life had been reduced to six to eight weeks on an offshore platform and a week off, during which time he either traveled the area sightseeing or just rented a motel, and ate and slept to suit himself. He'd never thought much about it before, because it was what he'd had to do to get over losing her. Now everything was different. Maybe it was meant to be that he hadn't put down roots. Maybe that was something they needed to do together. His parents had instilled money-handling skills in all their boys, so he could afford whatever they decided to do. He just needed her to get well.

He'd put in a call to his boss a couple of nights ago, updating him on what was happening and inquiring about the possibility of an onshore nine-to-five job within the company. He was still waiting for an answer.

Through the window, the looming darkness of the mountain against the night sky seemed almost ominous, but he knew it as home. As he was looking up, a bit of heaven fell from the sky, burning across his line of vision before it hit Earth's atmosphere and flamed out. He often saw shooting stars on the rigs at night, but they seemed more special at home. He was still watching the stars when he heard a soft moan and something rattling against the bed rail. He spun toward the sound just as Talia lifted her arm.

"I'm here, baby, I'm here," he said, and raced to her bedside.

Her eyelids were fluttering again. He could tell she was trying so hard to wake up. He took her hand, and when her fingers curled around his just as they had when he'd pulled her out of the wreck, he lost it.

And that was what Talia saw when she opened her eyes, the tears rolling down Bowie's cheeks.

"Alive," she whispered.

"Yes, thank God, you're alive," he said.

"Brakes," she said, just as she had earlier.

"Yes, I know. That's something for another conversation."

She squeezed his fingers to indicate understanding, and then licked her lower lip. "So dry," she said.

"You can have ice chips. Do you want one?" he asked.

She nodded, then winced.

He scooped one tiny sliver up into the spoon. She opened her mouth like a baby bird so he could place it on her tongue.

As soon as it was gone, she opened her mouth again.

He fed her a good dozen ice chips before she quit, and when she tried to move her head, she moaned instead.

"Hurts…"

"I'll ring the nurse," he said. "Just rest. I've got your back on this. I won't leave you alone."

She squeezed his fingers again.

"…you forever," she whispered, and then closed her eyes.

Bowie felt the words all the way to his soul as he watched her drifting back to sleep. She would heal, and then they would leave here to heal some more, and he would never leave her behind again.

Constable Riordan was pleased and not entirely unsurprised when the news about Justin Wayne's arrest spread through Eden like wildfire. People were in greater shock that the arrest had actually happened than learning what he'd done to cause it. In their eyes, that family had lived above the law for as long as they'd been here. It was about time someone finally paid.

Back in Chicago, William Frazier received a text from Leigh Youngblood that only added fuel to the fire his story was going to cause.

Justin Wayne arrested for attempted murders of my son Bowie and Talia Champion. Investigation continuing re: whether he'll be charged for Stanton's murder as well.

He responded with a message of his own.

Investigation building. Don't worry. Stay safe.

Dinner was over. Dessert had been served and eaten as if the earlier events had never even occurred.

Jack Wayne set down his empty coffee cup and pushed away from the table.

"I'm going out onto the terrace for a cigar. Anyone care to join me?" he asked.

"I have some work to do," Blake said.

"I'm going out," Charles said, and headed upstairs to change from his dress clothes to something more casual.

Fiona left without speaking to anyone, leaving Andrew and Nita on their own.

"I'm sorry tonight was so stressful after the wonderful afternoon we shared," Andrew said.

Nita gave his hand a quick squeeze.

"Thank you, darling. I'm going to indulge in a hot soaking bath before bed."

"Sounds perfect," he said, and gave her a quick kiss on the cheek. "You run on up to your room. I'll let myself out."

Nita patted his cheek, and when he helped her up, she slid a wad of bills into his hand and walked away.

Andrew followed her to the staircase, blew her a kiss after she reached the top, and then counted the hundred dollar bills on the way out of the house.

He was just about to get into his car when Charles came running out behind him. Charles aimed the remote at his own car, which automatically turned on the lights as it unlocked the door. Then he impulsively threw his arms around Andrew's neck, gave him a hard, lingering kiss and shouted, "Race you!"

A little taken aback, Andrew glanced up toward the second floor, but the windows were all dark. At that point, he grinned.

"Last one to the lake house is the last one to get a blow job, but no speeding," he said.

Charles laughed again, and then jumped into his car and sped up the driveway.

Andrew followed, because winning wasn't the point when you were getting paid either way.

Nita was standing naked at the window, lights off for a better view, watching Andrew leave and thinking of what a fabulous afternoon they'd had before all that unpleasantness with Justin.

She was just about to turn away when she saw someone running up behind him. Charles. Curious, she leaned closer to the glass. And when she saw Charles throw his arms around Andrew's neck and kiss him with unmistakable passion, she pressed a hand to the window in disbelief. Charles was gay? And when it dawned on her that Andrew had two Wayne clients instead of one, rage rolled through her in waves. When she saw that they were talking she dropped to her knees and opened the window just enough so she could hear what they were saying. The conversation was brief, but it rocked her back on her heels.

*Race you? Last one to the lake house is the last one to get a blow job?* What the fuck? As she watched them drive out to the road and turn in the same direction, rage blanked out conscious thought.

Within minutes she was dressed, purse and car keys in hand. She ran through the halls to the office, snagged an extra key to the lake house, then stormed out without telling anyone where she was going. It had been ages since she'd been to the lake house, but she could find it with her eyes closed. If she was lucky, she would catch them in the act and rain hellfire down upon both their heads. She would teach Andrew to two-time her with her own damn family, not to mention she was going to teach Blake's little boy how big a mistake he'd just made.

Charles was naked on the bed and waiting for Andrew when he heard the door open. Listening to Andrew's footsteps moving through the house toward the bedroom was a turn-on he hadn't expected. He couldn't just lie there waiting when he knew how good this was going to be, so he got up and met him at the bedroom door.

Charles was laughing as he reached for Andrew, but Andrew sidestepped the embrace and shoved him backward to the bed. Tonight Andrew was the man in charge, and Charles was loving it.

Nita's heart was pounding from shock and anger as she drove out of Eden, but the closer she got to the lake house, the more focused her anger became. She wasn't a Wayne for nothing, and payback was a bitch.

She turned off her headlights as she drove closer to the house, finally coming to a stop on the far side of Andrew's car.

The house was dark except for a light in the back, where the bedrooms were located. She turned off the dome light inside the car, so that when she got out it wouldn't come on, and then slipped across the yard toward the front door.

The sky was beautiful. There was a faint breeze coming off the lake. A chorus of frogs along the shore had been tuning up when she got out of the car, but they were silent by the time she reached the front door. It was the only warning Andrew and Charles were going to get, and they were undoubtedly too involved in the business of sex to pay attention.

Nita put the key into the lock. It turned soundlessly as she slipped in and eased the door shut, then paused in the darkened front hall to listen.

Charles's sudden and loud guttural groan startled her. Then it dawned on her that he was just being fucked, not murdered, and this was most likely how Fee must have felt listening to her and Andrew do the deed. Whatever.

She was actually ambivalent over the fact that Andrew was screwing around, because he was basically just a dick for hire. What pissed her off was that he was doing business with a member of her family, and that her nephew had no qualms about taking advantage of that. She imagined Charles laughing behind her back that they were both using the same paid whore.

Betrayal was a bitch, and she was about to break up the party.

She headed deeper into the house, maneuvering through the darkened rooms like a homing pigeon. By the time she got to the bedroom with the light beneath the door, she was pitched to throw one hell of a fit.

She turned the doorknob and shoved the door inward. It slammed against the wall with such force that it knocked a picture to the floor.

"You sorry-ass piece of shit!" she screamed, and picked up a vase from a nearby table and threw it at both of them.

Charles flew out of that bed as if he'd been shot, holding his hands over his crotch, like that would hide what he'd been doing.

"Aunt Nita! What the hell are you—"

She threw a paperweight that missed Charles and went straight through the window beside the bed. The sound of shattering glass punctuated the sudden silence, and it occurred to Nita that Andrew had yet to say a word.

"Well, hell, Andrew Bingham! What do you have to say for yourself?" she screamed.

"Nothing, actually. This is just business," he drawled, and began looking for his clothes.

"Have you no sense of decorum? What were you thinking, screwing multiple members of the same family? You're not half the stud you purport to be. Your hair is thinning, for God's sake." She didn't give him time to respond as she lit into Charles, who was desperately trying to get dressed. "And you, you little bastard! You knew he was mine!"

"You don't have the market cornered on an itch that needs to be scratched!" Charles shouted.

Nita stepped forward, grabbed him by the arm, and raked her fingernails down the side of his face and neck.

He cried out in pain, and then slapped her so hard she staggered backward, fell over a chair, and hit the floor butt first. The moment she went down, Charles grabbed his shoes and ran for the front door.

Nita got up cursing.

"You little bastard. I'll teach you to lay a hand on me!" she shouted, and chased after him.

Andrew was still smarting from her remark about his hair and disgusted with himself for letting it matter. He'd hoped to get a few more months out of this gig, but considering the legal mess the family was in now, it was probably a lucky break for him that it was over.

He heard the front door slam as Charles left the house, and then heard it slam again as Nita followed. He glanced out the window just in time to see both of them driving away. Now it was his turn to make an exit. He dressed, patted his pockets to make sure he had everything, then proceeded to go from room to room, recovering the video equipment he'd hidden here months ago. It had motion detector switches that turned it on, and a timer that turned it off after two full minutes of no activity. He'd changed the discs every week and had recorded plenty of his encounters with Charles. Never could tell when they might come in handy.

He snagged one camera from the bedroom, a second one from the living room, and the one he'd secured in the kitchen area last. Then he locked the house and tossed the key in the lake.

He drove all the way back into Eden with only one thought. Get his things from the hotel where Nita had put him up before she thought to have him locked out, and then get the hell out of Eden. His time in paradise was over.

# Seventeen

The race between nephew and aunt back to Eden was straight out of a Hollywood movie. Their head-lights were small bright patches in the vast darkness, leaving them with the misconception that they were isolated and beyond human law. The speed limit did not exist, and the two-lane road became their race-track. Before they cleared the lake area, Nita barely missed hitting a deer, and once they were out on the highway, rather than slow down, Charles kept his speed and ran over a possum with a sickening thump that made his gut knot.

They were neck and neck more than once, until they were forced to slow down because of oncoming traffic, but they always accelerated again through the next open stretch of highway.

Once Charles thought Nita was actually going to force him off the road, and then she took a curve too fast and fishtailed before spinning out. He looked up in the rearview mirror with a sense of relief that he was finally ahead, but when he looked again, her headlights were behind him again and gaining ground. At that point he pushed the accelerator all the way to the floor, and by the time he passed the Eden city limits his tires were screeching as he rounded every bend.

He needed to get home so he would have protection or face the reality of an actual fistfight with a woman twice his age. In desperation, he took a short-cut through a residential neighborhood, which cut off ten blocks, but he still didn't breathe easy until he pulled in beneath the portico and ran for the door.

Jack was on the phone in the office when he heard the front door slam. He looked up just as Charles raced past, caught a glimpse of the bloody scratches on his face and neck, ended his conversation and ran out into the hall.

"Charles! Stop! What the hell happened to you?" he shouted.

Charles slid to a halt, but before he could answer the front door flew open. Nita entered the foyer in an all-out sprint.

"Where are you, you little bastard?" she screamed.

Jack stared at his niece in disbelief. Her clothing was awry, her hair a mess, and the expression on her face was pure rage.

At that point Blake had heard the shouting and appeared at the head of the stairs. His saw his son's bloody face and his sister's manic demeanor, and came down on the run. "Did she do that to your face?" he demanded.

"Yes," Charles said.

"Oh, hell, no," Blake muttered, and grabbed her by the shoulders and started shaking her so hard they heard her neck pop.

At that point Charles panicked, afraid his father would break Aunt Nita's neck, and began trying to get between them to break it up, but he couldn't budge either one of them. His dad was furious, and Nita was now trying to claw her brother's face the way she'd clawed his.

When Fiona raced out of her room and stopped at the top of the stairs, she gasped and then screamed, "Uncle Jack! Make them stop!"

Charles yanked a bouquet of flowers from a nearby vase, threw it aside and then flung the water on both of them.

Blake turned Nita loose to wipe his eyes, and Nita slipped on the water and fell backward, whacking her head. She was moaning and Blake was cursing, when Charles silenced them all.

"Everyone! Shut the hell up!" he shouted. "All that's wrong with Aunt Nita is that she's pissed because she caught me and Andrew screwing."

Blake's mouth opened, but he couldn't think what to say.

Fiona started laughing and sat down on the top step to watch the drama unfold. "Oh my Lord! That's rich! What a hoot! Does he run a discount with two or more from the same family?"

Nita tried to get up and slipped again.

"Somebody help me up," she moaned.

Jack thrust out his hand, and when she grabbed hold, he pulled her to her feet.

"Nita, for God's sake, stop carrying on," he said. "Despite the unsavory aspects of this situation, the man was nothing but a high-dollar prostitute like all the men you drag home. At least this one didn't steal the family silver. He didn't owe you any allegiance and Charles was nothing more than another paying customer, although I will say, young man, you could have made a more thoughtful choice."

Charles wilted under his uncle's judgmental gaze.

Then Jack pointed at Nita.

"As for you, attacking your own kin like some wild animal? That should be beneath you. Until they heal, those scratches on your nephew's face will be a visual reminder of the poor decisions you've made in life."

Nita glared at Charles, who was glaring back. Commenting on the fact that he'd hit her, too, seemed pointless, since the truth was that she'd struck the first blow.

"Fine. I'm going to bed now," she said, and stumbled up the stairs, sidestepping her sister at the top.

Blake was a little taken aback by the sordid aspect of the situation his son found himself in; although, to be honest, he'd never thought one way or the other about what Charles did in his spare time.

"If you'll come upstairs with me, I'll put something on those scratches for you," Blake said.

"If I'm old enough to play with the big boys, then

I'm old enough to doctor myself," Charles muttered, and went upstairs to his room.

"Is it over?" Fiona asked.

"Your guess is as good as mine," Jack muttered, and went back into the office.

"Whatever," Fiona said, and left, as well.

A few moments later Frances appeared with a mop and a bucket to clean up the water, then left as quietly as she'd come.

Talia smiled as the wind coming in the open window of Bowie's car played havoc with her freshly washed hair. Finally being able to wash the blood out of it had been an emotional boost, and after three days in the hospital, it was heaven to be going home with the man she loved when they'd come so close to losing their second chance.

Bowie had the windows down and his sunglasses on against the summer sun's hot glare, and she thought that he was beautiful. Earlier, while they were waiting for her release papers, she'd asked if she could braid his hair like she used to do when they were young.

"Only if you sit down first," he had said, and helped her out of the wheelchair and back up on the bed before sitting down beside her.

He'd leaned back on his elbows, giving her access to the full length of his hair, which accounted for the thick black plait hanging over his shoulder now. The white T-shirt against his tanned skin made his shoulders look wider and his belly flatter. Talia loved how he wore his clothes, but she was more partial to when he wore nothing at all.

As if sensing he was under observation, Bowie gave her a quick glance.

"Are you feeling okay? Road's not too rough? Those bandages on your ribs aren't too tight?"

Talia was watching the way his lips moved as he spoke and remembering how they felt moving on her skin, but when she saw that he'd stopped talking, she realized she was supposed to respond.

"Everything is fine," she said.

"I promised the doctor that you would lie down as soon as I got you home," he said.

"I know, and I will."

A frown deepened the V between his eyes.

"It may seem like I'm fussing, but you came too close to dying because I brought danger to your door. I can't forget that."

"But the guilty party is in jail, right?"

He nodded.

"And they're charging him for your dad's murder, too?" she added.

"That's what I was told," he said.

She frowned. "You don't seem happy about that."

"I'm just not sure he's responsible for both crimes. He admitted to tampering with our brakes, but he swears he had nothing to do with Dad's death. I don't want to think that the real killer was handed a get-out-of-jail free card because it was so convenient to blame someone else."

Talia eyed the muscle jumping at his temple and

could only imagine how his whole family must be feeling.

"Life can be so ugly, can't it, Bowie?"

He hesitated to answer. He'd been raised to stay strong despite whatever was going on, but his father's murder had shaken his faith.

"Sometimes, yes," he said.

They rode a couple of miles farther in silence before Bowie reached for her hand and began absently rubbing her ring finger.

"Are you still my girl?" he asked.

"Always," Talia said.

"Do you want a fancy wedding?"

She shook her head.

"My heart doesn't feel like partying."

"That's how I feel, too," Bowie said.

"I just want to be able to lie down beside you each night and wake up next to you each morning," she said, and then her voice began to shake. "I thought I was going to lose you all over again. I thought I was going to die."

He couldn't bear that tremor in her voice and pulled over to the side of the road. He wanted her in his arms, but moving her in any way would only cause her more pain, so he settled for holding her hand.

"But you didn't, and we have the rest of our lives to be together. Are you going to be sad to leave Eden?"

"No. I planned to once before, remember?"

He rubbed her ring finger again.

"I remember. Someday all this will be a story we tell our grandchildren."

She gave him a look and frowned, as if he'd missed the most obvious point. "We have to make babies first."

He laughed, then put the car in gear and started driving again.

When they finally reached his family home and parked, they saw Jesse sitting in his rocking chair on the porch. He jumped up and waved, then came running down the steps as Leigh came out the front door.

Bowie grinned.

"Prepare to be loved," he said, and got out of the car.

Talia swallowed past the knot in her throat. This felt like a homecoming. Then her door opened, and Jesse was leaning in so he could see her face.

"Hi," he said. "I helped Bowie find you! I have sharp eyes!"

"And I am so grateful to you for that," Talia said.

Bowie gave his brother a quick pat on the back.

"Hey, Jesse. There's a suitcase in the trunk. Would you please take it to my room?"

Jesse grinned.

"Yes. Bowie's girl is going to get well here. I will be quiet, and I will help, won't I, Mama?"

Leigh slipped up beside him and gave him a hug.

"Yes, you will. Get the suitcase for Bowie and take it to his room now, okay?"

Bowie leaned in to help Talia out, but as soon as

she was upright, Leigh wrapped her arms around her, kissed her cheek and gave her a very gentle hug.

"Welcome home, daughter," Leigh said softly.

Talia's smile wobbled. "I've waited a long time to hear that."

"I regret the pain you've suffered because of us. I think you're due for some spoiling," Leigh said, and then led the way back into the house.

Bowie swept Talia up in his arms and followed his mother inside.

There was a cutting of honeysuckle in a vase near the front door, and the sweet scent was another facet of homecoming for Talia. They'd had lilac bushes at the house where she'd grown up, and this felt like a bit of serendipity from the Universe to prove that she was finally back on the right path.

Leigh glanced at the clock.

"It's a couple of hours 'til lunch. Why don't you rest a bit, and then Bowie can come get you when it's time to eat?"

"Yes, thank you, I believe I will," Talia said.

When Bowie carried her back to his bedroom, Jesse was standing at the foot of the bed holding an afghan like a bullfighter with a cape.

Bowie laid her down, careful not to bump her bruised and swollen knees.

Jesse covered her up.

Talia pulled the afghan beneath her chin and then looked up at them and smiled.

"You have no idea how tall you both look from down here."

Jesse grinned.

"Going now," he said, and quickly left the room.

"I'm going now, too," Bowie said, but left her with a kiss before he shut the door behind him.

The air in the room was cool compared to the outside heat. She could hear the hum of a central air unit somewhere outside as she took a deep breath and closed her eyes.

The gossip about Justin Wayne's arraignment two days ago was still fresh fodder in Eden when William Frazier's story hit the national media.

Leigh was in the kitchen making piecrust and thinking about what might appeal to Talia's palate when her phone signaled a text. She wiped her hands to check it and then read the post with a bit of disbelief that it was actually happening.

It's about to hit the fan, my friend. This is for Stanton.

She laid down the phone and grabbed the remote, aiming it at the TV on the sideboard. She and Stanton used to watch the morning news over breakfast, never thinking that one day they would be part of a lead story.

"Bowie! Come here, please!" she called, and Bowie came running from the other room.

"What's wrong?"

She pointed to the TV, and then moved to the chair where Stanton used to sit and stood behind it.

*I've still got your back, my love.*

When Bowie put his arm around her shoulders and pulled her close, she willingly leaned against him.

*And our sons have mine.*

Jack Wayne was at work, but he was just going through the motions. The disgrace of having a member of his immediate family imprisoned was humiliating, and for such a juvenile stunt. He still couldn't believe Justin had done all that in broad daylight. The least he could have done was wait until nightfall. When Barbara, his secretary, burst into his office without knocking, he didn't react with his usual disdain.

"Sir! You need to turn on the TV!" she cried.

He frowned as he reached for the remote. "What channel?" he asked.

"It doesn't matter," she said, and bolted.

Down the hall, Blake's secretary, Connie, was doing the same thing, only Blake was on the phone, so she didn't say a word. She just turned on the TV, handed him the remote and exited the room.

Back at the mansion, Charles had chosen to hole up in his suite rather than expose his wounds to public gossip, but after three days of self-imposed solitude he was bored with his own company.

He was stretched out on the sofa and channel surfing when he caught the breaking news alert. Seeing photos of his family flashing onscreen one after another with the headline "Scandal" made him turn up the volume. When the journalist began his report, Charles launched himself off the sofa, unable to believe the series of infractions, criminal activities and shady business dealings being listed. The final nails in the good will of public opinion were going to be the families they'd forced from their ancestral homes just to build a resort, the murder of a man who'd tried to stop them and the arrest of Justin Wayne on charges of attempted murder.

"Sweet son of a bitch," Charles muttered.

Within seconds the phone began to ring. He left it for Frances to pick up, pulled a couple of suitcases from the closet and started to pack, then remembered they'd been ordered not to leave the county.

Nita was on the phone with a New York City friend when the friend suddenly gasped and then changed the subject.

"Oh my God, Nita! Your whole family is on the news! What happened? What's going on?" she cried.

"I don't know what you're talking about," Nita said, and began running from one corner of her suite to the other trying to find the remote.

Then Fiona came running in unannounced with a look of horror on her face, and Nita froze.

"I'll have to call you back," she said quickly, and disconnected. "Fee, what the hell is going on?"

"They're talking indictments. They're saying we all share the guilt because we're sharing the profits. They said money is missing, and they're talking fraud and embezzlement and even issues with the FDIC because of a lending company we own."

"Who's 'they'?" Nita cried.

"It's all over the news," Fiona said, ignoring the question, and sank into a chair and started to weep. "We're ruined. We'll never recover from this."

Nita glanced out the window, absently noting a contrail in the sky as a chill rolled through her. She stood, the tears so close to falling that she couldn't see, and then turned to face her sister. "She did it."

Fiona blew her nose and then reached for another tissue. "Who did what?" she muttered.

"Leigh. She told us what she'd do if anyone else messed with her family, and what Justin did lit her fuse."

"But we're her family, too," Fiona said.

Nita laughed, and it was not a pretty sound.

"Like hell. We wrote her off nearly thirty years ago. We forgot she even existed, and then Justin killed her man and tried to kill one of her sons, and now she's schooled us on what it means to keep your word."

"What are we going to do?" Fiona asked.

"Make sure our trust funds are intact. Call our law firm to make sure you and I don't wind up included in any of these charges, and find out if we're ever allowed to leave the country."

Fiona's eyes were awash with tears, and when she nodded in agreement, they spilled over.

"I'm sorry I've been mean. Will you take me with you when you go?"

Nita sighed and, in a rare moment of emotion, hugged her sister.

"Of course, Fee. We have to stick together in this mess."

* * *

Andrew Bingham had gone straight to Charleston. The state capitol of West Virginia had its own kind of elegance, which he preferred. He had taken up temporary residence in one of the finer old hotels and spent the last few days resting, working out and going through the video files he'd recovered from the lake house.

It was a somewhat boring task for him, because everything he did was routine and precise, calculated for a client's greatest satisfaction, but as he watched, he realized there were a few things he should probably switch up. Being repetitive was the kiss of death to someone with his job skills, so he took time to watch all the recordings, deciding which ones he would keep. Those he cataloged and stored, while the others he set aside to be erased. He had to take stock of how much money he'd banked during his stint in Eden, then tie up loose ends before he moved on, preferably out of the country for a while. It would be great if the next job he landed was in Paris, but that wasn't going to happen unless he made himself available there.

He'd finished most of his lunch from room service and was down to the last five recorded sessions when he happened to look up and catch sight of Nita Wayne's face on TV. To say he was startled would have been putting it mildly. He upped the volume to hear what was going on and, as the story unfolded, began to realize how fortunate he'd been in leaving Eden before this broke.

He watched the piece all the way through, then turned off the TV and got up to refill his wineglass. Now that he knew what was happening with the Waynes, he was even more eager to get out of the country.

He grabbed a piece of Godiva chocolate from a dish beside the wine decanter, then settled in to view the remaining discs.

The next one he saw was of no importance, so he set it aside to erase and popped in the next. He noted the date and time as he hit Play, expecting to watch yet another episode of sexual antics that went along with the role-playing Charles liked.

To his surprise, the image that popped up was neither Charles nor himself, but another member of the family. He was thinking how easily he and Charles could have been compromised even earlier, and was glad it had been Nita who found them.

But then it dawned on him that the man on screen wasn't exhibiting his usual emotional control. Andrew watched him run across the room to the gun cabinet, take out a rifle, check to see if it was loaded, then run out of view, the skin crawled on the back of his neck.

The video timed out after no further movement. As Andrew made a note of the date and time, it dawned on him that this was the day of the murder.

"Oh my God! It was you," he mumbled.

Then he quickly made note of the date and time when the next recording on the disc was made, noting that it occurred about forty-five minutes after the first. He wasn't surprised when he saw it was the same man with the same rifle, this time racing frantically from one place to another, gathering objects, before he sat down and began to break down the rifle.

When the man began to clean the gun, Andrew realized he was cleaning the murder weapon.

"You sorry-ass bastard," Andrew said.

His heart was pounding as he watched the man clean every aspect of the rifle, put it back together, wipe it completely of prints, then return it to the gun case in plain view of the camera.

"Despite all your indignation, *you* actually did it."

The moment he knew what he had, he never had the impulse not to turn it over to the police. However, he sat for a moment thinking about what he needed to do first. He decided to burn a copy of the disc for safekeeping before slipping the original into a protective sleeve. He wrote the words Lake House, the date and time of the recording, and the word KILLER in caps, and put it in his suitcase, separate from all the others.

The bummer was that he was going to have to take a trip back to Eden. He didn't want to go, but considering the news report he'd just seen, this was too volatile and too important to trust to the US mail.

He called the front desk and asked them to prepare his bill, then began packing. If he didn't hit a lot of traffic, he would be back in Eden before dark.

A calm settled over Leigh once she knew the story was finally out. She heard Bowie on the phone discussing the news with his brothers, and while she had no regrets, she was surprised to find she felt no sense of satisfaction, either. Stanton was still gone, and no amount of legal retribution would change that.

When Constable Riordan called her later to tell her Stanton's body was finally being released to the family and that he was also releasing the pickup Bowie had been driving, it felt like the past days of tragedy were finally coming to an end.

"I thank you for the courtesy of your call. I'll have a wrecker pick up the truck and bring it into Eden for repair, and I'll notify the funeral home. Do I have to sign anything before they can pick him up?" she asked.

"Which one do you intend to use?" Riordan asked.

She told him.

"I'll make a note. They know what to do."

"Thank you," Leigh said.

She heard him disconnect and then laid the phone on the table. The walls of this house were closing in. She could see thousands of lonely hours ahead of her, and in a moment of panic she turned and rushed outside to the back porch.

Hit by the sunlight and the scent of pine, her panic subsided almost instantly. With a slow, shaky breath, she sat down in the porch swing and pushed off with her toes, remembering the day she and Stanton had hung this swing and all the time they'd spent in it over the years, making plans for the next day's work.

She heard a soft *cluck, cluck,* and made herself

focus on the present and what was in front of her, rather than what might be still to come.

The chickens were out of the coop, meandering about the backyard, searching the grass for bugs and seeds, and registering their disapproval with a squawk if another chicken got too close.

The faint breeze coming down the mountain cooled the beads of sweat on her forehead. She looked up at the infinite sky peppered with small white clouds and swallowed past the knot in her throat.

"So now I have to bury you. I hope you've mentioned to God, Whose infinite wisdom has often confounded me, that I completely disagree with you having to die."

A hen squawked loud and long.

"My sentiments exactly," she muttered, and pushed off in the swing again, giving way to the tears.

# Eighteen

Talia's first night at the Youngblood home was hectic and noisy, but after so many years of enforced solitude she was savoring every moment.

Baby Johnny still had tiny stitches in his lip and was soaking up every ounce of attention he was given with giggles and squeals.

"He's a handful," Bowie said, laughing at Johnny's latest antic.

"He's adorable," Talia said.

"Until you're the one chasing him down," Leslie countered.

"When they're your own, somehow the trouble doesn't seem as big," Leigh added.

Talia laughed with Leslie, but the sadness in Leigh's voice was impossible to miss. Jesse was down on all fours, and the baby was crawling under him. Bella and Maura were in the kitchen, quietly finishing up the supper dishes, doing what Leigh couldn't focus enough to do. Talia grieved Stanton's loss along with them, but she grieved more for Leigh, because she knew what it felt like to lose the only man you would ever love. She viewed the fact that she'd been given a second chance with Bowie as nothing short of a miracle.

Leigh seemed to be participating in all the post-dinner socializing, but in reality Talia knew she'd checked out. More than once she noticed Leigh's focus shift to a picture on the wall or the floor at her feet, and her behavior didn't change until Aidan brought up the story about Wayne Industries being under investigation, which sparked a whole new conversation.

"Yes, how the mighty have fallen," Bella said, coming in from the kitchen. "The charges against them seem overwhelming. How do you get out from under any of that without going to prison?"

"What I can't figure out is how some journalist in Chicago latched on to the story," Samuel said.

"I told him," Leigh said.

A shocked silence followed, then everyone began talking at once.

"How did you know to call him?" Bowie asked.

"He's one of our brokerage clients…and he liked Stanton," Leigh answered.

"Oh, wow, Mama, that's amazing," Michael said.

Leigh's expression darkened.

"What's amazing to me is that my brothers and sisters didn't take me seriously from the first."

The anger in her voice was unmistakable. Another moment of silence followed, and then Leigh took a deep breath and turned her hands palms up, as if physically handing her children more information.

"So, there's more stuff you need to know," she said. "Constable Riordan has released your daddy's body. He's already at the funeral home. I'll take clothes down tomorrow for them to dress him, but we will not be having an open casket funeral. It's been too many days. We will have a family viewing only, and then the casket will be closed. Riordan also released Stanton's truck. I sent a tow truck to take it back to Eden for repair."

"When are we having the services?" Bowie asked.

"This coming Friday at 10:00 a.m.," Leigh said. "I've already talked to our preacher. Services will be at our church on the mountain, but I'm burying him in the family cemetery here on the property. The Pharaoh twins will be here sometime in the next day or so to dig the grave."

"And the family dinner afterward?" Leslie asked.

"I think I want it here," Leigh said. "We can put the tables outside and set the food out all over the kitchen. People will come and go. It will be fine."

"You could have it at the church and skip all the mess," Samuel said.

"I know, but considering the fact that I'm going to bury my husband on this land that morning, I don't want to go off and leave him alone. At least not so soon."

The image of a new grave in the old cemetery hit all of them hard, and the silence that ensued was uneasy, except for Talia. She knew exactly what Leigh meant.

Talia had gone off and left her daddy at rest beside her mother only to come close to joining them hours later, and there was something she hadn't told Bowie and probably never would. All during her drug-filled days and nights of sleep, her daddy had been with her in her dreams. A part of her attributed that to his recent passing, but there was also a part of her that wanted to believe his spirit had stayed behind with her, just like she'd stayed behind with him.

"Then we'll have it here," Bowie said. "Don't worry about the logistics, Mama. We'll make it happen."

Leigh nodded without speaking, settling instead for looking at the beloved faces of the family she and Stanton had made.

*We did good*, she thought, and when Johnny toddled toward her begging to be picked up, she pulled him into her lap, buried her face in his soft baby curls and held him close.

Bowie kept a close eye on his mother, and one on his woman, as well. When he saw her put a hand on her ribs and wince, he knew she was hurting.

"Where are your pain pills?" he whispered.

"On the bedside table, and thank you."

"Be right back," he said, and kissed the side of her cheek.

Talia watched the sway of that long black braid against his back as he strode out of the room and wished they were in a bed somewhere making love.

He came back with a glass of iced tea and the pills, then sat back down before he handed them to her.

"Here you go, baby," he said. "And whenever this all gets to be too much, just say the word and I'll take you back to bed."

She swallowed the pills with a sip of tea, and then handed him the glass. He took a drink, then set it aside and pulled her close.

It wasn't long before Bowie noticed she was nodding. The pain pills were working. While everyone else was still talking, he picked her up and carried her out of the room.

As broken as Leigh felt about her life, there were no words for how happy she was for them. His absence from their family and the solitude of his single life had bothered her, but no longer.

When he came back, he stopped beside Leigh's chair and laid a hand on her shoulder.

Both the span of his hand and the gentleness in his touch reminded her of Stanton. She looked up.

"Can I get you anything, Mama?" Bowie said.

"No, but thank you for asking."

He picked up the tea glass and carried it back into the kitchen. The dishwasher was already running, so he rinsed it and set it aside. After a quick glance into the living room, he slipped out onto the back porch. Like Talia, he was weary of the day.

The drama that had ensued here after they'd seen the report had been its own storm. He'd seen shock, then resolution, on his mother's face as they'd watched that first news report together. Only now, after learning about her part in it, did he fully understand what had led to those emotions.

He walked off the porch and out into the yard, then looked up. The sky was black, the stars brilliant points of light so very far away. Rationally he knew what he was looking at was little more than an echo of what had been, that the brilliance he was seeing was no longer a living fire, but tonight he accepted the heavenly light in simpler terms.

He remembered another night like this when he and his brothers were all little. They'd begged and begged to sleep out under the stars, until finally their mother relented. Then they spent hours making their camp, carrying quilts and pillows, dragging food, flashlights and finally a weapon apiece to fight off wild animals. He'd chosen a baseball bat, and then Jesse had cried because he didn't have a weapon. Their mother had soothed the tears and given her baby the pick of anything from her drawer of spoons and spatulas. He'd chosen a little spatula she often used to fry eggs and come out ready for battle. They'd played until dark, eaten all their food, made countless trips back in the house to tell Mama and Daddy good-night and then, when all was said and done, had been too afraid to stay outside to sleep.

Looking back, he was certain his parents had been keeping a close eye on all five of them, because when Jesse and Aidan ran inside crying that a bear was going to eat them, their dad had been ready with his own sleeping bag and a gun.

He'd taken the two little ones back outside, moved all five bedrolls into a circle so that their heads would be touching in the middle, and tucked them all in. Then he'd unrolled his own sleeping bag, positioning it so that the boys were between him and the house. They slept then, confident that nothing could hurt them with Daddy on guard.

By daybreak they were up and running wild, filled with the elation of having slept the whole night outside. He remembered the fried ham and biscuits their mama made for breakfast that morning, giving them one last camp meal to end their adventure. They ate sitting in a circle, listening to Daddy spinning tales about the wild animals he'd fought off while they slept.

His heart hurt. He was struggling to find a new level in the family without his father's presence, and he knew his mother's pain was so much worse.

And yet, in all that loss and pain, knowing Talia was sleeping in his bed felt like a gift from God. He kept remembering something his Grandma Youngblood used to say about the Lord giving and the Lord taking away. It was the Universal search for balance, always in motion as it attempted to reach equilibrium.

The back door opened. He turned toward the house and saw all his brothers coming toward him.

"We didn't know where you'd gone," Samuel said.

"We didn't want you out here by yourself," Michael added.

"They made me come with them," Aidan said, which made everyone laugh.

Jesse laughed, too, filled with the joy of still being one of the boys.

A group hug ensued, and then the night wrapped them up in silence as they stood together beneath the stars.

It had taken a while for Bowie to get Jesse calmed down after everyone had gone home, so he'd pulled out the Daniel Boone book and read another chapter, giving Leigh time to shower.

He was sitting on the bed with Jesse when he heard the water come on in the bathroom across the hall, and when he heard his mother crying he read louder.

It was just shy of midnight when Bowie finally got to take his own shower. A few minutes later he eased into bed beside Talia and settled the covers over both of them, taking care not to wake her. He thought it would be hard to fall asleep, and yet he was asleep within minutes.

He was dreaming that they were dancing, and that Talia was standing on his feet as they moved across the floor. She had locked her hands behind his neck. His hands were at her waist, and she was laughing and laughing, when all of a sudden the laugh morphed into a scream.

He woke with his heart pounding, only to realize it wasn't a dream and Talia was screaming in her sleep.

He jumped up and turned on the light. "Talia! Sweetheart! Wake up!"

She gasped, then choked, and was trying to catch her breath when Leigh burst into the room.

"Bad dream?" she asked.

"Yes," Bowie said.

"Bless her heart," Leigh said. "I'll make her a cup of hot chocolate to wash it away."

Talia was crying and struggling to sit up when Bowie lifted her into his arms, then walked over to a big easy chair by the window and sat down with her close against his chest. With all the bruises on her knees and legs, and the broken ribs, he let her lean on him, rather than holding her too tight.

"It's okay, baby, it's okay," he kept saying. "It was a dream, just a dream."

Talia knew it, but the shock and the sensation of falling was still fresh in her mind. In the dream she'd even felt the rush of air against her skin as she was tumbling.

"I wasn't in a car. It was just me. I fell off the mountain, and I kept falling and falling and falling, and then you woke me. Oh my God, it was so real."

"It was a dream, and it's over. Mama is making you some hot chocolate—to wash away the dream, she said."

Talia groaned. "Oh, no! I woke her, too? Did I wake Jesse? Is he okay?"

"Mama needs someone to baby, honey. Let her do her thing. As for Jesse, he sleeps through just about everything."

Talia went limp against him, waiting for her heartbeat to return to normal.

A couple of minutes later Leigh was back, carrying a small towel and a steaming cup of hot chocolate. "I put marshmallows in it," she said.

"That's what Mother used to do," Talia said, and burst into tears.

"Bless your heart," Leigh said, as she sat the cup aside and pulled a blanket from the bed for Bowie to cover Talia with. Then she leaned over the both of them, gave each one a kiss on the cheek and left the room.

Talia cried until her eyes were swollen and the chocolate had cooled. She drank it lukewarm, sharing some with Bowie until the cup was empty and the hollow feeling in her belly was gone.

"Do you feel like you're ready to lie back down?" Bowie asked.

"I want to go to the bathroom first," she said.

"I'll get you there, then you call out when you want me to come get you."

"I think maybe I can walk," she said, but when she stood, her knees were so stiff and painful that the few steps she took were more than Bowie could stand to witness.

He carried her across the darkened hall and into the bathroom, waited until she was steady enough on her feet to get to the toilet, and then slipped out the door. A couple of minutes later he heard the toilet flush and then water running in the sink. He was waiting for her to call him when she opened the door.

"I'm ready," she said softly.

He carried her back to bed, turned off the lights and stretched out beside her once more. There were a few moments of silence, and then he heard her sigh.

"I love you, Bowie."

He smiled. "I love you, too," he said.

"When we get married, I don't care where we go or what our house looks like. As long as you're there, I'll be happy."

"Sounds perfect to me," he said.

"I want babies," she said.

His heart skipped a beat at the thought of his child in her belly.

"So do I... Pretty little girls with curly hair and sassy smiles like their mama."

"I've lost my sass," Talia said.

"You'll get it back," he promised.

She didn't say anything more, and when he heard her breathing change to a slow and steady pace, he knew she'd fallen asleep.

The next time he woke it was morning and Talia was lying on her side watching him sleep.

"Good morning," she whispered.

He managed a sleepy grin.

"Good morning to you, too, sunshine."

She touched his face, then ran her fingers through his hair, loving the feel of the silky strands sliding between her fingers.

"You have sexy hair," she said.

He chuckled. "The hell you say."

She nodded.

"And you have a sexy body," he said.

She made a face. "I have a skinny body," she muttered.

He frowned.

"No, you don't. You're perfect—like a gorgeous car that just needs a tune-up."

She laughed.

"I'd almost forgotten what man-speak sounded like."

He grinned. "Want me to see if anyone is in the bathroom?"

She nodded.

He brushed a quick kiss across her lips and rolled out of bed, and so their day began.

Andrew chose his clothes carefully that morning. Good gabardine slacks, a pale blue shirt and a beige linen sport coat. He chose a pair of brown alligator shoes to add a little flash and made sure his short curly hair was moussed into place. On a good day his reputation was questionable, but being connected in any way whatsoever with the now infamous Waynes was dicey, and the thought of presenting himself at the police station with his information was unnerving. By the time he felt presentable it was almost 9:00 a.m., and his belly was churning. If only he could get this done without any ensuing notoriety he would be grateful.

He checked out of the motel, intent on leaving Eden after he got the video into the proper hands, and headed for downtown. He knew where the police station was located and arrived there without an issue. He grabbed his laptop, patted his pocket to make sure the disc was there and got out of the car.

It appeared to be the beginning of another sunny summer day, although it had yet to get hot. A stray cat ran across his path as he headed toward the station. He made the sign of the cross and whispered a quiet prayer of thanksgiving that the damn thing wasn't black, then hastened his stride.

Once inside, he walked up to the receptionist at the front desk, a thirty-something woman with gray roots and red hair. He wanted to suggest another color to offset the reddish cast of her skin and tried not to stare.

"Good morning," the woman said. "How can I help you?"

"I need to speak to Chief Clayton."

"Your name?" she asked.

"Andrew Bingham."

"Is he expecting you?" she asked.

"No. Just tell him it's about Stanton Youngblood's murder."

"Are you from some newspaper?"

He frowned. He hadn't driven all this distance to be grilled by a receptionist.

"I'm not going to discuss why I came with anyone but him. Just tell him it's about the killer."

"They already have the killer in custody."

"No. They don't," he said, and watched the shock spread across her face.

"Have a seat," she said, pointing to a bank of chairs against the wall, then grabbed the phone.

Andrew didn't bother sitting down, which was just as well, because he heard footsteps approaching at a fast pace. Then a door opened behind the reception area.

It was Clayton.

"Come with me," the chief said shortly, and led the way back to his office, then waved at a chair on the other side of his desk. "Take a seat."

Andrew sat.

"Who are you, and what the hell do you mean, we don't have Youngblood's killer?"

"My name is Andrew Bingham. Up until a few days ago I was Nita Wayne's guest at your local hotel, and on call at any time, night or day, to appease her sexual whims."

Clayton blinked. "You're a gi—"

"I prefer 'professional escort,'" Andrew said. "At times I was also an escort for Charles Wayne."

Clayton frowned. "Okay, fine. You got paid for sex. Now speak your piece."

Andrew nodded.

"It has been my habit for many years to record my activities with clients. Not for blackmail. Never for that. But as a kind of insurance against winding up in a serious situation not of my making, if you understand my meaning?"

Clayton shrugged. "I'm listening."

"The regular meeting place where Charles and I... indulged was the Wayne family lake house. In fact, it was Charles who suggested it, because he said the family never went there anymore. So he gave me a key, and at agreed-upon times we met and we played, and unknown to him, I recorded our activities. The equipment was motion-activated, so all I had to do was show up and let the party begin. A few days ago I had a falling out with both Nita and Charles, so I packed up my things, including the video equipment, and left town. I've spent the past few days in Charleston, going through the recordings, and in doing so I came across a piece of video that you need to see."

Clayton threw up his hands. "I have no intention of watching two guys boink each other."

Andrew frowned. "That's not what's on the disc."

"Then what is?" Clayton snapped.

"It's video of the man who, I'm quite certain, shot Stanton Youngblood."

Clayton leaned forward.

"The hell you say! You aren't trying to tell me you have video of the murder?"

"No, sir. But what I do have is video taken on the morning of the murder, showing a member of the Wayne family running into the house, taking a rifle out of a gun cabinet and leaving just as quickly. Forty-five minutes later the same man comes back, breaks down the rifle, cleans it, then puts it back in the gun cabinet."

Clayton's eyes narrowed. "Show me."

Andrew nodded, opened his laptop, slipped the disc into the slot, hit Play and turned the screen toward the chief. It didn't take long for Chief Clayton to get the gist of what he was seeing, and it was obvious he was as surprised as Andrew had been by who it was. The minute the video was over, he reached for the phone and called Constable Riordan.

A few moments later Riordan answered. "This is Riordan."

"Chief Clayton here. I have just been given evidence that I would say clears Justin Wayne of Stanton Youngblood's murder."

"No," Riordan said, and then sighed. "Well, hell. When are we going to catch a break on this mess?"

"Oh, we already caught it," Clayton said. "My evidence gives you the identity and damning evidence of the killer's culpability, and if I remember the transcripts of your interviews of the family, this completely refutes his alibi. Grab a pen and paper to take down the info you'll need for an arrest warrant. I'll be waiting for you here at the office. You can see the video for yourself before we bring the sucker in."

"Who is it?" Riordan asked.

Clayton spilled the beans, and after he'd hung up, he leaned across the desk and shook Andrew's hand.

"You did a good thing today, Mr. Bingham. I hope you don't mind waiting here a little while longer. Constable Riordan may have a question or two for you himself. Since his office has the lead in the murder case, you will officially turn over your video to him."

"No problem," Andrew said. "In the meantime, may I ask for a cup of coffee? I didn't eat breakfast this morning. A little anxious about coming here and all."

"I'll get your coffee. Feel free to enjoy the donuts and sweet rolls on the table at the back of the room."

"Thank you," Andrew said, and went to get something to eat as the chief poured him some coffee.

The Pharaoh brothers arrived right after breakfast with the backhoe to dig Stanton's grave, but they also came prepared with pickaxes, should the need arise. Sometimes mountains were more rock than dirt.

Leigh's heart skipped a beat when she saw them coming. One more step toward making Stanton's absence horribly final.

"Want me to do this?" Bowie asked.

"No, but thank you," she said, then stuffed a tissue in her jeans pocket and went out the back door, past Talia, who was sitting in the porch swing.

"Where you goin', Mama?" Jesse yelled, as Leigh walked past the garden.

"To the cemetery," she said. "You keep picking the berries, okay?"

"Okay, Mama. Picking berries," he said.

Talia saw the stiff set to Leigh's shoulders and the fact that her hands were curled into fists, and looked away.

Bowie came out carrying a glass of cold water and handed it to her.

"Drink up, honey. It's already getting hot out."

She took a big drink and then cradled the glass

between her hands as condensation began to coat the outside of it. "I feel so sad for what's happening."

"We all do," he said, and then eased down on to the swing beside her. "I have news," he said.

"Is it good?" she asked.

"Yes, very."

"Then tell me."

"I've been offered an onshore job by my company. Supply engineer. It's coordinating what both offshore and dry land rigs need, and then facilitating getting the goods to them. I have the experience. The pay is good, the hours are regular, and I'll be based in New Orleans and home every night."

"Oh, Bowie! This is wonderful!"

Her delight and excitement were evident on her face.

"It's going to be a new start for both of us," he said.

"Do you have a deadline for when you have to be there?" she asked.

"Within the next two weeks. We'll be here for the funeral and still have time to do some house hunting before I start work."

"Rather than rush the house hunting, why don't we just settle into an apartment, preferably with a short lease, and then take our time finding a permanent home?"

Bowie grinned. "You wouldn't mind that?"

She threw her arms around his neck.

"I don't care where we are, as long as we're together, remember?" she said, and kissed him, then didn't turn loose.

The kiss went longer and grew more heated until Bowie stopped with a groan.

"You might want this, but you can't have it, and neither can I," he said. "Just get well."

"We could pretend."

He laughed.

"We moved way past that stage when you turned sixteen."

"I've been missing you for so long," she said.

It was the quiet tone of her voice that made him look closer.

"What's wrong?"

She hesitated for a moment before she answered.

"I guess I'm afraid this is all too good to be true. I wanted this for so long and thought it was lost to me. Getting you back, and with the dream, seems too good to be true."

Bowie hated the fear he heard in her voice. "What dream are you talking about, baby?"

"The one where we live happily ever after."

Bowie took her hands and held them against his chest.

"What do you feel?" he asked.

She shrugged, uncertain what he meant. "I feel you."

"What else?" he asked.

"How soft your T-shirt is and how hard your muscles are."

"What else?" he asked again.

"I don't know what you mean," she said.

He held her hands tighter against him. "Close your eyes, then tell me what you feel."

He waited.

Suddenly her eyes were open and she was smiling.

"Your heartbeat. I feel your heartbeat."

"As long as my heart beats, it beats for you. We aren't *going* to be happy. We already *are*. Even in the middle of such sadness and uncertainty, we already have each other. Now, no more fear about our future. We're good to go, okay?"

"Okay."

"Love you," he said softly.

"Love you more."

"Well, I know that. You have to," Bowie said.

Talia laughed. "Why do I have to love you more?"

He stood.

"Because there's so much more of me to love," he said, and blew her a kiss as he headed for the garden to check on Jesse.

She was still smiling when he started tilling the ground between the rows of sweet corn.

A short while later Leigh came back to the house, then stopped at the porch swing and held out her hand.

"Come inside with me where it's cool, honey. The day is already way too hot."

Talia eased herself up and went inside. Only after the cool air hit her did she realize how good it felt. "Can I help you do anything?" she asked.

Leigh looked pale and shaken. Watching them dig her husband's grave had been gutting.

"You've already given me something wonderful. You brought joy back into my son's life. As tragic as Stanton's loss is for this family, you are the gift that none of us saw coming."

Talia hugged her. "You're going to make me cry again. Seems like these days that's all I do."

"These days will pass," Leigh said softly. "They won't pass quickly, but they *will* pass, and we will be all the stronger for it when they're gone."

# *Nineteen*

Riordan was worried about Clayton's revelation being too good to be true until he, too, saw the evidence Andrew Bingham had produced. He didn't care how it had happened, because he now had what he needed, and instead of putting one member of the family behind bars, he was going to put two.

"We appreciate your honesty and your good intentions in coming forward with this evidence," Riordan said. "I have your phone number. You've given your deposition. If there are any other questions that arise, we'll contact you."

Andrew nodded. So much for leaving the country right now; however, Florida would be a good second choice.

"Will I have to testify or anything?" he asked.

"I seriously doubt this will go to trial. Purposefully going after a gun shows intent. Cleaning the gun afterward and wiping it clean of prints speaks to an understanding of guilt. And the victim was run down like prey and then shot in the back, which eliminates the excuse that it was an accident. No matter what reasoning the killer can come up with, it will never excuse premeditated murder. However, thanks to you, my job is almost done. The rest will be up to the courts."

"So I'm free to leave?" Andrew asked.

Riordan nodded.

Andrew straightened his jacket as he stood, and then shook their hands.

"Gentlemen, I won't say this has been a pleasure, but it *has* been enlightening."

He left with his laptop, gratefully leaving the damning evidence behind. It was time to plot a course for sunny Florida.

Riordan looked at Chief Clayton and grinned. "What do you say we go arrest ourselves a killer?"

"I appreciate the offer to ride along. I'm ready when you are. Where do you think he is right now?"

"I checked. He's at work."

Clayton nodded. "Then let's do it."

Blake had just finished a call to one of their overseas subsidiaries, trying to calm the panic and uncertainty rolling through every aspect of their financial empire. He glanced at the clock, then thought about seeing if Charles was free for lunch. Things had been a little strained between them since the incident at the lake house, and he wanted to make sure his son knew he had his back.

He was a little put out with his Uncle Jack for behaving as if Justin no longer existed. Despite what he'd done, he was still family, and then he remembered they'd done the same thing to Leigh with far less reason.

Deciding a face-to-face invitation was a better choice than a phone call, Blake left his office to find Charles.

He stopped at his secretary's desk.

"Connie, I'll be out to lunch for a couple of hours," Blake said. "I don't have any afternoon appointments, but if there's an issue or another call from one of the companies, have them call my cell, okay?"

"Yes, sir. Have a good lunch," Connie said.

"Thank you," Blake said, and walked out into the hall, then headed left to Charles's office.

This was Charles's first day back at work after the fight with Nita, and he was still self-conscious about the scabby streaks on his face and neck. When his father walked in, he was genuinely glad to see him.

"Hey, Dad. What's up?"

"I came to see if you wanted to go to lunch with me."

Charles grinned.

"Yes. Absolutely. Is Uncle Jack coming, too?"

"I haven't asked him yet. Do you want him to tag along?"

"As long as no one talks about the splash we made on the national news, I'm good," Charles said.

"I'm so sorry all of that is happening," Blake said.

"So am I," Charles said, as he began logging out of his computer and locking up his desk. "Sometimes

I can't believe all this chaos is real. One day we were just doing our thing, and then all of a sudden we're caught up in the middle of a nightmare."

Blake frowned. "Well, a man *was* murdered. That's what started it."

Charles shrugged. "But we didn't know him."

"Well, actually the rest of us did, just not you."

Jack walked in at that moment and patted Blake on the back. "I'm going to lunch. Do you two want to come along?"

Charles glanced at his dad and nodded.

Blake got the message. "Sure, Uncle Jack. We'd love to."

They walked down the hall to the elevator and moments later exited into the lobby of Wayne Industries.

A janitor was using a floor polisher on the white marble tiles. The guard in the lobby was on the phone, but he quickly hung up and smoothed a hand down the front of his uniform when he saw them coming. A pizza delivery boy was coming in the front entrance with a half-dozen boxes of pizza. Some people were obviously staying in for lunch.

Then Charles saw the police cars pulling up at the front of the building and pointed.

"Hey, Dad. What's going on?"

Blake sighed. "Who the hell knows," he muttered.

Jack frowned. "Does this shit never end?"

They watched Constable Riordan, Chief Clayton and a trio of officers enter the lobby, but when the officers suddenly fanned out as they approached, Blake's gut knotted.

"Dad?" Charles said as he took a step back, his voice suddenly pitched higher than normal.

"We're fine," Jack said.

Blake wasn't so sure. This was too reminiscent of Justin's arrest. What the fuck did the cops know?

The lobby guard looked nervous, but he stayed behind the desk.

Riordan gave a nod, and the officers headed for the Waynes.

Blake saw the handcuffs and panicked. What's going on?" he said.

Jack Wayne glared and then shouted, "I demand to know the meaning of this."

Riordan produced the arrest warrant. "Jeffrey Jack Wayne, you are under arrest for the murder of Stanton Youngblood. You have—"

Blake gasped. "You have to be kidding!"

Charles was shaking, afraid they were all going to be arrested before this nightmare was over.

"You have my alibi. You have nothing to back this up. Blake, call our lawyer. *Now!*" Jack demanded.

Riordan finished reading Jack his Miranda rights as the officers handcuffed him.

"Actually, we do have proof," Riordan went on. "A most revealing video of you less than an hour before Stanton Youngblood was murdered running into the lake house to get a rifle, and then a follow-up video of you coming back forty-five minutes later, when you sat down and calmly cleaned the rifle before putting it back in the gun case."

The shock on Jack's face was obvious. "You don't! You can't! How—"

Blake was shaking. "Is this true? You have proof?"

"Yes. It was actually turned in to my office first, so we've both seen it," Clayton offered.

Blake turned on his uncle in disbelief.

"From the start, you tore into all of us, trying to pin us down with alibis, making it look like all the trouble we were in was because of something one of us had done, when all the fucking time it was you? Why? Just tell me why?"

Jack shrugged. "He ruined everything."

"But it wasn't that big an investment!" Blake cried. "We've lost far more money on bigger projects before, and one way or another we've always recouped it."

"I guess you may as well hear the truth from me, rather than hearing it in court. I transferred money from offshore accounts, and from accounts the board never got a chance to approve, and I manipulated some assests through East Coast Lenders in order to buy up the loans from the bank and force those foreclosures."

"But you aren't in charge of all that! *I* am," Blake said. "I handle the investments. How did you do that without me knowing?"

Jack lifted his chin in a defiant gesture.

"How do you think I did it? I forged your damn signature, you idiot. I would have put the money back. But then Leigh and her hillbilly husband blocked the project when they made sure the last two pieces of land we needed were unavailable, and with the annual audits less than three months away, there was no way to cover up a ten million dollar shortfall without major embarrassment."

Charles's shock morphed from fear to disbelief and then anger.

"You murdered a man because you were going to be embarrassed? We have billions. It would have been a simple matter of moving money around!" he cried.

Jack glared. "But I would still have been removed as CEO of Wayne Industries. It was the principle of the thing!" he shouted.

"I've heard enough," Riordan said, and led Jack Wayne away.

Blake started to take a step, and then staggered.

Charles caught his father by the elbow and quickly guided him out of the lobby to his car. "Get in, Dad."

Blake obeyed without comment.

Charles drove all the way back to the mansion in silence. He couldn't look at his father, knowing there were tears on his face. That wasn't how their world worked.

"We're here," he said, as he parked beneath the portico.

Blake fumbled with the door handle before he finally got it open, and then he followed Charles inside.

Frances was carrying a fresh bouquet of flowers to the table in the foyer as they entered.

"Oh, Mr. Blake, Mr. Charles, did Cook know you were coming home for lunch?"

"We didn't come home to eat," Charles said. "Are my aunts here?"

Frances nodded.

"Would you please ask them to join Dad and me in the library?"

"Yes, of course. Do you want anything to eat or drink?"

"Not now, Frances, but thank you," Charles said, and led his father down the hall and into the library.

Blake sat in the nearest chair as Charles headed to the bar. A minute later Blake took the shot of whiskey Charles offered him and downed it neat.

"What are we going to do?" Charles asked.

Blake didn't respond. He didn't even act like he'd heard him.

Charles tried not to panic. It wasn't like his dad to be so indecisive. "All right. We'll talk about it when your sisters arrive," he said.

Blake leaned back in the chair and closed his eyes.

A few minutes later Charles heard footsteps on the stairs and promptly poured Aunt Fiona a shot of whiskey, neat, and Aunt Nita a glass of wine. They were going to need it.

Fiona was fresh from a massage and still in her dressing gown as she sauntered into the library.

Nita was still in a state of defiance, and was experimenting with makeup and hair color. She looked ghastly to Charles, but since he was still pissed off at her, he was secretly pleased that she looked like a tramp.

"What's going on?" Fiona asked, and then frowned when Charles handed her the whiskey.

Nita took the wine without comment, but her senses were on alert. Blake looked like shit, and the air was so charged with energy she could feel it. "Blake? What's happening?" she asked.

"Dad doesn't feel well," Charles said. "Uncle Jack has been arrested for that man's murder. The authorities have video proof of him going into the lake house to get the rifle, then bringing it back and cleaning it later."

Fiona moaned and covered her face.

Nita frowned.

"There was video equipment set up at the lake house?" she asked.

Charles shrugged. "It seems so."

"Did you know?" she asked.

Charles rolled his eyes. "Hardly."

Nita downed her wine like it was water and then set the glass down so hard it shattered.

"You know he did that," she muttered.

Charles's shoulders slumped. She was talking about Andrew, saying that Andrew had been the one who turned their uncle in. "Yes."

"Well, shit," Nita said. "Why didn't he try to blackmail us with it? He knows we would have paid."

"Maybe he was afraid it would shorten his life," Charles muttered, thinking of the people recently targeted by the family.

Nita sighed. "Who knew the slick bastard had a streak of honesty? But more to the point, where does this leave us?"

"I don't know, but I need you to see to Dad. I have to go call the lawyer and let him know Uncle Jack has been arrested."

The sisters looked at each other and then at their brother.

"What's wrong with him?" Fiona said.

"He just quit talking," Charles said, and headed to the office to make the call.

It was late in the evening.

The Pharaoh brothers were gone. Jesse was feeding the chickens, and Bowie was at the barn when Constable Riordan drove up to the Youngblood home.

Leigh was in the kitchen making supper, and Talia was in the living room, stretched out on the sofa and looking out the window. "Leigh! Someone just drove up!" she called.

Leigh wiped her hands and turned down the fire on the chicken she was frying. She saw the vehicle through the window and recognized the constable's car.

"It's Constable Riordan," she said, and hurried to open the door just as he began to knock. "Good evening," she said.

"Excuse me, Mrs. Youngblood. I know it's late in the evening for a house call, but I have some important information."

"Come in," Leigh said, and then introduced Talia.

"Constable Riordan, you remember Talia Champion."

Riordan nodded at Talia. "Yes, I do, and may I say how happy I am to see you alive and healing," he said.

"I don't remember your help in rescuing me, but I am very grateful," she said.

"Have a seat," Leigh said.

"No, no, I won't stay that long, but Chief Clayton and I both agreed that it was only proper that you hear this news from one of us. And since I was on my way back to the office, I volunteered."

The back door slammed, and then they heard footsteps moving quickly through the house.

"That's Bowie," Leigh said, with a smile. "He enters and exits a house just like his daddy."

"What's going on?" Bowie asked.

"I came to tell you that we arrested the man who killed Stanton today. He confessed after the fact, but it didn't matter. We have proof."

Leigh's chin came up, as if she was bracing herself for yet one more blow. "So it wasn't Justin after all."

"No, ma'am, it was Jack Wayne."

Leigh blinked. It was her only physical reaction.

Bowie felt blindsided. He'd laid the steak knife they'd taken away from Justin across that man's plate. It was a good thing he hadn't known then. He would probably have put it in his back, instead.

"Did he say why?" Leigh asked.

Riordan wished she hadn't asked that, but he wasn't going to lie. It would all come out later anyway.

"It appears Wayne forged Blake's signature to embezzle money from quite a few accounts in the family company. It was to help facilitate a series of questionably legal foreclosures that removed a number of local homeowners from property the Waynes' partners in the development of a resort here on the mountain wanted, and he was angry that when Stanton paid off your relatives' loans and protected two key pieces of land, he made the resort impossible. Once the investors pulled out, his financial misdeeds were going to be found out."

Leigh was stunned, shaken, but also filled with disbelief. "I can't imagine the board would have had him arrested."

Riordan sighed. "But they would have removed him as CEO, and he couldn't have stood the embarrassment."

Leigh moaned. "Killing Stanton wouldn't have changed any of that! Oh my God. He did it out of spite?"

Riordan shrugged. "I can't say exactly what was in his head, but I'm so sorry for your loss."

Bowie saw his mother's eyes lose focus, and then she was falling.

He caught her before she hit the floor. Despite the pain, Talia quickly got up from the sofa so Bowie could lay Leigh down. She went to get a wet washcloth. She wrung it out, folded it up, and came back and put it on Leigh's forehead.

In that vulnerable position, Leigh looked more

like the teenager who'd run away with the boy she
loved than the woman she'd become.

"I'm sorry," Riordan said. "Is there anything I
can do to help?"

Bowie shook his head. "We've got this, but thank
you for taking the time to come tell us in person."

The back door banged again, but this time the
steps were slower and halting.

"It's Jesse," Bowie said.

Leigh was already rousing, and she began trying
to sit up. "I just got dizzy. I'm okay," she said.

"Sit!" Bowie ordered. "I'm going to get you a
drink of water."

Riordan was heartsick for this family on so many
levels.

"If there's nothing I can do to help, then I'll be
getting out of your way," he said, and let himself out.

"Who's that?" Jesse asked, as the door swung
shut.

"Just Constable Riordan," Bowie said. "Go wash
your hands real good—and use soap. We'll be eating supper pretty soon."

Jesse glanced at his mother, but when she smiled
and nodded, he went to do what he'd been told.

"Help me up," Leigh said.

"No, ma'am. You stay seated a bit longer," Talia
said. "I can stand at a stove and turn chicken. My
knees are sore, not broken."

"And I'll help her," Bowie said. "You sit there and
make the calls you need to make."

Leigh had been blindsided, not by who'd done it,

but by the shallowness of the reason. It was a petty
gesture from a man who'd lived his life with too
much of everything.

"Sweet Lord, give me strength," she whispered,
and began calling her sons.

After that she had to call Stanton's sister and
brother. Then the news would spread, and gossip
with it, but it didn't matter. Her sweet man was gone,
and no amount of grief or righteous indignation was
going to change that.

# *Twenty*

The church service was a blur for Bowie, and when it was over, instead of going home, the mourners all lingered, wanting their moment with Leigh Young-blood.

When the family came out of the church, Leigh didn't get into a car but stayed and let them come to her. Because they were burying Stanton on family ground, most of the attendees would not be at the cemetery, so they swarmed around her, all sincere in their sorrow, too many people all saying the same thing: "We're so sorry for your loss."

As the widow, Leigh bore the brunt of so many kindhearted people not knowing when to stop talking, and accepted it with grace. Last night, during a heart-to-heart talk with God, it had finally hit her that she had to let go of the way Stanton had been taken from her. He was just as dead as if he'd died in a wreck or from a lingering disease. Other women bore the same loss, and with just as much grief. She wasn't unique. She wasn't special. Her loss wasn't worse. She had to let go of the rage, because it was not her cross to bear.

Stanton's sons, with Jesse among them, stood in their mother's shadow, never very far away should the need to step in arise, tending to their own families while making sure she didn't need to be rescued.

After a while Bowie had moved through the crowd, whispered in his mother's ear and then led her away.

Now the hearse was on the way to the Youngblood property, where the body would be laid to rest. It was a silent trip on a narrow winding road, with only family and a few close friends as escorts.

Talia had a horrible sense of déjà vu. She'd been in this same car only a few days before, and here she was again, right behind the hearse.

Leigh had Jesse at her side. What none of them had expected was Jesse's grasp of death. Despite all the things the war had taken away from him, Jesse still remembered his friends dying and was sad again for them as well as for his father.

It was close to noon by the time they arrived at the Youngblood home. At Leigh's request, they got out at the back of the house. Bowie took Jesse and, together, they began directing people where to park.

Leigh went straight to the porch swing and sat down. It would take a while for everyone to get there, and then for the pallbearers to gather. The day was sweltering. Sweat was already beading on her upper lip as she leaned back and closed her eyes.

Talia was far more mobile now than she'd been on
her arrival at the house, and she slipped past Leigh to
go inside. Two of Leigh's friends from church were
in the kitchen. They had volunteered to stay at the
house and accept the food that people kept bringing,
and now they were busy heating up casseroles, and
slicing cakes and pies. One long table out on the front
porch held nothing but desserts. The entrees were inside, laid out on every table and surface imaginable.
It was how sadness was marked in small communi-
ties. Feeding the grieving was a way of expressing
condolences, and today was no exception.

"Could I have a cup of something cold for Leigh
to drink?" Talia asked.

"I'll get some lemonade," one of the ladies said,
and quickly returned with some in a paper cup.

"Thank you," Talia said, and went back outside.

She sat down in the swing beside Leigh, and when
Leigh opened her eyes, Talia handed her the cup.

Leigh took it and drank thirstily.

"That was so good," she told Talia. "Thank you
for thinking of me."

"None of us can think of anything else," Talia
said. "My heart hurts for you."

Leigh slipped her hand beneath Talia's elbow, then
set the swing in motion.

"I don't remember a thing that the preacher said.
Was it a good sermon?" Leigh asked.

"It was perfect," Talia said.

Leigh nodded, but her gaze was focused on the
Pharaoh brothers' rig parked out by the cemetery.

When all was said and done, they'd had to cover the casket. She'd already seen Stanton's body dressed in his finest clothes inside it. She didn't want to have to watch them cover him with six feet of West Virginia dirt, but life wasn't about what you wanted; it was about what had to be done.

She reached over and clasped Talia's hand.

"I am so terribly sorry for the pain and suffering you've endured, but very grateful that you were here with me these past few days. I know it must be especially difficult for you, since you just buried your father."

"My father's passing was a gift," Talia said. "I grieved his loss years ago and wouldn't wish him back the way he was for even a single second."

Leigh nodded in understanding.

"You know, honey, I always wanted a daughter, and yet every time there was a new baby, it would turn out to be another little boy. Finally I settled with God and told Him, Thy will be done. Five boys turned out to be perfect. They grew up just fine and have since given me the daughters I always wanted."

Talia held those words close in her heart.

"Thank you for that. It's been a long time since I had a mother, so I'm grateful for your presence in my life."

Leigh leaned over and kissed Talia's cheek, then watched the growing number of cars driving into the yard, and saw Bowie directing them to park in rows. It wouldn't be long now.

"Bowie was my firstborn, as you know. Mothers

aren't supposed to have favorites, and I don't, but he's so much like Stanton, except for that black hair, which he gets from me. If I squinted my eyes just right, I could believe it was the father and not the son I'm seeing."

"We'll come home far more often than he did before," Talia said. "I promise."

"I'll hold you to that," Leigh said.

As Leigh watched, the pallbearers began to gather. Her four oldest sons; Stanton's brother, Thomas; and his brother-in-law, Carl.

"Where's Jesse?" Leigh said. "He's going to walk with me."

"Over there, with Samuel," Talia said.

Leigh took a slow, shaky breath. "I guess it's time."

Talia stood, and when Leigh stepped off the porch and back out into the sunlight, Talia was holding her hand.

A few moments later they unwound themselves from the gathering crowd and fell into line behind the pastor, who began leading the way to the cemetery just visible through the trees.

Directly behind the pastor, the pallbearers walked with the casket, and behind them, Leigh with Jesse, who was now holding a bouquet of flowers someone had given him. Talia fell in with the daughters-in-law, and behind them came the rest of Stanton's family. Friends came last, moving in an orderly line, and somewhere along the way a man began to sing. The clear notes of "Amazing Grace" swelled up into the air, floated above the heads of the mourners and dispersed out on to the mountain.

Talia watched the pallbearers as they stepped in unison, strong shoulders, broad backs and, in the Samson-like tradition of their father, their long hair loose and hanging far below their shoulders, as they carried Stanton Youngblood to his grave.

Prayers were said.

Someone was crying. Talia couldn't see for the tears.

She heard another brief passage from the Bible being read as a blessing to the man in the casket now being lowered into the ground.

When Leigh stepped forward and picked up a handful of dirt, it seemed as if everyone held their breath. When she tossed it into the grave and it hit the top of the casket with a splattering sound, they exhaled as one. Jesse threw the flowers he'd been carrying into the grave and then turned away in tears. Talia saw Bowie catch him and hold him like a baby against his chest, patting his back and whispering to him over and over.

Someone in the crowd began to sing. Someone different this time. A young woman with a mountain twang to her voice singing "I'll Fly Away." By the time she reached the first chorus, the air was filled with voices joining in.

The songs were nothing Leigh had planned or expected. Just a simple gift from friends and neighbors to a grieving widow, hoping to soothe her heart with a reminder of the heavenly path Stanton was already on.

* * *

It was nearing 2:00 p.m.

The meal was in full swing, and the occasional sound of gentle laughter could be heard out in the yard. Healing sounds. Sounds of life happening and people moving past the grief.

It would take Leigh Youngblood far longer to reach that place, but she was grateful for the presence of family. Even though the thought of eating was impossible, she'd gone outside to walk among the mourners, a chance for one last thank-you to all of them for helping her lay Stanton to rest.

Bowie was sitting on the edge of the porch, talking to a friend from school when his friend suddenly pointed. "Here comes one more," he said.

Bowie recognized the man coming up the drive on foot.

"Excuse me a minute," he said, and headed toward his mother, who was facing the house and had no idea her brother was approaching.

Blake was certain that this was one of the scariest things he'd ever had to do. He wasn't even sure he would make it off the mountain alive, and truthfully, the way he'd been feeling for the past few days, it would be a kindness if his misery would end here and now.

He saw Leigh almost immediately. Even though her back was turned, she was impossible to miss.

And then he saw one of her sons and stopped,

waiting to see if he would even be allowed to speak to her.

He watched the tall, black-haired man slip his hand beneath his mother's elbow and then whisper in her ear. He knew she must be shocked by the way she stiffened, and then she slowly turned to face him.

They stared then, sister and brother, until the thirty years of exile and the heartbreak of what had been done to her found another place to be.

She moved toward him with her son at her side as three more of her boys came running to join her. They said nothing, but they clearly weren't letting him talk to her alone.

"This is not a place where you will ever be welcome, so what are you doing here?" Leigh asked.

Blake's voice was shaking when he spoke.

"I didn't come to say I'm sorry, because there's no way to apologize for murder. We had a family meeting after Uncle Jack's arrest, and in a unanimous decision, the only thing we could think to do that would count for anything was to give the land back to everyone who was forced from their homes, along with money enough for them to rebuild what was torn down. Although it counts for nothing to you, we did it in your husband's name. His name is listed as the owner of each property, and it's his name that's on the release giving back the land to each family for the sum of one dollar. He wanted to save them. It seems only fitting that the credit for it happening goes to him, as well."

Leigh reached for the son closest to her and held

on. She could not show weakness to a Wayne. She hadn't back then when they'd cast her out of the family, and she wasn't going to do it now.

Blake was still talking.

"We don't know if any more of us will wind up under arrest, but it doesn't matter. We're leaving Eden. All of us. And we won't be back. We've deeded the house and the land to the city. I wish to God I could change the past. I wish to God none of this had happened."

He stood for a moment, waiting, but Leigh stared him down, then turned and walked away.

Blake looked at the faces of the men standing before him. His blood and yet not.

"It's time you leave now," one of them said.

Blake turned around and started walking back down the hill to where he'd had to park his car, and the farther he walked, the faster his steps became, until he was running.

He was out of breath, blind with tears, and shaking like a whipped dog by the time he reached the car. He didn't know who he was anymore, but he didn't like who he'd been. He drove off the mountain with a knot in his belly and never looked back.

Ten days later, Talia stood beside Bowie in the shade of three oak trees near the corner of Leigh's house, watching a dragonfly dive-bombing the water in a vine-wrapped birdbath. The breeze was just enough to cool her skin and push the hem of her pale pink sundress against her knees, and to play with the loose wispy curls she'd left down around her face.

His hand was warm against the middle of her back. His dark slacks and white shirt made him look taller and tanner.

Talia was watching Bowie's face as the pastor spoke, and she saw a faint sheen of tears in his eyes. She heard Johnny's baby laughter and his mother's anxious hush, then she heard the pastor say her name.

"Talia Champion, do you take this man to—"

Everything else faded except the look in Bowie's eyes.

"Yes, forever," she said, unaware she'd cut the preacher off in mid-vow.

There was a faint thread of laughter throughout the small gathering. The preacher cleared his throat and turned to Bowie.

"Bowie Youngblood, do you take this woman—"

"I do," he replied.

The preacher sighed. He'd never been interrupted quite like this before, but he supposed the vows still took. However, he wasn't going to be denied the perfect ending. His voice rang out like the crashing of cymbals at the end of a long refrain.

"Bowie and Talia Youngblood, you are now man and wife. What God has joined together, let no man put asunder. And as pretty as she is, young man, I suggest you kiss your bride."

All the breath went out of Bowie at once. He meant to tell her he loved her more than life, but he couldn't find the words, so he kissed her instead, in the presence of God, hoping their missing family members were there with them in spirit.

She smiled as she put her arms around his neck, and then it was done.

Her lips to his mouth.

Heart to heart.

Forever.

# Epilogue

It had taken Talia less than a day to learn that hot in West Virginia and hot in New Orleans were two entirely different things.

Her ribs were the last thing to heal, and while she wasn't as tightly bound as before, she still had to be careful. No lifting anything too heavy and no tight hugs.

Bowie had helped her hang up all her clothes on the first day in their temporary new home, and then they'd made love first on the bare mattress, then later after she'd put on the sheets, and then that night they'd made love again simply because they could.

The heat here sapped what strength she had regained, so during the hottest part of the day she stayed indoors in their new apartment.

She'd brought everything with her from home that she wanted to keep and had put the house up for sale. She had her mother's china and hutch, the sideboard that had belonged to her Aunt Jewel, the old desk from her daddy's office on the railroad, and bits and pieces of the history that made her who she was; but she'd only unpacked the bare essentials, because they were already in constant house shopping mode on every day Bowie had off.

She'd recently gotten a phone call from Chief Clayton, letting her know that Justin Wayne had taken the insanity plea and in return had been sentenced to a mental facility, with intermittent evaluations to assess his ability to blend back into society. Bowie was disgusted, but she was too happy now to hang on to the past.

A day or so later Leigh called to tell them that Jack Wayne had also made a deal. Rather than go to trial and face a death sentence, he'd opted for life without parole.

Bowie had heard the tension in her voice.

"How do you feel about that, Mama?" he'd asked.

"It's going to be hell on earth for a man like him to be in prison. I'm fine with him being in hell."

And that was when Bowie had smiled.

"That sounds like the Mama I know and love."

He'd heard her sigh. "I'm getting there," she'd said. "Jesse says hello and to bring him another baby to play with."

Bowie laughed.

"Do me a favor and get him a puppy instead. We're just fine like we are for a while."

Talia couldn't get enough of life, or food, or Bowie. It was as if she'd starved not only her body but her soul during the time they'd been apart. She was discovering the joy in the world all over again.

Bowie said she was regaining her sass. It was all as they'd first planned it to be, just a few years late. She still couldn't believe it sometimes and spent long hours late at night watching him sleep.

She'd bought another car with the insurance money from the one that was wrecked, and ventured out in the mornings to a neighborhood supermarket to shop for groceries after Bowie left for work.

On weekends they house hunted, and made love again and again, and in the third month of their residence in the apartment, they finally found what Talia knew right away was The House.

It might have been all the black wrought-iron fencing around the small courtyard in front.

It could have been the lush, green landscaping with jasmine blooming at the gates and bougainvillea spilling from the limbs of a massive oak in the tiny front yard, and wisteria hanging from the eaves at the back of the house.

It was most likely the ancient two-story red brick house itself, with its black shutters and black trim, on the quiet little street in the neat little neighborhood.

But it was for sure the feeling of home as the Realtor unlocked the door and they stepped inside for the very first time.

"Oh, Bowie! This is it," Talia said.

He laughed. "We haven't seen anything but the living room," he said.

"It won't matter what the rest of it looks like. We can fix what needs fixing, but you can't fix the feeling, and it feels like home."

"Then we better do this right," Bowie said, and took her by the hand and pulled her back out onto the porch.

"What are you doing?" she asked.

"I'm carrying you across the threshold," he said, as he gave her a quick kiss and swooped her up into his arms.

The Realtor was smiling and gladly held the door open as Bowie carried her back into the house.

"Welcome home, my love."

Talia smiled as Bowie set her back on her feet, and then, from the corner of her eye, she saw something swoop in the door from outside.

It was a robin. Once again, her messenger.

"Oh, look, Bowie!"

The Realtor frowned, watching the red-breasted bird fly up to the newel post of the stairway, then to the mantel of the fireplace before it lit in a patch of sunshine on the shining hardwood floors.

"I guess it came in while I was holding the door," the Realtor said. "If we're lucky, it will go out the same way."

"It's a sign. That's our blessing, Bowie. This is it. This is home!" Talia said, and then ran to open the door.

She swung it wide and then stood back as the robin took to the air and flew back out into the light.

Bowie walked up behind her and kissed her just below her ear.

"Even though the robin has spoken, we may as well look at the rest of the place while we're here, okay?"

Talia laughed as she took his hand.

"Yes, we may as well."

\* \* \* \* \*